Jesters

Jesters

DAVID MARKISH

Translated by
Antonina W. Bouis

HENRY HOLT AND COMPANY
NEW YORK

Published in the United States by
Henry Holt and Company, Inc., 115 West 18th Street,
New York, New York 10011.
Published in Canada by Fitzhenry & Whiteside Limited,
195 Allstate Parkway, Markham, Ontario L3R 4T8.
Originally published in Israel under the title *Shuty.*

Library of Congress Cataloging in Publication Data
Markish, David, 1938-
[Shuty. English]
Jesters / David Markish; translated by Antonina W. Bouis.
—1st American ed.
p. cm.
Translation of: Shuty.
ISBN 0-8050-0444-0
1. Jews—Soviet Union—Social life and customs—Fiction.
2. Soviet Union—History—1689-1800—Fiction. I. Title.
PG3483.2.R54S5813 1988 87-37455
891.73 44—dc19 CIP

First American Edition

Text and map design by Jeffrey L. Ward
Printed in the United States of America
1 3 5 7 9 10 8 6 4 2

ISBN 0-8050-0444-0

Contents

Jesters and Jokers

As opposed to jokers—people as a rule trite and smug—professional jesters seem tragic to me. And court jesters, if they are not mad, are doubly tragic.

Jesters is a novel about Jews in the court of the Russian czar Peter the Great: Lacosta, Shafirov, Divier, and Ambassador Veselovsky. And though of these four only Lacosta was a professional, they were all jesters of the great czar-experimenter. And even today, anyone raised to the top of a totalitarian regime is either jester or joker.

The four Jews of my novel are historic personages, who lived and died about two and a half centuries ago. I suppose that the only fictional character in my book is the dwarf Kabysdokh, a colleague of Lacosta's. However, Peter had dwarfs in his retinue, and the details of the fictional dwarf's stomach problems are true.

I gathered material on Peter, his people, and his era—on everything that could be called the "revolution from above"—in libraries in America, Europe, and Israel. In Geneva I held the glass from which Peter drank at Lefort's housewarming for his palace in the German Suburb. In Paris I had the good fortune to leaf through a book about Peter's Azov campaign, published in Russia in 1703. I collected so much astonishing information that it could not all fit into the novel. But I am sorry that I was unable to go to Russia and work in the archives and libraries of Moscow and Leningrad.

My research and preparation took nearly a year. I am grateful to the American organization the Memorial Foundation of Jewish Culture, which supported me in my work.

N
RUSSIAN EMPIRE
KINGDOM OF SWEDEN
Olonets
SAINT PETERSBURG
Novgorod
Suzdal'
MOSCOW
EAST PRUSSIA
BALTIC SEA
Smolensk
Tambov
KINGDOM OF POLAND
Marienburg
WARSAW
Kiev
Poltava
Yavorov
Taganrog
Carlsbad
DNIESTER
PRUT
WALACHIA
BLACK SEA
DANUBE
TSARGRAD
OTTOMAN EMPIRE
MEDITERRANEAN SEA

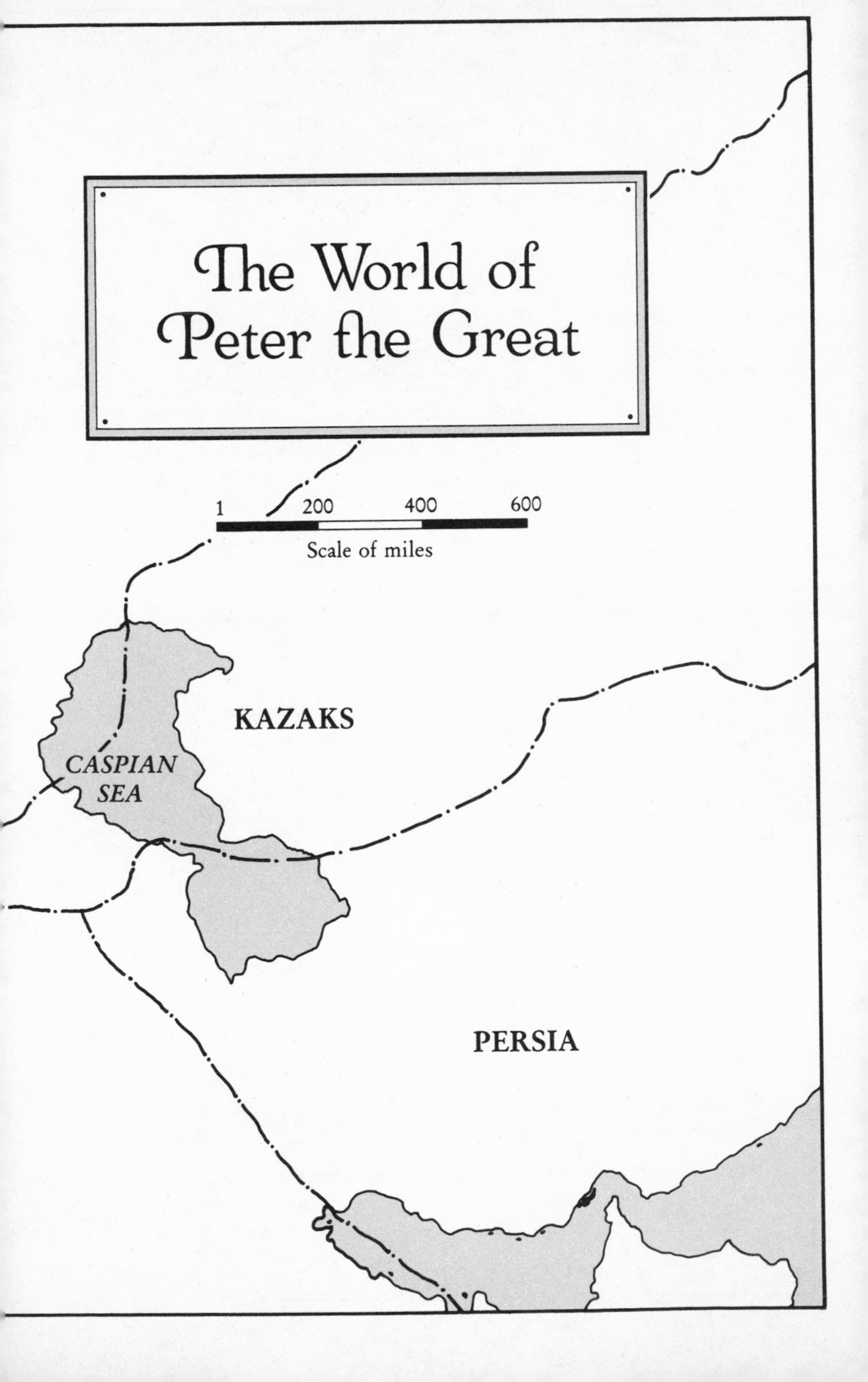
The World of Peter the Great
1
200
400
600
Scale of miles
KAZAKS
CASPIAN
SEA
PERSIA

I

The Hat

1689

They don't sell Polish honor in the Polish Rows of Moscow's oldest section, Kitai-Gorod; they sell cloth and fur, clothes and chopped wood, sledges and wagons no matter the season (a good man prepares his sledge in summer and his wagon in winter), wine from under the counter and pies from the stand, and whatever else comes handy and God grants: pitchforks, rawhide, oats, fiery potions and love potions in a rag, dried foot of sand crocodile, which is a cure for the terrible disease leprosy. Legend has it that once upon a time, in the olden days, real Poles with mustaches and wearing *kuntushes* traded here, but now only the name remains from those times, and the sellers in the Polish Rows are Russians and Tatars, Jews and cannibals and swamp creatures—all mixed together; once in a while you come across a Polack too.

The Rows were good and crowded. Back in the Time of

Troubles, under the False Dmitri, the Poles had gotten their hands on this place, and it hadn't come completely unstuck yet. You could see the Kremlin from here, and St. Basil's on the Square; and after the intoxicating sight of a morning execution and mortal torture, crowds of people flowed from the Execution Block to the Polish Market Rows: if they'd come all this way at the crack of dawn from all over Moscow and nearby villages to stare at the executioner's artistry, then they might as well peek in at the bazaar, since it was right there, take a look at the merchants and their wares, buy some nails, have something hot to eat. . . . There is no better advertising for a bazaar, tavern, or brothel than a torture square situated nearby: the sight of someone else's suffering and death prompts you to spend money, to drink and make merry.

Evreinov's shop stood not far from the center of the Rows—it was one of the wealthy shops of a wealthy merchant. Clothing for men, women, and children, cotton and broadcloth, silk and velvet, with gold or silver embroidery or plain, was neatly spread out inside the spacious, sturdy shop and piled in a tempting jumble on a counter by the entrance to be looked at and fingered by passersby. At the counter, in front and to the side, was the ever-present sitter—short and stocky, with sharp but lazy-looking eyes, a young man called Peter Shafirov. He did not have co-workers or assistants; he managed the shop alone. The merchant Evreinov valued the commercial and other talents of this young man, and with reason: Shafirov had a thorough knowledge of math and Italian bookkeeping; spoke English, German, and Dutch fluently; and had not once been caught stealing.

The sitter was dressed modestly but not poorly: he wore an ample, baggy caftan of brown broadcloth, beneath which showed navy blue trousers, stuffed into leather boots that had known better times. Gazing at the crenellated wall of the

Kremlin and the onion-dome cupolas of St. Basil's, glimmering in the frosty air, Shafirov tapped his cold feet on the greasy, thawing spring clay, which had been mauled by thousands of bast shoes, boots, and bare feet and mixed with horse manure, straw, and wood shavings. April that year was fresh, with cold, Marchlike mornings and nights. He should go into the shop and get a sheepskin coat to toss over his shoulders, but he didn't want to budge, to take his eyes from the red fortress teeth cutting into the tender blue sky. Just stay in the sun—and think. How could he not think? He had already learned twenty new French words that morning, and he had another twenty yet to learn. . . . In Red Square they were making one robber sit on a stake, flogging another, and burying a woman alive—that meant a big crowd, which would arrive at the bazaar in an hour, no sooner. . . . Was it really true that Czar Peter had not left Anna Mons's bed, in the German Suburb, for four days and had not gone to his young bride? No wonder they called her Peter's Gates.

It was cool, too cool; he'd get a chill soon. Shafirov pulled his caftan closer to his chest and kept a suspicious eye on a shabby pie vendor who had appeared out of nowhere, waiting for him to pass the counter piled with clothing: his fingers were probably greasy and his hands dirty. But the vendor, grinning widely, was in no hurry. He leapt over puddles in his bast shoes, splashing mud high and far, either dancing a jig or just keeping warm, while he drummed the fingers of one hand on the tray that hung from his neck and held a reed pipe to his mouth with the other. Catching Shafirov's anxious glance, the vendor spat out the pipe, and jumping and dancing more furiously, chanted:

Some buy shoes, some buy pies!
If you're wise, buy two pies!

If you're feeding kith and cousin,
Come and buy pies by the dozen!

Was that damned vendor dancing in the puddle on purpose? Globs of mud flew in all directions, the thick black ooze making a streak on the hem of a velvet caftan on the counter.

"Hey, you!" Shafirov hissed and headed for the dancer.

"That's me!" the vendor sang and hopped out of the puddle. "Want some pies?"

I've got cat, dog, hare, and frog pies!
Chase them with vodka, they'll leap down to your belly!
Chase them with water, you'll be skinny and weak like jelly!

Stepping out of the puddle and wiping the mud from his boots, Shafirov leaned back against the counter. He couldn't stand boisterous people. This wastrel with the reed pipe, all skinny and raggedy, disgusted him. A fellow like that would pick your pocket with one hand and punch you in the face with the other for no reason at all.

The wastrel was now hopping around and playing his pipe on dry land, and people came out of the stores to gape at him. Shafirov spat into the puddle and turned away.

"If there's no water in the lake," the vendor sang, holding his pipe,

That means the Jews their thirst did slake.
Yid, Yid, Yid, Yid,
Look at what he did.

Shafirov did not react to the offensive ditty: even a man half blind would see that he was a Jew, and mentioning his father's baptism would only make the situation worse. In cases like this, he followed the good advice of his father, Pavel Filippovich, formerly Pincus: keep silent and pay no attention. Young Shafirov felt more Jewish than Orthodox Christian, although he did not follow the strict and burdensome rules of his father's old religion. On Saturdays his father locked the door, covered his head with a white shawl with black trim, turned to face the wall, and prayed to the old, tried-and-true God. Both father and son knew that converting was necessary, otherwise they could give up any thoughts of advancement in Moscow, where Pavel Filippovich, still Pincus back then, had arrived from Polish Smolensk.

Shafirov did think about advancement. He thought soberly, calculating this way and that, weighing his possibilities and those of others, taking into account his Jewishness, so clearly written all over his face, and his father's conversion; his own knowledge of languages, and his father's connections in the embassy office, where he worked as a translator of books and documents; and, in particular, the unobtrusive but solid commercial ties of Veselovsky, his aunt's husband.

So Peter Shafirov considered his sitting in Evreinov's shop not pointless, but profoundly temporary. And he could not be upset or made to forget his ambitions by the vendor's stupid songs, or any other songs. All things being equal, the pie vendor wore bast shoes and a torn shirt, while he, Peter Shafirov, was pacing in front of the counter in boots and caftan. He should not forget that and put himself on a par with the beggar.

The fool gave Shafirov a brazen farewell wink and finally went dancing on his way. His high voice cascaded from the end of the rows:

Hey, you baptized men, come and get pies while you can!
Hot and fair, buy a pair!

He should be an officer with a voice like that, thought Shafirov. He took the mud-spattered caftan from the counter and went inside to clean it.

He had carefully scraped off all the mud when his attention was caught by a slight, light rustle or a shadow slipping along the counter; he dashed out of the store with a speed his stocky build belied. The spindly legged vendor was scampering away from the counter, looking over his shoulder, and perched on his round head was a fine, brand-new rabbit fur hat with flaps.

Shafirov shot a quick glance at the empty spot on the counter, raised the standard cry of "Stop, thief!" and gave chase. The vendor was prepared for this possibility; he whirled away from his pursuer and, racing like a horse, jumped right in the middle of the wide puddle and began shouting: "Hey, good people! The Yids are harassing a Russian; they're sucking our blood! Come here, people! Help! Fire!"

The vendor had calculated correctly. Shafirov, who stopped for an instant before following the thief into the puddle, noted the cleverness of his enemy's strategy: it brought people running from all ends of the marketplace, and it would not be hard for a Russian fellow to hide in a crowd hostile toward a dark-haired sitter with a hooked nose.

In fact, a crowd quickly surrounded the puddle in a tight ring. Shafirov stepped into the puddle, and as he reached out to pluck the hat from the thief's head, the man spun around him, holding his tray in front of him, and shouted in a singsong, to the crowd's approving hum:

I'm a merry honest lad,
Not a Uke and not a Tatar.

JESTERS

Not a Jew and not a Turkman,
But a pure Russian man.

The Evreinov store's hat was kept just out of reach by the vendor's tray. Shafirov grabbed the edge and pulled hard. The neck strap broke, and the pies fell in the mud. The crowd grumbled angrily. Taking a full swing back, the vendor struck out at Shafirov's head—but the sitter blocked the punch with his shoulder, and the vendor's fist might as well have struck the side of a horse. Shafirov, locking his fists together, struck the vendor in the solar plexus as heavily as with a log.

"They're beating our people!" the vendor cried. He punched the sitter below the belt and rushed over to the counter, where, with one smooth motion, he swept all the caftans, coats, hats, vests, and underpants to the ground. "Honest people, come and get it! If you need it, want it, take it!"

The crowd, chattering in excitement, rushed forward. Shafirov lunged ahead of them, dove for the clothing, and threw it into the shop. The vendor ran over and gave him a swift kick in the rear. Heavyset Shafirov did not fall, he simply swayed, then he turned sharply, grabbed the vendor by the throat with one hand and pulled the hat off with the other, and stuffed it inside his caftan. Now that he had gotten the stolen goods back, he felt calmer and more confident.

But the unsuccessful thief, bereft of both his pies and the hat, grew furious. He wrapped his wiry arms around Shafirov, tripped him, and they fell to the ground, rolling and kicking at the crowd's feet. The crowd, breathing hard in concentration, watched the fight. Their sympathies were with the feisty, attacking Russian, but they gave the Jew his due for his lupine hold and stubbornness.

Two men—one no older than the combatants, the other in middle age, both in German dress—stood to one side and watched in rapture. The young man was half a head taller than his tall comrade and gnawed thoughtfully on his thumbnail. In his right hand he held a thick walking stick topped with a heavy, ornamented silver head, its end resting on his boot toe; it served as a cudgel when necessary.

"I wager a dozen bottles," the older man said with a heavy French accent, "that the beggar will win. He has no choice. If he loses, he'll have to pay for the hat too."

Without listening, the young man jerked his head, on its long, still boyishly slender neck. A broad-shouldered fellow in a well-cut coat appeared at his side, a bit behind him, and stood at attention.

"Who's that?" he asked, without taking his eyes from the fight.

The stout fellow stood on tiptoe and whispered with servile fervor in the young man's ear.

"The Jew is the merchant Evreinov's sitter. The thief isn't known yet. Do you want me to take them, Your Majesty?"

"Think of it, a Jew fighting for someone else's property," muttered the young man. "Break it up! And bring them to me!"

The stout fellow, followed by two others in matching coats, pushed apart the crowd and hurried across the puddle to the fighting men.

"You're right, Your Majesty," said François Lefort, when they strode quickly from the Rows. "That's the way to pick servants, two at a time. And so that one hates the other from the start. They'll serve you better."

"You take them first, watch them," Peter said. "They might come in handy, Franz, my heart. One is merry and brazen, the other as stubborn as the devil. Eh? Will you take them?" Peter looked at him closely, as if he thought refusal was a possibility.

"I'll take them," Lefort agreed without hurry. "Why not?"

"And if they turn out to be useless," Peter said, bringing his stick with a whistle through the air, "what could be simpler? One gets flogged for thievery, the other to keep him company, so that he doesn't feel lonely."

"They will get a beating not for theft or for company, my good friend Your Majesty," Lefort said and glanced at Peter to see if he was listening, "but because possibly you were mistaken about them. Sovereigns are allowed to make mistakes, but the punishment must be borne by servants. That is the law!"

"You're right, my heart, you're right!" Peter said and smiled gratefully. "The sovereign sets up an experiment of benefit to the country, most definitely beneficial. Then it fails to come together, nothing is set out correctly to begin with, or the material at hand is either raw or rotten. But the experimenter can't punish himself for that! Or give up the experiment completely! When you chop wood, the tree feels pain but the ax feels warm."

Lefort nodded in agreement but said nothing. He knew the czar well and knew that one could disagree with him only to a certain point. But he had never read or heard that any king had considered his reign harmful to the country. Then he thought how good and comfortable it would be to die in his own bed in his own house in the German Suburb—at least a year or two before the czar's grand innovations and experiments came to an end. Lefort's chances weren't bad—he was twenty-three years older than Peter. To die peacefully, not on the block—and let them figure out this barbaric masquerade for themselves.

"Your efforts, sire, will make Russia great," Lefort said, staring straight ahead. "And if that beggar and that Jew are flogged—well, let them scream and weep."

Seized by the czar's secret guards, the Jew and the beggar were for now neither weeping nor screaming; the beggar was thinking of escape, the Jew of intercession by his uncle-by-marriage Veselovsky. The guards watched them closely, with powerful fists ready; no sooner had the beggar stepped over the puddle to try to move to the side than he received a heavy blow, an extra-heavy blow, on the neck. The guards tied the hands of the two captives behind their backs and led them out of the marketplace and into a waiting wagon hitched to a powerful gray mare. There was no straw in the wagon, and it was uncomfortable to sit with their hands tied.

"You viper," said the beggar, spitting a gob of pink phlegm over the side of the wagon. "It's all your fault. . . . You broke my tray, and all my pies scattered! and now . . ."

"And now you'll be flogged," Shafirov interrupted grimly. "You shouldn't steal."

"Shouldn't steal!" The beggar's bulging blue eyes popped. "Who are you to tell me whether I can steal or not? Every Yid who comes along thinks he can tell me . . ."

"They'll let me go," Shafirov said in a monotone, "and they'll send you down to the mines. I may be a Jew, but you're a peasant, an empty-headed, impoverished peasant."

The beggar, panting, tried to shove Shafirov with his shoulder.

"Hey you!" the driver said. "Watch it, or I'll use the whip on you!" And he let them have a stroke, but only one, and not full strength. Shafirov, who was sitting closer to the coach box, got less of the blow.

"Compared to the Jew, the Russian always gets the worse deal," the beggar said, explaining the injustice calmly. "You're wearing a caftan and you didn't feel it at all. You stole the caftan from the merchant, right?"

Shafirov did not respond. With anxiety and fear, he observed that the driver had turned from the Kremlin and its offices, and he watched the wagon rattle on toward the German Suburb.

"Where are they taking us?" The beggar had noticed too. In those days the prison named for the adventurer from Geneva, François Lefort, had not yet been built in that area.

"They'll just throw you into the Yauza River, that's all," Shafirov predicted. "And they'll let me go."

He felt a certain inner surge, as if before a difficult and wearying trial upon which his life depended. Were they being brought to the Germans? Well, the Germans were gathering power, the czar was promoting them. . . . Shafirov knew in that instant that his days sitting in Evreinov's shop were at an end.

They were brought to the clean, well-swept courtyard of a large and very clean house, neatly painted light blue, with glass-paned windows and checked curtains tied back at the bottom. They were prodded in the back, brought through the yard almost at a run, and pushed into a tall stone shed. The door was locked behind them. They went into separate corners and silently watched each other.

Less than a quarter of an hour later, the lock rattled and the big strapping fellow from before appeared in the doorway. Without a word he untied their hands, pushed the two men together, and stood to one side. After that, bending over, Lefort stepped across the threshold, held the door, and let the czar in.

"Well, who won?" Peter asked, stopping abruptly in the middle of the shed.

"I did!" shouted the beggar and fell to his knees.

After a moment's thought, Shafirov got on his knees too.

"He won in speed of response," Shafirov said. "At the marketplace I would have choked him half to death, because I outweigh him by fifty pounds."

"You lie, pig's ear!" the beggar shouted. "Even half dead I'd bite through your throat!"

"Why only half to death?" Lefort asked with interest.

"The punishment for killing is too high," Shafirov explained readily. "And I haven't had time to learn French yet."

"You know languages?" Peter asked quickly.

"He knows Jewish!" the beggar interposed.

"I know Yiddish, yes," Shafirov agreed.

"What else?" Peter asked impatiently.

"Dutch, English, German. And Polish."

"Admirable. . . . Well, what about you?" Peter poked the beggar's shoulder with the end of his stick. "Did you steal the hat?"

"I'm Moscow-born," the beggar shouted, squirming to get over to kiss Peter's foot while still on his knees. "Take pity on my youth! I take, not steal. I sell pies, and he broke my tray!"

"What more do you have to say? Haven't thought of anything yet?" Peter laughed. "What's your name?"

"My pa called me lousy Aleksashka when he switched me," the beggar said with a fake sob.

"He didn't use the switch enough," Lefort said with conviction.

"Oh, he did, a lot!" Menshikov insisted. "My father, Danila Menshikov, was a hard man, may God rest his soul."

"Are you afraid of me?" Peter asked suddenly, looking from one man to the other.

"Very much!" Menshikov answered for both.

"Why?" Peter asked.

"You're so young and so terrible," Menshikov explained. "And your stick is so big. Just horrible!"

Now Peter was looking at Shafirov.

"The master is wrathful," Shafirov said. "But it is not his wrath I fear—I fear that I might displease him, God forbid . . ."

"Here is your master," Peter said, pointing at Lefort. "You will serve him. And if you," he said, his stick reaching out for Shafirov, "lied about speaking tongues—I'll have your tongue pulled out!"

Turning sharply on his heels, Peter strode toward the door and kicked it open. Lefort followed him out.

"Who was that?" Menshikov asked, suddenly much braver, of the stout fellow by the wall. "An officer or something?"

"Czar Peter, you fool," the fellow said on his way out.

Shafirov smiled happily.

II

The Pirate from the Island of the Holy Infant

1697

Tsykler hated being stuck in Taganrog, at the end of the earth, running the construction of the harbor. He figured, and not without reason, that his next assignment would be a real dead end, deep in Siberia. Having served the Russian throne for thirty years and having reached the rank of colonel of the Streltsy, Tsykler realized that his career, which had begun so well, was now over: Czar Peter would not forgive his secret ties with the late Ivan Miloslavsky and Peter's rebellious sister, Sophia. The ties, if you thought about it, were completely understandable: Sophia promised Colonel Tsykler much, and Peter—nothing. It didn't have anything to do with Peter's love of things German (Tsykler, after all, had been born in Bremen, not Kaluga) or with Sophia's love of old Russia. Tsykler was equally indifferent to both old Russia and new. But the fact that some drunkard and procurer like Lefort got to show off his general admiral's uniform irritated Tsykler mightily. He might drink no less than Lefort, but he could bring Czar Peter a dozen clean and sturdy German girls instead of one Anna Mons. But fortune did not smile on Tsykler. He was in Taganrog, while Lefort was in his new palace in the German Suburb. And that was disgusting and offensive to the point of making Tsykler's blood boil.

"He's afraid," mused Tsykler, all alone in Taganrog in his solid little house. "Czar Peter is afraid of me, that's why he's kept me so far from Moscow. He knows I'm not an old fool like Avraam." Tsykler wouldn't write letters, he wouldn't lecture him: "Don't give in to earthly pleasures, Czar, don't go to the German Suburb, listen to the advice of your mother, and your wife, and the boyars . . ." Old man Avraam had recently written his last letter, given Peter one last bit of advice: he was hauled up on a rack at the Preobrazhenskoe palace, and all his veins were pulled out, one by one, while Czar Peter lectured him: "Look, old man, this is your central vein, and this is an auxiliary one. Keep looking, maybe you'll learn anatomy before you die."

Tsykler's old friends, not yet removed from Moscow—the boyar Alexei Sokovnin, the boyar Matvei Pushkin, and criminal court clerk Silvester Poltina—sent word with trusted emissaries that the czar was planning to take lousy Lefort, and the Yid Shafirov, and that filthy Aleksashka Menshikov, and the devil knew who else to visit the Germans and the Dutch to learn new things and to recruit new people; and after this embassy he would banish from his court all the people who had served him, like Tsykler. They also informed him that the Swedes were displeased by Peter's curiosity and that Sophia trusted Tsykler wholly and completely.

Sophia's trust meant an acknowledgment of his past services and a future reward, besides being pleasing in purely human terms. But it carried a price in the implication that slipped around between the lines and between the words: "Colonel Tsykler, kill the czar, undermine the embassy!" He understood and accepted it without regrets: he wasn't the first to whom the offer had been made, and it wasn't the first time it had been made to him. The earlier candidates had not succeeded: the flesh from their heads, placed on stakes, was eaten by Moscow crows. The one to succeed would be the last one, the lucky one.

It wasn't yesterday that people began wondering whether it was fate, chance, or a combination of circumstances that directs the course of human events—and they wouldn't stop wondering tomorrow. Why was that one killed to lie rotting in the earth, while this one lives, in glory and closeness to the king? Who knows?

Tsykler plotted where, when, and how to kill Czar Peter, made secret plans, and had a variety of advantages over his intended victim. Nevertheless he was apprehended and tortured horribly, and he confessed to everything and betrayed everyone.

Peter directed the interrogation—passionately, ruthlessly, and bloodily. As his assistant he took Stepan Medved, called Vytashchi, which meant "drag it out." A master of the knout, a jester, a man not completely normal, Vytashchi alternated between unbridled merriment and sophisticated tortures. Peter and Vytashchi had something in common. Peter, who enjoyed talking, almost never conversed with Vytashchi—he observed him closely, studied him the way he studied almost everything in life, and also silently, with varying success, played chess with him.

Vytashchi appeared before Peter at Preobrazhenskoe with the executioner's box under his arm. The young czar was not completely sober; his cheek twitched more than usual, and so did his head on the strong, muscular neck.

Shoving Vytashchi in the back, Peter chased him to the cellar, to the torture chamber. There on the far wall of the large, dank room, Tsykler hung on the rack. His body was limp, and his arms, screwed to the crossbeam, had pulled out of their shoulder sockets. Vytashchi walked around the man and looked questioningly at Peter.

"The knout!" barked the czar, his words like a lash.

Unhurriedly removing Tsykler from the rack, Vytashchi placed him on the box and with a flourish, but still trying not to miss, splashed cold water from a leather bucket on him. Tsykler groaned hoarsely; his arms hung lifelessly. Squinting and chewing on his lip as he thought, Vytashchi tied the colonel by the neck to the angled sawhorse and then tightly bound his legs below the knees. The czar, hands clasped behind his back, rocked back and forth and impatiently watched his master of the knout at work.

Straightening the knout—a thick wooden handle and a leather strap with a rawhide tail as hard and sharp as bone—Vytashchi took a running start, jumped up, and as he exhaled with a drawn-out "He-ey!" lashed out. The blow was weakened: Vytashchi had not calculated the run and leap properly, and the tail of the knout struck the wall, leaving a deep scrape, as if by a nail.

Peter ran up wildly and pushed aside the executioner.

"Give me!" He tore the knout from his hands.

With great interest, professional interest, Vytashchi, knocked to the ground, watched how his sovereign measured the knout in his hand, backed toward the wall, and then, with a headlong running start, jumped in place, like a gigantic rooster, drew a full circle over his head with the knout, and struck. Tsykler screamed harshly, from the depth of his lungs; on his white back, from shoulder to shoulder, a thick welt appeared, like a bloody rope. Stepping back and running again, the czar repeated the blow.

"Two!" Vytashchi counted approvingly. "After the fifth blow, change knouts, sire: the tail will get soggy, and the blow will be soft."

Tossing aside the knout, Peter walked over to the sawhorse and, with a jerk of his head, spat at the bound man.

"Cur!" the czar said and wiped his mouth with the sleeve of his caftan. "Who sent you? The Swedes? Or did Miloslavsky prompt you from his grave? I'll get him underground too!"

After a brief look at Tsykler and his back, Peter bent over and poked his finger curiously into the open wound: was it far to the bone? No—it was close.

"Well, come on!" Peter turned to Vytashchi as he wiped his finger on his trousers. "Take the knout. Now you see how it should be done."

The executioner obeyed and diligently reached for the knout. He not only feared the czar, he loved him.

Peter kept his promise, and not without inventiveness: the coffin of boyar Ivan Miloslavsky was unearthed, opened, and carried to Preobrazhenskoe in a rubbish wagon hitched to six pigs. Alongside the procession ran four court dwarfs, two of them black, bells jingling. It was a long way to run; the dwarfs grew weary, stumbled, and fell. Behind the wagon, in an open cart, rode the chief of the secret police, the jester Mock-Prince Caesar Fedor Romodanovsky, drunk as a pig, with the face of a monster, bulging eyes, and protruding mustache. In front of the cart the jester and master of the knout Vytashchi strode haughtily, hurrying the dwarfs with a royal staff topped by a goat's head. The entire procession was thickly surrounded by Preobrazhensky troops and people thirsty for spectacles.

Author of the scenario, Czar Peter awaited the cortege at Preobrazhenskoe, near the scaffold, which for the occasion had gutters and holes cut into the flooring. On the scaffold, face up on a wheel set on a sharpened log, lay Tsykler, arms and legs broken. With flickering consciousness he tried to divine whether it was day or night, whether it was a bright moon in the sky or a cold sun. He was still alive, and that was bitter.

The crowd around the scaffold greeted with shouts the appearance of the rubbish wagon bearing the coffin. Cursing, the dwarfs climbed up into the special bird gazebo built for them at the top. The pigs drew the wagon under the scaffold and were unhitched at last.

The assistant executioner of the Preobrazhensky secret police climbed up on the wheel and turned Tsykler over onto his chest. Tsykler passed out from the pain, and when he came to he saw below him the high-ranking Alexei Sokovnin and court clerk Silvester Poltina, mutilated by torture, being beheaded. The blood poured along the gutters and out the holes.

Then, at Peter's sign, they pulled Tsykler down from the wheel, settled him comfortably on the wooden blocks, and first chopped off his right arm and left leg and then, after a short while, his left arm and right leg. Then they chopped off his head.

There was a lot of blood. It poured in streams along the gutters and fell into the coffin placed under the scaffold. The desiccated remains of Ivan Miloslavsky floated in the coffin as if in a pig's trough.

Finishing with one business, Peter without hesitation moved on to the next: on March 2, 1697, two days after Tsykler's execution, a thousand sledges of the Great Embassy moved from Moscow to the northwest, to the border. There were translators and cooks, guardsmen and physicians, counselors, toadies, priests, bakers, jester–master of the knout Vytashchi, and four dwarfs, rested and full of energy. At the head of the embassy was François Lefort; Czar Peter did not wish to be on show and traveled semi-incognito as Peter Mikhailov, head of a detachment going to learn naval craft. Those who were supposed to know about this, knew for sure; those who weren't, guessed.

Having gone through Riga, Mitava, and Königsberg, the embassy headed for Amsterdam. Peter's chief goal was Holland—with its wharves, manufacture, and powerful East India Company. Amazed by the solidity and dependability of Western life, Peter planned to study everything and learn as much as possible. He was supported by his active and knowledge-seeking nature—and he didn't put much faith in his subjects, whom he considered sluggish, lazy, and thieving. Hating Sophia and her Streltsy, Peter came to hate all of Russia's past—and he rushed, like an artillery bomb, to Europe, to its innovations. He was set on an "experiment" of renewal and, naturally, decided to head the experiment himself. And in order to do that he had to become privy to all the nuances of the business, test everything with his own teeth and tongue, feel everything with his own hands, not completely trusting either his people or foreigners: once he got started, there would be no one to ask for advice, nor would there be time for that. It was in that spirit that he had tested Tsykler's wound: was it far to the bone?

He felt almost as cozy in Amsterdam as he did in the German Suburb. He studied and researched everything he had planned to study and research back in Russia and beyond that almost everything that was new to him and seemed useful: the brewing of beer, the preparation of condoms from fish bladders, the making of the hooks for catching fish, the manufacture of glass. But first and foremost was the wharf, the building of ships—from keel to deck and from bow to stern. His happiest time in Amsterdam was the day of naval maneuvers performed especially for him. The frigate *Peter and Paul*, built before his eyes and with his participation, took part; he sailed near it in command of his yacht.

That autumn day had begun quite pleasantly for the czar; from early morning the sun was warm and sparkled through the breaks in high clouds, the sea was almost calm, the mail had come from Moscow with a letter from Anna Mons (Peter, as he read it, suddenly wanted to grab her, hold her, and push her down) and a missive from the loyal monster Romodanovsky. Everything was fine at home too. After reading the letters Peter quickly breakfasted on thickly peppered roast meat, which caused a burning in his chest, so he tried a new medication. It helped, but not very much. The czar drank a glass of anise vodka, felt a pleasant relief, and decided to withhold from the pharmacist his invitation to come to Russia; he didn't like the medication; he would have to find something stronger in London.

After breakfast came Nicholas Witsen—tall, straight-backed, in a snowy wig. He sat down in a low wooden chair, spread his knees wide, placed a black wooden walking stick between them, and leaned his broad chin, so wide you could hang a bucket from it, on the stick's silver head. The Amsterdam burgomaster, one of the directors of the East India Company, liked the strange Russian czar, and perhaps without any mercenary reason. Peter, however, doubted the burgomaster's altruism: man is weak and thieving, and that fact should never be forgotten.

"I am extremely happy to see Your Majesty in good

health," Witsen said gallantly, shaking the curls of his wig.

What about my heartburn! Peter thought and said with a sigh, "Yes, yes, Mister Burgomaster . . . I see you come with good news: what about craftsmen for our metal foundries? Have you found them? Do you have them?"

"Yes and no," Witsen replied evasively, and Peter frowned. "They don't know a word of Russian, and that is a great obstacle, if not the only one. . . . But I do come with good news."

Peter paced the room, recalling what else he had asked Witsen to do besides finding and hiring metalworkers: acquiring instruments for military doctors and the latest system for making fireworks.

"The Jews of the city of Amsterdam," Witsen continued, "ask permission, Your Majesty, to come to Russia, to settle there, to set up merchant offices and begin to trade."

"And that's your good news?" the czar said and laughed out of the corner of his mouth.

"The Jews do much to help the city of Amsterdam flourish," Witsen explained. "And for the first instance they present Your Majesty with one hundred thousand gulden."

Peter was preoccupied and rocked back and forth on his feet. One hundred thousand gulden was no small sum, and if he let the Yids in, he could always throw them out again.

"Jews in a government are like a spare treasury," Witsen argued. "There is no harm from them, and in case of need you can always borrow money from them at low rates."

The black dwarf called Kabysdokh rolled out from under the table, where he lived in a wooden crate. Howling and hopping, he climbed out of his red silk trousers and ran around the room, holding his small penis in his black fist. As if he had completely forgotten Witsen's proposal, Peter watched the antics of his dwarf.

"The Yids are coming!" shouted Kabysdokh. "Save me! They're cutting! And mine is so little!" He opened his fist. "And they'll shorten you too, Sovereign! Oh! Help!"

How much did they pay him to represent them? Peter thought with a burst of anger as he looked over at the politely smiling Witsen. "I won't get into a cabal with Yids; oh, no, I'd rather shake up the monasteries, and then my own merchants will cough up too."

"Even though Yids are known to be artful tricksters throughout the world," the czar said, kicking the dwarf away, "they will not get much from my Russians. . . . And then Kabysdokh here is afraid of them."

Hiding behind Peter's legs, the dwarf made indecent gestures at Witsen.

"Mister Shafirov thinks . . ." Witsen began, watching the dwarf thoughtfully.

"Thinks, thinks!" Peter interrupted with a sharp movement of his arms. "Naturally he thinks that they should be let in. Good for Shafirov: he's supporting his own! He wouldn't be worth a copper if he didn't."

Witsen stayed a bit longer and then made his bows. He had been to Russia several times, he knew Russian, and it sometimes seemed to him he knew Russians—but still he could not understand Czar Peter. Banging his stick on the clean black stones on the street, he thought about why the czar had refused the Jews. Every reasonable ruler—and Witsen considered Peter a reasonable man, albeit unrestrained—would have welcomed additional capital into his country, be it Jewish or even Chinese. You don't find a hundred thousand gulden lying around in the streets, and that was only an advance.

But in one fell swoop, at the urging of some vile dwarf, the Russian sovereign refused money in hand as well as guaranteed income in the future. Regrettable, regrettable! Deplorable, deplorable! And that was without mentioning Witsen's commission going out the window. Well, all right, he could have understood if the czar were a Jew hater, but he had Shafirov, and the Veselovsky brothers were moving up in the diplomatic corps, most likely they would soon take important positions in the embassy. A mystery!

On the way to the sea Peter considered Witsen's proposal. He felt neither hatred nor scorn for the Jews—nothing special. Likely to steal? And who wasn't! Take Aleksashka Menshikov, as Russian as one could get—he'd grab whatever came to hand. There was no distinction on that score between people, whether they were baptized or circumcised. But still, Jews were foreign, even more foreign than Tatars, or the Dutch or Germans. Jews lived in a shell, and their souls did not attach to anything Russian. Truth be told, there was nothing special to get attached to—there was nothing much good in Russia—but just compare the Russian Shafirov with the Genevan Lefort! For Franz, my dear friend, our most vile shit has become his own, while Shafirov, that Yid lout, secretly mocks the Russians. If he only laughed openly—but no, he does it on the sly, among his own kind. As for the facts that his tongue is sharp and that he could outtrick the devil himself and leave him without horns—that's why we keep him.

Catching sight beyond the earthen dike of the swaying masts of the *Peter and Paul*, the czar forgot about Witsen and Shafirov. He did not, could not explain to himself why he preferred naval military games to games in fields and woods, why the very sight of the sea brought peace to his heart and put him in a mood that bordered on piety. He did not know, though he did honestly try to figure it out.

Shafirov observed the maneuvers from shore. He was given to seasickness, could not bear movement on a ship; even the sight of calm seas brought on nausea and dizziness. However, giving the czar's love of naval exercises its due, he felt it necessary to come to the shore and watch waves and ships. He was not the only one to think so, and he was not the only one to come: almost the entire staff of the embassy was situated along the shore on the dike. Some looked with interest and others with boredom at the sea, at the *Peter and Paul,* at the yacht and the other ships and boats. The czar liked an audience, and a nonappearance could have dire consequences.

Sitting in a folding chair on the dike and watching with a polite smile, Shafirov thought about Witsen's morning visit to Peter. The czar's refusal soothed Shafirov: deep down he had not wanted a different answer. If Peter let the Dutch Jews into Russia, Shafirov would willy-nilly become responsible for their words and deeds and would have to answer to the czar, as an expert and coreligionist, even a former one. And Shafirov had no doubt that sooner or later, and probably sooner, there would be something to answer for: he knew his Jews, knew their hardness in dealings, their secrecy, and he knew that the Russians would look askance at all that. Besides which, the Amsterdam Jews had used the goy Witsen as their emissary and not him, former Jew Shafirov, depriving him of the opportunity to earn a good bribe. . . . So let them stay in their Amsterdam, thought Shafirov, slightly miffed, as he gazed at the sea.

And on the sea the frigate *Peter and Paul* sailed around the boats and yachts like an elk among wolves. He could see sailors climbing up the ropes, raising and lowering sails. Then the czar's yacht came alongside the *Peter and Paul,* and Peter and his men climbed aboard. The yacht was pitching. Shafirov felt a wave of nausea and surreptitiously turned away. The jester Vytashchi was strolling along the dike, as bulky as a wardrobe. The black dwarf Kabysdokh, imitating Vytashchi's clumsy movements, stuck his pointy, feline tongue out at Shafirov.

The mock battle was coming to an end. Peter's flag was raised on the frigate. Shafirov sighed with relief and got up from his chair. He could go congratulate the czar.

Peter was in a rage. He broke the heavy carved chair, threw the hapless dwarf Kabysdokh out the window when he made the mistake of coming out of his box, and smashed Menshikov's nose with his fist when he tried to console him. The congratulations on his victory were postponed; the congratulators now huddled and whispered and made signs in the embassy guesthouse outside the czar's study.

The czar's wrath was justified: six Russian volunteers, noble ignoramuses, had made a poor showing in the maneuvers, especially in the boarding attack, and had responded insolently to the czar's rebukes.

"We no longer wish to wave axes on a wharf or climb ropes above the deep seas. And it's unbecoming to you, Czar; you're not a carpenter, after all."

Upon hearing such talk, Peter shook his head horribly and ordered the criticizers put in chains right there on the shore. "Into chains with them! Deliver them to Lefort!"

Now the shackled men were sitting in the cellar of the embassy palace, the wounded dwarf lay in the corner of the courtyard, Menshikov was holding ice wrapped in a cloth to his nose, and Peter was wildly pacing his study from wall to wall in expectation of Vytashchi. They looked for the jester and master of the knout all over the city and at a run: the czar did not like to wait.

Vytashchi was found in a tavern, assiduously celebrating the czar's victory. On the way to the palace, prodded in the back and the sides to hurry him up, he joyfully told his finders about the lousy life abroad and how he wanted to go home to Moscow. The meat had no gristle here—you couldn't even chew it like real meat, and the water was too sweet, and they didn't even bake rye bread here. . . . No one ever listened to Vytashchi unless there was extreme need or they were forced to—and so he took advantage of the situation.

As soon as he saw the czar, Vytashchi grew frightened. The pieces of the broken chair lay on the floor, and with a creepy sensation the master of the knout realized that a heavy leg of fumed oak could break a skull. Vytashchi hung back in the doorway, afraid to step into the room, close to Peter.

"Get carpenters," the czar said, with a whistle in his breath, "and have them build a scaffold by tomorrow, here in the courtyard. . . . What's the matter with you?"

"Fear," Vytashchi admitted.

"Ah." The czar suddenly smiled and laughed. "Tomorrow before lunch you will bring the fools out of the cellar and chop off their heads, so that others will not follow their example. Go, take care of it! And tell the people waiting outside to come in: it's allowed."

The congratulators poured in noisily and swamped the study. Everyone spoke at once, unwilling to give primacy to the others. Peter smiled and glowed.

Against the far wall, behind the congratulators, stood a muscular, well-built young man in sailor clothes. In his strongly tanned or naturally dusky face showed large dark eyes, like black stones, surrounded by soft lashes. His hands were small, strong, and also dark. His whole demeanor—his gaze, his sensitive, wary pose, the gold bracelet with a blue stone around his thin, almost fragile wrist—was imbued with something exotic, foreign. He was modest but not shy, and his modesty seemed put on rather than natural. It was hard to place him: a Persian or Armenian perhaps.

Peter noticed him over the sea of heads and beckoned. The young man came over, moving with the agility of an animal, and bowed without bending his back.

"You ordered me to appear, Russian Sovereign," he said in Dutch.

"You're the sailor from the *Peter and Paul*?" Peter asked, staring at the man with interest. "Are you the one who pushed my assistant into the sea during the boarding attack?"

The young man gave a slight nod of assent.

"Here's a taler," said Peter, taking the coin out of his purse. "You're a good seaman, you fought well. . . . Have you been one long?"

"With the Dutch, two years. Before that I was a ship's boy on a Portuguese pirate's brig, in the South Seas."

The congratulators grew quiet and stared at the young pirate, some with curiosity, some with horror. Peter breathed noisily and happily.

"Then you're Portuguese?" he continued his questions. "Will you come serve me?"

"I'm Sephardic," the young man said, and the czar's brows moved up questioningly. "Antoine Divier, Portuguese Jew. I'll come serve you."

Snorting in satisfaction, Peter sought out Shafirov with his eyes, called him over, and asked in Russian, "He's a Yid? Talk to him in your tongue."

"Sh'ma Yisrael . . ." Shafirov said drily: he did not like being reminded publicly of his Jewish ancestry.

". . . adonoi elohenu adonai echad," Divier responded by rote.

The onlookers listened tensely.

"Well?" Peter demanded impatiently. "Is the pirate a Yid?" He relished the word *pirate*.

"Yes, without doubt," Shafirov confirmed. And added, not without solemnity, "I tested him."

"And have you been a pirate long?" Peter had switched back to Dutch.

"Six years, Sovereign," said Divier, as if talking about the most ordinary things. "Since I was a child. I know that work well." It was hard to tell from his response which work he meant: sailing or piracy.

Suddenly Peter put both hands on Divier's shoulders and felt the striated, rock-hard flesh beneath his fingers and the sailor's jacket.

"Is your hand steady?" asked Peter, staring into Divier's eyes.

"It's steady, Sovereign."

"I may give you good work, Anton Divier," the czar said, using the Russian *Anton* instead of *Antoine.* "Very good work."

Menshikov pushed his way through the crowd to Peter. His nose was swollen but no longer bleeding. The czar gave him a tender look.

"Nicholas Witsen asks to see you," Menshikov reported. "He has two underburgomasters with him. Do you permit him, *Min Her*? They're out in the courtyard."

"Let them in," said Peter and thought about those one hundred thousand gulden: maybe he should accept them?

His black stick ringing solidly on the white floor, Witsen entered the study. The crowd parted. The underburgomasters in black caftans stood behind him like wings; this was solemn.

"Your Majesty," Witsen said and coughed into his hand, "has ordered six young men to be executed tomorrow morning. I beg of you: do not do this, Your Majesty!"

"What's it to you?" Peter shouted, turning red. "They are my men!"

"Do not do this in Amsterdam," Witsen repeated.

"They *may* deserve death—but here people are not executed without a court hearing. Such hurried execution could cause talk that would be unpleasant for you, Your Majesty, and for the whole Russian embassy."

Stepping lightly, Lefort entered the room. Meeting the czar's eyes, he smiled understandingly and heartily.

"Here's the ambassador," Peter said, indicating Lefort. "Have you spoken with him, Witsen?"

"He did," Lefort said confidentially, coming over. "There will be a scandal, Your Majesty. They don't understand here: the people are out of hand, they don't know authority."

"They don't know the knout," Peter grumbled and turned to Witsen. "That's what you should have said, that you have your own customs here, instead of all this do they deserve it or not. . . . They deserve it, Nicholas, and they should be executed for the greater good!"

"Then send them to Russia, Your Majesty," Witsen said. "Execute them there."

"Let them remain here for now," Peter decided. "I wasted money on them. Anton!" He sought Divier in the crowd. "Set them to work tomorrow for Master Paul, the shipbuilder, and watch them like a hawk. Watch them!"

And then, later, when Witsen had left with Lefort and the congratulators had departed, Peter kept Divier and said once more, "For now your work is to watch, Anton. You won't be able to turn those rags"—the czar kicked the floor vigorously, for the bound criticizers were down there in the cellar—"into pirates. But I want to knock the nonsense and free thinking out of them with hard work; the lesson will be for their own good. . . . And you," he asked with harsh curiosity, squinting at Divier, "would you have executed them?"

"I would have," Divier said unhesitatingly. He sensed that this was the answer the Russian czar expected of him, and he saw no reason to give another. He did not know why the Russians were in the cellar, nor did it interest him in the least. What were they to him—relatives, acquaintances? They were put there, and there they sat. They could be executed, or better still, set to hard labor—as on the pirate island of the Holy Infant, where under heavy guard prisoners felled tropical forests, built bastions and houses.

"A soldier must do what an officer tells him," Peter said, staring off into a corner. "The people, what the czar commands. Then there will be good and benefit for the homeland. . . . But one lousy sheep spoils the whole herd!" Peter kicked the floor angrily once more. "That sheep has to be torn to pieces in public! Remember that, Anton Divier!"

"I will, sire," Divier said and bowed his fine head.

III

A Jewish Joke

1698

Above wintry London glowed an astonishingly pure, silvery sky. The corridors of stone streets were clear and resonant, and the square in front of the Royal Mint rang beneath the wheels of the occasional early morning carriages as if it had been cast in metal.

Shivering in the cold, the warden of the mint threw off his nightshirt, blew on his numb fingers, sat up on the edge of the bed, and pulled stockings over his stiffened legs. His stomach made it hard to bend over, and he groaned and panted. He saw no sense in wearing stockings—they gave almost no warmth, tore easily, cost a lot, and it was time-consuming and disgusting to pull them on every morning—but he could not refuse to wear them: he would be considered completely mad, and perhaps fired. Leibniz, for one, would be glad of that. Damn that Leibniz!

Finished at last with the stockings, he rose heavily from

the bed, put on wide breeches and a baggy coat, and straightened slowly to his full, short height.

"Leibniz is a scoundrel, a blackguard, and a thief!" the warden said out loud.

For many years now he had said that phrase every morning—just as he pulled on his stockings.

The warden looked older than his fifty-six years: he was jaundiced, sick, and lonely. His lifelong argument with Leibniz had cost him his health and now infuriated him out of habit; if Leibniz had had a fatal stroke, the warden of the mint would have felt robbed. Of course, there was no point in dreaming of a stroke: that damned Leibniz was hale and hearty.

Once he was dressed, the warden laughed grimly and clapped his hands. No one appeared, just as he had expected. Then, picking up a hollow, thin-walled brass ball that he had once used in an experiment on free-falling bodies, he went from his bedroom to his living room, opened the door, and carefully set the ball rolling down the narrow stone stairs that led to the first floor. The house was filled with a cascading brass racket, to which the warden listened with satisfaction.

A short time later a sleepy servant came up to the living room with a bowl of oatmeal and a pitcher of milk on a tray. In his free hand the servant carried the brass ball, which he placed, under the warden's eagle eye, in exactly the same spot from which it had been picked up.

On the tray beneath the bowl, the warden discovered a letter on expensive paper. It was from Charles Montague, the enterprising relative of his late wife who had obtained this royal appointment, this house, and this foolish servant who had brought the ball, the oatmeal, and the letter from Charles Montague. Charles Montague-appointment-house-servant-ball-oatmeal-letter from Charles Montague-Charles Montague-appointment-house. . . . As he swallowed the porridge, the warden angrily shook his slightly spinning head: nonsense, slippery brilliant nonsense—a circular connection between the ball, the foolish servant, and the enterprising relative of his wife. A connection between animate and inanimate objects, between cause and effect.

"My dear Sir Isaac Newton," wrote Montague, "I beg you not to refuse me a favor: to receive the Russian czar Peter, who is traveling incognito and who has expressed an interest in the achievements of our sciences. Do not be annoyed or confused by the peculiarities of the monarch's behavior—I have been told that he is trying to appear simpler than he is. This undoubtedly is a simpleminded Asiatic trick and one must be prepared for it."

Spoon poised in the air, Newton mused, Why was Montague, an enterprising man, sending him an Asiatic Russian czar, and a strange one to boot? In Russia, as it was known, there were no scientists and no science. Maybe it had to do with politics, and his relative was planning to line his pockets? Or maybe this strange czar was no czar at all but an impostor and adventurer, who would ask to see the machines and then rob the mint, and he, Isaac Newton, would be accused of being a conspirator? Maybe, maybe. . . . He should not rule out the possibility of this being a plot of that damned Leibniz, who sent the Asian, with Montague acting as his intermediary. Montague, by the way, always avoided a direct response to the question: who was first to discover and study infinitesimal quantities, Newton or Leibniz?

In the end Newton doubted that Leibniz had planned this conspiracy, and he angrily finished drinking the milk and got up from the table. The coming visit upset him; without resorting to the noisy ball, he called his servant. And while the servant moved indolently (damned servant! damned mint!

damned Charles Montague!) to clean up the room, Newton stayed at the window, peering out on the street through the cold glass in rhomboid lead frames. He had no idea what he would talk about with the Russian czar, but he was eager to take a look at him. Catching himself with this desire, Newton pressed his forehead against the glass and smiled: that meant nothing human was alien to him, that meant his enemies were lying when they told everyone in the world that he had gone mad ages ago and that all his discoveries were the fruit of an inflamed brain and not worth a plugged nickel. With the exception of course of those that the bandit Leibniz ascribed to himself. And Houck too.

The visitors arrived in a seedy-looking carriage with an unmatched pair of horses. Ah, yes, incognito, Newton recalled. But which of them is the czar?

Three men strode toward the house, a very tall one in front with a heavy stick, unbuttoned coat, and no wig. Looking over the house, the tall man spoke to an impeccably dressed fat man. The third, with a large, handsome face displaying an extreme degree of exhaustion, walked a bit to the side and was laughing about something. Just at the door the tall man turned, said something, laughed, and punched the handsome one in the ribs—apparently as a joke and not because they were fighting. A second later the worried Newton heard a confident knock at the door.

"Open up, open!" He waved his hand at the servant who appeared on the doorstep. "Well!"

The fat man, who introduced himself as Mr. Shafirov, spoke in English.

"My lord"—and he bowed in the direction of the tall man, who was unceremoniously looking around the room: table and chairs, buffet, corner shelves—"has heard a lot about your inventions in the area of the movement of objects; in particular of artillery bombs. We would like to hear your explanations—in a general form, naturally."

Shafirov was carefully choosing his words, intending this very evening to write down a description of the man who had discovered the laws of nature, on whose head they said an apple fell and prompted his scientific ruminations.

"And who is this gentleman?" Newton asked about the handsome one. "An expert?" He had not yet decided who was the czar here.

"No, no," Shafirov mumbled, unable to describe Menshikov's position. "He is just . . . an accompanying figure."

"I see," Newton said and studied Menshikov. He suspected that Menshikov was not an accompanying figure but the main character in this scene, while the tall man was his bodyguard. Shafirov didn't count at all: he was clearly Jewish and therefore could not be a Russian czar, even incognito.

"I see," Newton repeated thoughtfully, looking at Menshikov, whose foggy eyes were fixed on the hollow ball, the only object in the room whose function was hard to determine. Feeling Newton's stare, Menshikov looked up and smiled. Newton doubted his supposition: Menshikov had a folksy smile, not a regal one.

"Nice ball," Menshikov said. Shafirov did not translate.

Meanwhile Peter had finished his examination of the room and went up to the table, noisily moved a chair, and sat down. Cocking his head slightly and extending his arm with the walking stick, he stared without blinking at their host. He always looked that way after a sleepless night or before falling into a rage, but only in his fifth decade would it become habitual. That's the czar, Newton decided. He really is strange.

"Well, let him begin," the czar said, nodding to the translator. "But not too complicated, my head is bursting."

"I told you," Menshikov whined, with a tear in his voice, "I told you, *Min Her*: after last night we should have gone to the baths to soak instead of to this old man."

"We caroused and that was enough," Peter noted grumpily. "I see you're worn out, Alexander."

"Why shouldn't I be!" Menshikov shrugged in agreement. "The girls are much nicer in Amsterdam. Here—how can they be like that? They're wolves, not girls. . . . Let's go to the baths, Your Majesty."

Newton understood only two words from the entire conversation, and those with difficulty: *"Min Her."* He was amazed to the point of fear and chills up his spine: if the tall man really was the czar, how could he allow himself to be addressed that way and by whom, and if he wasn't the czar, who was he and why was he here? Besides which, Newton was now certain that all three men were not completely sober at this early morning hour.

"Well!" Peter struck the floor with his stick. "Why is he silent? Shafirov, translate!"

"How do you like London?" Newton asked, cursing Charles Montague in his heart and desiring but one thing—for the dubious guests to leave as soon as possible. "You, as I understand it, have come from afar."

"We like it very much," Peter said. His throat was parched; he was thirsty. "Shafirov, ask him if he knows artillery work."

"Ballistics is not quite my field," Newton said, frowning painfully. "As you know, I am the discoverer of a number of laws of mechanics and optics. As for a certain Leibniz, if you have heard that name . . ."

"Can he set up our cannon system or not?" Peter interrupted, impatiently tapping his long thin foot shod in a crude shoe. "If he can, tell him I want to hire him to work for

Russia. . . . Don't mope, Alexander, my heart! We'll go straight to the baths from here, bear up."

"Can you call what they have here real baths?" Menshikov complained bitterly. "What can they know about it? . . . Shafirov, be a friend, ask him if they have good steam baths here or not."

Newton heard the question and turned gray. There were no more doubts: the scoundrel Leibniz had sent these blackguards, these hooligans, to humiliate him, to turn him into a laughingstock. The whole world was against him, he was all alone, but he would bear up, his discoveries would immortalize his name, and only bastards and fools did not realize that yet.

"You are fools!" Newton shouted, lifting his head high and regarding his visitors angrily. "You are base—you and your Leibniz! Baths! How dare you! To talk to me like that! Get out of here!"

"He doesn't want to come work," Shafirov translated. "Let's go, Your Majesty . . ." As he passed Newton he asked in a low voice, practically pleading, "Sir Newton, forgive me for God's sake, but is it true that you were sitting in the garden and an apple fell on your head?" He had wanted to ask that from the very beginning, but no appropriate moment had come.

"Out!" howled Newton. "Apples! Ignoramus! Leibniz's calumnies!"

There was no need for a translation. As he passed the hollow brass ball, Menshikov bent down and flicked his fingers enviously over its surface.

"What a nice ball," he said with a dreamy smile. "Ask him if he would sell it." He took out his purse and jingled the coins.

Newton turned from gray to purple. Flecks of foam appeared in the corners of his mouth.

"Ball!" Shafirov barked. "Can't you see the man is having a fit?" He sincerely regretted that the historic conversation had taken such a turn.

Sweeping down the narrow stairs out onto the street, Peter took a deep breath of fresh sea air.

"You have an angry master," Peter said, mixing English and Dutch words, to the indifferent servant hanging around by the door.

"He's cracked," the servant observed without any expression and made circles with his finger by his temple. "A long time now, ever since the fire when some of his books burned."

"Rotten old man," Menshikov added his opinion.

Shafirov controlled himself and gave Menshikov a scornful look.

Oh, it's hard to understand the Russian soul, thought Shafirov bitterly to himself. Take Sir Newton, he's a great man, and he didn't understand.

The amusing misunderstanding with the London warden of the mint did not upset anyone except Shafirov and Menshikov, who had had his eye on the hollow brass ball but soon forgot about it. The members of the embassy were wholeheartedly pleased with the new life abroad, so interesting and unusual. The only ones with real complaints were Vytashchi, who missed tough meat, and his short colleague in the jester department: Kabysdokh had been granted one-sixth the average living allowance, and he felt this was insultingly little.

Nevertheless, things were not moving smoothly for the embassy: Peter had not come to the West to learn how to handle an ax, repair watches, or dance in the Dutch style. The czar had set himself the goal of strengthening his position on the shores of the Black Sea—and since he was not strong enough to handle the Turks alone, he had gone to Europe to seek allies for a new anti-Turkish coalition. The Europeans were in no hurry to hitch themselves to the same wagon with Russia: the Russian czar did not seem a serious man, he did not inspire confidence. Besides which Turkey did not cause Europe undue trouble, and there really was no point in worrying over the fate of the Cathedral of Saint Sophia, which the Turks had turned into a mosque. The real issue was Russian interests, and there were no takers for a Turkish adventure on that score. The Europeans were much more concerned about the division of the Spanish inheritance.

Peter thought about striking at Sweden and coming out into the Baltic. He would not have found allies for that enterprise in gallant Holland or friendly England, while the ceremonious Austrian Emperor Leopold would at the first hint (it would have been impossible to speak openly with him of war on Sweden) warn Charles XII of the unbalanced Asian's dangerous ideas.

But an opening to the sea was Peter's life goal. Russia's rivers and ponds were too cramped for his sweep. And there were only two seas possible: the Black and the Baltic. Turkish and Swedish. The Turkish was well defended from Russian expansion; that left the Swedish. All that was required was allies.

To his later regret, Augustus II, king of Poland, high noble and debaucher, finally agreed to become Peter's ally. At private conversations over dinners that turned into drunken breakfasts, with breaks for healthful male amusements, the two young men formed the Northern Alliance. War with Sweden was preordained.

The day after the farewell banquet, after the exchange of presents and swords, flighty Augustus forgot the number of points in the unwritten agreement, their order, and in part, the contents. But the image of Peter remained—a marvelous fellow, merrymaker, inventive and rich. Peter remembered every unwritten letter, every unmarked period.

Romodanovsky had written: the Streltsy were rebelling again. Shein had broken the rebellion near New Jerusalem and the ringleaders were punished. The rank and file were sent into exile and to faraway garrisons. There was proof of Czarevna Sophia's involvement in the uprising.

"The family of Ivan Mikhailovich Miloslavsky is growing. I ask you to be strong in this," wrote Peter in response. "There is no other way to put out this fire. . . . Even though we regret to leave our important business, because of this reason we will be with you before you know it."

Naturally, he preferred drunken revels with the acquiescent Augustus, dragging him into the coming war with Sweden. However, he could not even think of a serious war without solving the problem of the insubordinate and undependable Streltsy once and for all. As he wrote his reply to Romodanovsky, Peter knew what he would do upon his return to Moscow: he would gather all the living Streltsy, exiled and free, young and old, and would hang them, chop off their heads, break them on the wheel. He would liquidate the Streltsy department. He would end the Streltsy business for all time: you needed a purge, a bloody purge of the nation before a war. Future rulers of Russia would thank Peter for this bloody lesson.

He had to hurry. Peter saw the purge as useful work, and certainly pleasant—but not at all easy. It had to be carefully prepared, so that it would be an all-encompassing action and an edifying spectacle. So that people would not just speak of it with horror, but be horrified just remembering.

As he approached Russia, Peter thought over how to choreograph the purge: through which gates to bring the Streltsy, which wagons to use, where to erect the scaffolds, where to place the wheels, the stakes, to whom to entrust the general administration. He ought to bring the grumbling boyars into the work: let them sweat for their homeland, chopping off Streltsy heads. And whoever refused could put his head on the block. . . . Purge—what a good word, fresh and stormy! Let there be a great purge, a cleansing royal storm.

Just before the border, in the Polish town Kolerovo, Peter made his last stop. He had put several days' distance between himself and the embassy, urging on the horses pulling the closed carriage day and night. In the carriage were his bosom friends, headed by Aleksashka Menshikov, food, a traveling chest, a two-headed infant in a jar (a gift from the English king), and also the dwarf Kabysdokh and Antoine Divier. Peter had remembered the pirate when he was getting into the sleigh and had called for him, and now he was glad. . . . Everything would have been fine if not for the Streltsy. The constant thoughts of the descendants of his enemy Miloslavsky spoiled the czar's mood, making his neck and head twitch. He would grow grim and not let anyone near him.

The little town lost at the very edge of flighty Augustus's territory was famous not for its vodka or its wenches but for the Church of the Weeping Madonna. This Madonna, according to experts, had been weeping for many years now, her holy tears dripping into a vessel placed to catch them, and anyone could dip his fingers in them. A fancier of the bizarre, Peter had decided to examine the church, and that was why he had chosen Kolerovo as the site of their stopover.

After the sparkling August sunshine, the church interior seemed as chilly as a vault and as dark. Dozens of pilgrims from neighboring villages and towns sang hymns and blocked the way. Candles flickered in their hands, splotches of golden light wandering along the black walls. Blinking, Peter grew accustomed to the semidarkness and strode from the threshold into the thick of worshipers. Menshikov hurried after, squeezing through and stepping on feet and hems. He was confused: what if the Madonna really was weeping? For some strange reason he recalled the stern face of his late father, Danila Menshikov, and got ready to cross himself—his fingers were pursed—to bow and maybe even to fall to his knees. But as he watched the czar striding freely, as if in a crowd at the market, he felt a sense of relief, changed his mind, and released his fingers. Shafirov crossed himself and prayed for them all. He did not move his lips, and so no one could hear his prayer: *"Sh'ma, Yisrael, adonoi elohenu adonoi echad."*

Coming right up to the artfully painted wooden statue, Peter squinted and peered. Mary's figure, life size, was raised on a pedestal, crisscrossed with parchments and ornamented at the corners with gilt carving in the shape of grape leaves, berries, and winged cherubs. Her severe, clear eyes looked into the distance, over the heads of the worshipers.

Peter turned and winked at the subdued Menshikov.

"She's crying, *Min Her,* Menshikov said, his voice quavering.

A tear rolled out of the Madonna's right eye and down the waxed surface into the vessel. A hubbub arose in the front rows of worshipers and passed like a wave over the church to the exit. Menshikov was beside himself.

"Wait a minute," Peter grumbled suspiciously. "What about the left eye?"

But the left eye grew moist and a tear rolled down into the bowl.

Peter gave the figure another close look—the folds of the robe, the nimbus over the head—gave the musing Menshikov a light shove, stuck his finger in the bowl, and headed for the door.

"She's crying, *Min Her,* Your Majesty," Menshikov said stubbornly, even reproachfully, once they were outside in the sun. "The tears just roll down . . ."

"I saw!" Peter barked. "The tears are sweet, not salty! This requires research! . . . Get candles ready, plenty of them—we'll come back in the evening. And a ladder!"

Before evening a dusty coach hitched to a pair of horses drove along German Road into the town. Besides its driver, the coach carried two men: Antip Gusakov, assistant to the czar's resident in Hamburg, and the Jew Lacosta, whom he had hired to work in Russia. Lacosta sat patiently in the back, on a trunk containing his worldly goods: two pairs of underwear, his father's Sabbath coat, a feather pillow, books of Holy Scripture and the Babylon Talmud. In his arms he held a child, a one-year-old girl, carefully wrapped in a towel or curtain. The girl wrinkled her nose and sneezed, and Lacosta blew dust from her face and chased away flies.

The coach stopped in front of an inn, the driver and Gusakov jumped down, but Lacosta remained on his trunk. It was better to stay in the fresh air with the child, especially since there was no bouncing or jostling now. It would take time before they fried the eggs, in that pork fat of theirs. . . . When bitter necessity forced Lacosta to hire out to distant Russia, he gave up on traditional kosher ways, thinking rationally that it didn't matter what a Jew had in his stomach but what he had in his head and his heart. You could eat matzo year round and not get a step closer to God. Having become free thinking not yesterday or the day before, Lacosta had been subjected to virulent attacks from Orthodox Jews, and if he hadn't taken this job they would probably have damned him, expelled him from the synagogue, and thrown him out of their community.

In the twenty-five years of his life, Lacosta had lived through quite a few unpleasant shocks, but this shock, unsurprising and, one would think, laughable by today's progressive standards—this shock would have been the most painful of them all: Lacosta did not want to fall out or sever ties with his ox-stubborn, strange, and unseemly looking people. "We were slaves in Egypt and You led us from there with a strong hand." Lacosta wanted to repeat that formula every year at the Passover table, and to sing the heartwarming song about the little goat—that was the extent of his traditional relationship with God. But his personal relationship was boundless, and sensing it, Lacosta felt joy. Jostled on the trunk, with his child in his arms, he did not look into the foggy northern future—but he mused that this road also led to the One who ordained it. And the kosher keepers of Hamburg could do nothing about it.

They had done everything they could already: they had bankrupted Lacosta's business. Thanks to them all his commercial endeavors burned completely, not even leaving ashes. Not literally, of course: Hamburgers respected the law, there wasn't a hint of arson in their city. The Jewish companies simply refused his intermediary services. He started a honey business—fanatical believers avoided his store. His brilliant, golden plan of payments and compensations was mocked and vilified—so now he was bringing it to the Russian czar. And then that horrible story with his wife . . .

In a word, Lacosta's business had turned off the main road and rolled into the bushes. And Lacosta did not see God's strong hand in that at all but only the hands of his kosher persecutors. The easiest way would have been to return—or at least pretend to return—to keeping all those funny and ridiculous traditional rules. But the conflict with the community had taken on a spiritual and principled character, and

Lacosta did not want to go against his principles. God would not approve of going against his principles for financial success. Actually, deep in his heart, Lacosta bitterly thought that there was only a one-way connection between man and God and that he could not receive any signals from Him. He had to seek approval and disapproval of his actions only in his own soul.

Lacosta's thoughts were interrupted by the driver, who knocked loudly on the trunk with his whip. Lacosta quickly got up, clutching the child to his chest, and clumsily jumped down.

Gusakov was agitated and businesslike.

"Well," he said, "well, here's what I have to say: Czar Peter is stopping in this very town! Eat up and we'll go: maybe we'll be permitted an audience. Whatever he asks, you answer sensibly; speak Dutch, he likes that. And whatever words you've learned in Russian—say them too. You tell him, Antip Gusakov found me to serve Your Majesty. And I'll tell him beforehand, properly, who you are and what you can do. Got it? This may be the moment when your fate is decided, and mine too."

What can I do? thought Lacosta, not without slyness, as he strode behind Gusakov, carrying the child down the hot and dusty streets, past the now-empty marketplace, past the stinking filthy pond, toward the church. If I were the czar, I wouldn't hire me.

The lancet door of the church was shut. A guard sat on a round rock near the wall.

"What do you want?" the guard asked without getting up. "No one can go in!"

"Get up!" Gusakov demanded, thrusting his chin out. "Don't you know whom we're here to see?" And with a flourish, he threw down a coin at the bewildered guard's feet.

The church was bright, lighter than it had been during the day. Two dozen fat candles burned with a steady flame, illuminating Czar Peter, who stood musingly at the top of a ladder near the figure of the Madonna. Menshikov, head up, held the ladder in place.

"What do you want?" Menshikov asked in a whisper, looking over his shoulder. "Who let you in?"

"I'm bringing a financial adviser, Your Majesty," Gusakov explained, his tongue suddenly numb. "From Hamburg. I am Gusakov, your servant, assistant to the resident."

Carefully stepping on the narrow rungs, Peter turned slowly.

"Financial adviser?" Peter repeated, looking down. "From Hamburg? What's that in your arms?"

"A child," Lacosta said. "My child. She's only a year old." He waggled his fingers in front of the child's face.

Peter laughed. His head shook, and the ladder shook. Menshikov held on for dear life.

"That's how you're going to Russia?" Peter had stopped laughing and questioned him sharply, angrily. "You're dragging a child around with you? Where's her mother?"

"She ran off, Your Majesty, because I was unlucky and lost all my money," Lacosta said with a sigh. "It was such a blow. . . . But just look what a marvelous child she is, what a perfect child!" He took a step toward the ladder and lifted the girl up higher for the czar to see. His tight-fitting traveling costume stretched on his back; the old threads could not take the strain, and the fabric separated under his arms.

Menshikov snorted, and Peter laughed once more.

"She did the right thing, leaving you, if you're such a fool," Peter said. "Put down your arms, or you'll lose your pants, too. . . . So what kind of advice do you want to give me, if you couldn't give yourself advice? Do you think that only fools live in Russia, stupider than you? Or am I supposed to pay just because you're a German?"

"He's a Yid, Your Majesty," Gusakov spoke up. "He has a Yid plan, a financial one."

"So," Peter said, nodding his head. "So . . . What's the matter with you, are you all mad? Or are you here to drive me crazy? A Jew with a child, a wife leaves a fool, some sort of plan. . . . I'm not in the mood for laughter today." His thoughts returned to the Streltsy, and the great purge, and the fact that he would need a lot of money. "Well, what's this plan of yours? Be brief."

"The plan is simple, Your Majesty," Lacosta babbled. "But clever. Judge for yourself: every man treasures his property, isn't that so?" He paused briefly, and Peter shrugged his shoulder, as if to say, well, yes, everyone does, even a fool knows that. "House, cattle," Lacosta went on inspiredly, "wagon—the owner could lose any of these: the house could burn down, the cattle die, the wagon be stolen. A man worries that he will lose what he's earned, that his children"—and Lacosta gave his child a loving look—"will be beggars. This fear for his possessions does not let a good man rest."

Lacosta stopped again and looked at the czar, who was listening with interest. "We will buy that fear and sell it to our benefit. This will be a voluntary tax on fear, an insurance tax! Property owners will bring us money themselves, every year they'll bring it—say three percent of the value of their property—and if anything should happen to it—fire, flood, death, theft—we pay them the full one hundred percent. And they could insure their lives to benefit their heirs. . . . I made some calculations: the net profit is sixty percent, maybe even sixty-five."

Peter was laughing. His large, heavy body shook, and so

did the ladder Menshikov was clutching desperately. Peter's eyes filled with tears.

"You mean you think that a Russian will give you money," he said through his laughter, "before his house burns down or his cow dies? He'd rather drink it away in a tavern with his buddies! They may pay up in your Hamburg, but we have a saying: 'A man won't cross himself before the thunder claps.' You're alive, not stiff yet, and you're supposed to pay just in case. . . . You've made me laugh, financial adviser, whatever your name is . . ."

"Lacosta, Your Majesty," Gusakov prompted, smiling pathetically.

"Lacosta," Peter repeated. "Financial adviser . . . Whoever hired you should have his head chopped off."

Gusakov felt weak, as if he had been hit on the head, and leaned against a column.

"Not every house burns down, Your Majesty," Lacosta said, with his last hopes. "And floods happen rather rarely. . . . So we'll have money left over." He had the feeling that he would be making the trip back to Hamburg very soon.

"Yes, that's a real Yid plan you have there," Peter said, right into the Madonna's face. "A good plan. But it suits us like a saddle does a cow. Maybe in a century or two . . . Come on up here!"

Lacosta handed the child to Menshikov and climbed up the rickety ladder to the czar.

"Look," the czar said. "Is she weeping?"

"No," Lacosta said after a quick look at the Virgin's face. "Wood can't weep. A man can weep looking at wood."

"She cries, she does!" Menshikov spoke up. "Don't listen to Jewish heresy, *Min Her*! If the Lord wills it, iron will cry too!"

"Yes, but the Lord doesn't waste Himself on such jokes,"

Lacosta said with a wary glance at Menshikov. "Why would He want to? You think He has nothing else to do but create a circus in this little town?"

"So, she doesn't weep?" Peter asked in an instructor's tone. "Then what is this?"

"Water," Lacosta said. "They poured water inside. There must be holes. May I look?"

"Stop!" Peter said huffily. "I'll look."

The pinholes were found by touch. The czar pulled carefully on the nimbus, twisted, and removed the upper half of the head. The inside of the head was filled with water, in which swam fast-moving little fish.

"Now I understand," Peter said with satisfaction as he put the head back on. "The fish swim, creating turbulence, splashing the water into the holes. Aleksashka—give the priest three rubles: he came up with a good idea!"

Lacosta climbed down and took the child from Menshikov, who made a show of wiping his hands on his trousers.

"Well, what am I supposed to do with you, adviser?" Peter looked Lacosta over again. "Send you back to the Germans with your plan, eh?"

"Right, *Min Her*!" Menshikov agreed. "We have enough Yids of our own."

"Once in a deep lake," Lacosta said, gently rocking the child, "they found a heavy trunk. The people came from all around, and the prince came: they had found a treasure, gold! They just had to bring the trunk up from the bottom.

" 'Any Jews here?' the prince asked. 'This is our trunk, and no matter what is in it, none of it belongs to Jews. So all you Jews go to your houses, there's nothing for you here!'

"So the Jews left, discussing the meaning of their wise man's comment 'It's all for the better.'

"The goyim got undressed and began diving for the trunk

in the icy water, and many drowned. They finally got the trunk out, and everyone wanted to be first in opening it. So they fought, and many were killed, and widows and orphans wept on the hill. Finally, close to nightfall, they opened it up—it was filled with cobblestones and sand.

" 'Those damned Jews!' said the prince. 'They didn't drown in the lake, didn't get killed in a fight, didn't lose a whole day, and got home first!'

"I'm leaving, Russian czar, and along the way I'll think about the comment of our wise man 'It's all for the better.' "

Peter laughed, throwing his head back. His large, strong teeth glistened under his bristling mustache.

"It was the Jews who threw the trunk in in the first place!" said Menshikov. "It's so easy—the Jews did it."

"Just a minute!" Peter said before Lacosta could take a step. "You made me laugh, told me a funny story . . . Listen, Lacosta, will you come serve me as a jester?"

"I will, Your Majesty," Lacosta accepted without hesitation.

"What does he know of that work!" Menshikov said, pursing his handsome lips in dismay. "What can he do? What does he know? . . . What kind of a jester can a Jew make?"

"I know what I will do," Lacosta said. "I'll cry."

"Whatever for?" Peter asked, awaiting the answer impatiently.

"Because when a Jew cries," Lacosta explained, "the goyim laugh."

The czar ordered Antip Gusakov docked a month's salary: he was a poor judge of people, mistaking a jester for a financial adviser.

IV

The Great Purge · 1698

Lacosta was happy to meet Divier: say what you will, they were the same sort—he was a Jew, and a pleasant one at that. At the first opportunity the new jester trustingly told Divier all about his problems: the wife who left him, the failed insurance plan, the argument with the Hamburg Jewry. The former pirate listened sympathetically, especially to the last part: while stubbornly considering himself a Jew, he had no doubts about which was tastier, a rare steak or a profoundly kosher one, and he took out his grandfather's tallith and skullcap from the prayer bag only once a year, on Yom Kippur.

"Does it matter to a Jew how he serves a Russian czar?" Lacosta said to him. "Jester! A jester is really an actor in the court theater, a soloist. A jester has much less responsibility than, say, a financial adviser. Isn't that right, Antoine?"

"Exactly so," Divier agreed with military concision.

"Czar Peter seems to be a charming man," Lacosta pried, peering into Divier's face. "He gave me permission to wear ordinary clothes, and not an actor's costume. That is noble of him. I would have felt uncomfortable in a costume."

"Well, of course," Divier said with a nod.

"Will you be a seaman in his service?" Lacosta asked. "After all, that's not a bad job either."

Divier could not answer that question even for himself: he did not know what Peter was going to assign him. He waited patiently, without tormenting himself with guesses. He would be told when the time came. There was no difference in how you make money: piracy in the South Seas or keeping surveillance on exiled Russian ignoramuses. One thing was perfectly clear: the closer to the czar, the more money. Divier intended to work conscientiously and hard in exchange for the czar's largess. He realized how lucky he was: if he hadn't knocked the czar's assistant overboard during those maneuvers, he would still be clambering the ratlines of the *Peter and Paul*. Instead, he was traveling in a covered coach behind the Russian czar. Now he had to solidify his luck, fasten it steadily, like a sail. And that's what he would do when they told him, fasten the lines! He had the strength. . . . But he would not want to be a jester, not even for the czar.

The coaches traveled fast, and the czar grew noticeably grimmer as they approached his homeland. Kabysdokh was constantly around his feet, like a cat or dog. The black dwarf did whatever damage he could to his rival, Lacosta: he put beetles and caterpillars in his food, stuck his tongue out at him, and one time crept up, lifted his leg, and urinated on his shoe.

"Give him a good blow on the neck," Divier advised. "But don't mutilate him. He's a useless fellow and should just stay in his box."

Divier had acted swiftly in dealing with the dwarf, who had pulled a nasty trick on him the first day of their trip, sprinkling ground pepper into his snuff. Divier picked up the dwarf by the scruff of the neck and held him over a roaring fire until his clothes began smoking and the dwarf screamed bloody oaths. Divier felt no hatred and was not punishing the dwarf for his action—it was simply that Kabysdokh bothered him the way a nail in your shoe, not a very sharp one, does. He might have killed the dwarf, if not for fear of incurring Peter's wrath for breaking his toy.

Unlike Divier, Lacosta saw a human being in the dwarf, albeit a nasty one. Hitting him on the neck was not easy, if only because of his repugnance. Explaining something to him was truly impossible: Kabysdokh hissed and spat in response to any attempt at conversation.

"Right on the neck," Divier repeated his advice. "But not too hard."

"He's so repulsive, such a pathetic person," Lacosta said.

"No!" Divier countered. "He's not a person. He's just a trifle, for amusement. . . . And then, what's he to you? He's not family, he's nothing. Just take this stick and hit him on the neck, if you don't want to use your hand. And if he bothers you that much, you should get rid of him completely."

"But how?" Lacosta asked bitterly.

"Throw him in the river at night," Divier said with a shrug. "He's a stranger to you, after all."

"Better I just don't pay any attention to him," Lacosta decided.

The domes of the Moscow churches appeared before evening. The lazy August sun lay on the golden cupolas, igniting the tall crosses with the slanted bottom crosspiece. The dark river slid past the fortress wall. Low wooden houses filled in the valleys and the riverbank. At the very first city gates, a blackened and desiccated human head was impaled on a stake.

"Hello, dear fellow!" Kabysdokh shouted to the head. "We're back!"

"It's all alien here," Lacosta whispered, leaning toward Divier. "It could be Tatary, or China. And there's just the two of us."

"Well, Shafirov too," Divier said, staring coldly at the head. "He's one of us as well."

They did not linger in the capital: Peter gave orders to continue to Preobrazhenskoe.

The Streltsy were herded to Preobrazhenskoe, to the Secret Office, in chains, kept in cellars and dungeons. The miraculously surviving leaders, three of them—Artushka Maslov, a troop leader, and the Streltsy Vaska Ignatiev and Efremka Gagin—were in the torture chambers of the Romodanovsky house.

The czar directed the search and investigation personally. He practically never left Romodanovsky's—he was there night and day, catching naps and grabbing snacks, spending most of his time in the chambers. His diligence paid off: under torture the Streltsy admitted that Czarevna Sophia carried on secret correspondence with the rebels from her cell in the Novodevichy Convent and incited them to act against Peter. It was she who had started the rumor that the czar had died abroad and that there was no point in expecting his return. . . . However, the letter itself had disappeared, and Sophia, with a wild stubbornness that equaled Peter's, denied its existence. You could understand her: if Peter found the letter, his sister would lose her head.

In Romodanovsky's entry hall lived a trained bear on a silver chain. No sooner would a guest enter than the bear, licking his chops with his long, scary tongue, would walk over on his hind legs carrying a mug of the strongest vodka. Whoever lost his nerve or didn't want a drink was mauled by the bear, who sometimes tore people's clothing. When he came up from the damp cellar, Peter was glad to have a warming drink and wondered at the bear's learning. Once, when the bear tore Peter's caftan and shirt and scratched his shoulder for not being quick enough, Prince Romodanovsky ordered the bear taken away—but Peter countermanded him.

In the cellar, next to the torture chamber, lived another bear, a white, savage one. He was set in action when the rack and the whip did not work and the prisoners were stubborn. No one survived an encounter with the polar bear, as big as a wagon. Falling into his paws and his jaws was more terrible than the rack.

In undertaking the purge, Peter started an action of great scope, edifying and urgent. Streltsy were arrested all over Russia, brought in from all corners of the country. There was neither the need nor the possibility to weigh each one's personal guilt: Peter could not tear himself into thousands of pieces. But he would not entrust the questioning and torture to anyone else; he did not want to involve anyone at all in his relationship with the old ways, with the Streltsy, with Sophia. The purge had to be his own, Peter's Great Purge.

The czar called twice for Divier, who had been ordered to direct all his energies for the moment to studying Russian. Sitting in the corner of the chamber, which stank wetly of blood and shit, Antoine Divier watched without interest as Peter and Vytashchi pulled out fingernails, whipped and branded enemies of the state. Blocking out the screams, Divier thought about how rich Russia must be in people, whose lives the czar wasted with such profligacy. For each of these little men, instead of being executed, could be put to useful work at almost no expense: raising floodlands, laying military and trade roads, building bridges. A hundred such little men, with an allowance for lost lives, were needed to erect a large stone house, a thousand to lay half a mile of road. . . . Yet Peter cut and slashed, stealing from himself. Cutting and slashing, unable to stop himself, like a Russian muzhik on a spree in a tavern.

Having kept Divier half the night, Peter, barely able to stand with exhaustion, would send him back.

"Go, Anton," the czar said, using the Russian form of his name. "Do you feel sorry for them?" He nodded toward a man writhing on the rack.

"No, sire," Divier replied truthfully.

"They're rebels, thieves!" Peter shouted, his head jerking, and Vytashchi recoiled in horror from the frenzied czar. "They're all against me, all these dull, thieving people! I'll beat the nonsense out of them, I will! . . . Go on, Anton."

If the whole country is against you, thought Divier, as he walked through the night in Preobrazhenskoe toward the house allocated to him, then you should send every tenth man to do useful work, far from his home. And whoever thinks of rebelling or running off—that's the one to punish, so that others won't think of imitating him. Then in ten years or so, Russia won't be worse off than other lands, and the czar will have many fewer enemies. Otherwise, it won't work: you can't put everyone on the rack, and there's no point in it anyway.

Peter finished the investigation in a little over a month. Two-thirds of the Streltsy brought to Moscow were not questioned: their fate had been predetermined. In the course of that month, the czar thought through a plan. The condemned men would be brought to the place of execution in black carts, two at a time. Each man would hold a lit candle. The executions for everyone would be simple: chopped heads or hanging. This intentional simplicity, grim and drab, and the swiftness of death would have a powerful effect on the people: never before had Russian czars dealt with their enemies so directly—without drawing and quartering, without the wheel. And this had a terrifying innovation about it, the spirit of the times. And so that Muscovites would not forget about the Great Purge—and visitors would learn and teach others once they returned to their far corners—Peter ordered the corpses to be left on the streets and squares for half a year, until spring.

For himself and his closest aides, Peter chose Red Square. The day before the execution, a corridor was built—two rows of fifty-two blocks, each two elbows high. Peter tested the height himself: he got on his knees and placed his head comfortably on a block and gave his approval.

The morning of the appointed day, hundreds of black wagons moved from Preobrazhenskoe to Moscow. There was no wind, perfect weather, and the candles burned steadily in the condemned men's hands. Thousands of Muscovites, herded from all over the city, stood in silence along the road and crowded the squares around the chopping blocks and scaffolds.

At the Pokrovsky Gates some of the wagons were separated from the flow and sent to Red Square. An ax blade on a long, comfortably curved handle was dug into each block, white and redolent of pine resin. At the first block, sleeves rolled up to his elbows, stood Peter.

The black carts moved gracefully, artistically. The Preobrazhensky Guards pushed the crowds and opened a narrow passage that led through the square to the blocks, to the czar. He was triumphant and, it seemed, sad.

The first cart stopped at the czar's block, and the others stopped behind it. The guards quickly removed the Streltsy from the carts and tied their hands behind their backs. The candles were tossed in a heap, for lack of specific instructions.

Artushka Maslov, the squad leader, was brought to Peter, poked in the back, and had his black shirt torn from him in one swift move.

"Well, come on," Peter said softly, his cheeks twitching. "Get ready."

Maslov crossed himself slowly, got on his knees, and placed his head on the block. An ant crawled along the fresh-cut grain of the wood, dragging its resin-sticky feet, and Maslov moved his head out of the ant's path.

Peter hefted the ax in his hand and looked around. The crowd was moaning softly. The executioners, their eyes on the czar, stood with axes over their heads.

"Aleksashka, Shein, Volkonsky, pick up an ax!" Peter shouted. "Everyone will chop! You, too, Zotov! And you!" Leaning back from his long waist, he watched, without blinking, as his order was obeyed. "Hurry! Hurry it up!"

"Chop without holding back, sire," Vytashchi whispered behind him. "It'll go by itself."

He swung back, took a deep breath, and aiming for a hand's width below the nape, struck. The head separated from the body with amazing ease, and the ax dug deep into the block. Bending over to pull out the ax, Peter noticed the ant floundering in blood and knocked it off with a flick of his fingers. Then he straightened, took a breath, and wiped his sticky fingers on his trousers.

The block was redolent of pine forests and blood.

Someone ran up from behind and hauled off the kicking body.

The guards were dragging a struggling Efremka Gagin to the block. Watching the struggle, Peter turned and beckoned to Divier.

"Here, Anton," Peter said and handed him the heavy ax. "You chop! Come on!"

Divier took the ax and looked it over methodically. He could refuse, say the hell with it, and go back to Amsterdam. He could take a swing and lower the ax on the block. Just one time. Who were these people in black, what had they done? Whatever it was, they were foreign, not his own. His own people went to synagogue, shouted and argued there about God knew what. He wouldn't have chopped their heads off; his hand would have trembled. But these Russians were foreigners, strangers, as foreign as everything else here. Like the black head on the stake over the gate the day he arrived. Just one time! The Russian czar was testing him. If he kills his own Russians, why shouldn't a foreigner kill foreigners? Just one time will guarantee work, career, money. What, hadn't Anton Divier seen blood in his time, hadn't he killed people? But that was in battle . . .

"Well?" He heard Peter's hoarse voice.

He tested the ax blade on his nail and got up on the block.

That evening they celebrated Lefort's housewarming in his palace in the German Suburb. Peter drank much and was merry and kind. He embraced his host and then took him by the ears and brought his face close to his own, nose to nose.

"Franz, my heart, what's the matter? You seem to have been working since daybreak. You look bad! Are you sick?"

François Lefort had been sick for a month now: a metallic taste in his mouth, liver trouble, loss of energy. The palace, built of red brick, with high ceilings and marble floors, made him very happy—but a letter had come from Geneva, and everything was turned to ashes. It was from his brother, who sold real estate.

"Dear François," wrote his brother, not too warmly. "I

have sad news for you: our mother died quietly in her house and was buried in the city cemetery, in the family vault. Our entire family, all the brothers and sisters, and Jean, and Uncle Arnold were present at the funeral . . ."

In an armchair by the fireplace in the small sitting room, wrapped in a plaid, Lefort tried to remember who Jean was. As if it made a difference who this Jean was, in fact. Unable to recall, he grew very depressed.

"You are no longer young, François," his brother continued.

> You have spent almost your entire life abroad. We know that you have some savings and that the Russian czar patronizes you and has made you an admiral general. This astonishes us all: for neither as a child nor as a youth did you show any interest in military exercises, and according to your own letters, you were Czar Peter's teacher of Dutch. How did you become an admiral general, if Russia, according to our information, has no sea, and Geneva, as you remember, is situated on the shore of a lake? . . . This worries our family, and some of its members feel that you have become an adventurer.

Lefort broke off reading the letter here, ladled a cup of hot rum punch from a bowl, and gulped it down. So, an adventurer. And that almost scornful "as you remember." . . . An old adventurer. Well, why not? It was partly true. If his brothers, Uncle Arnold, and that mysterious Jean could have seen him after the Azov Sea victory, his triumphant return to Moscow: the carriage in the shape of a seashell, the silly triumphal arch, the drunken jig of Mock Prince-Pope Nikita Zotov—they would have been shocked. And if they had learned that their merry François, the admiral, had never set foot on a ship in his life—they would be struck dumb! . . . Teacher of Dutch, who procures for his young student the maiden Anna Mons from the German Suburb. And the grateful student bestows the admiralty on him and wants to turn all of Russia into the German Suburb . . . Who was that Jean, damn his eyes?

"None of us," wrote his brother, "including Uncle Arnold and naturally, Jean, can believe that you do not think about coming back to us in your old age, that in your heart, once so kind and responsible, there is no more love for your home. Come back, dear brother, come back! No matter what your savings may be, you can count on participation in our family business—real estate. Fortune is fickle and health is irreplaceable. The time has come for us to reunite and end our days in peace and tranquillity, near the graves of our loved ones."

Lefort finished the letter, leaned back in his deep armchair, stretched his legs toward the fire, and thought. The valet who came to announce the arrival of his first guests did not dare disturb him: he seemed to be asleep. But he was simply lying there with his eyes shut, seeing Geneva, and the mountains above Lake Leman, and his brother, and that worrisome Jean, whom he could not remember. How good it would be if his new palace were on the shore of Lake Leman, and not in Moscow's German Suburb! Illness had given Lefort a new sensitivity; with two fingers he lightly pressed tears from the corners of his shut eyes and smeared them on his cheeks. Then, wearily and bitterly rubbing his face with his large hands, he got to his feet.

Passing through the formal living room and the ballroom, Lefort came to his guests. The czar had not yet arrived, and the host, bowing right and left, listened to delighted comments and congratulations, and then went out onto the broad stone porch. Coaches and carriages rolled up one after another, and important guests, tripping on their long, formal clothes, were coming up the marble steps. Generalissimo Shein, Prince Dolgoruky, Prince Romodanovsky, Golovnin, the Naryshkin brothers, young Gagarin, boyars, Duma leaders, ambassadors . . .

Peter drove up in a two-wheeled car and ran up the steps, pushing aside the heavy noblemen. The czar had changed clothes after the execution—he now had on a simple German coat, black, and without ornaments or galloons. Next to him, sharp-eyed Menshikov in his crimson half-caftan, green satin pantaloons, and high curled wig looked like a luxurious prince.

They came to the table noisily appreciating the exotic fare and foreign wines. But when they were seated, they grew still, not knowing what to drink the first toast to, and wary at the sight of the large sheep shears that Peter put down with a thump on the tablecloth before him.

"Why so glum?" Peter asked, narrowing his eyes. "This morning we worked well for the welfare of the homeland, got rid of the contagious disease for all time. Now we can move forward, learning from those who are wise. . . . I drink to you, Franz, my heart, to your house, and to the fact that it stands in the middle of Moscow!" Raising his glass—a wide, low chalice filled with vodka—Peter looked at it in the light. The Lefort crest was engraved on it: an elephant on a shield festooned with ribbons.

"I had it made specially for today, Your Majesty," Lefort explained. "The elephant is 'fort,' that is, strength, the fortress. That's where Lefort comes from."

"My heart, I give you my eagle to add to your crest," Peter said. "The eagle and elephant are good together. It's beautiful . . ."

Lefort smiled gratefully through his tears. He was sorry that his brother couldn't see all this. And even more sorry, more bitter, that it was all happening in Moscow and not in Geneva.

After the vodka they drank Rhine wine, and then sweet Romany. They ate pork, aspic with pickled lemons, chicken drumsticks with gold paper frills on the ends. They had raisins, prunes, honey pastille, and Persian halvah. The ladies were getting impatient, whispering in anticipation of the dancing.

"Shein!" Peter called, banging the shears on the table, "come here!"

The generalissimo rose heavily from the table and walked unsteadily; his feet got caught in his long-sleeved velvet coat.

"Give me your hands!" the czar commanded, and Shein obediently extended his hands. Clipping quickly, Peter cut off the coat's sleeves, which came below the fingertips, and then cut the bottom at the knees. "Where can you see anything like this in Europe?" the czar said. "This is a joke. You have to expect misadventures all the time: you'll break a glass or dip into the soup. Save the cuttings, you can have a pair of boots made."

Romodanovsky followed Shein, and then the Naryshkins. They came without a murmur, silently. The sovereign mangled their precious festive garb, taken from family trunks, the clothes of their boyar fathers and military leader grandfathers. He cut to the quick, shearing off the ancient freedom of local princes and willful fighters. But it was better to lose clothing than one's head.

Kabysdokh the dwarf rushed over, grabbed the shears from the czar's hand, dove under the table, and began shortening the guests' garment hems. Peter laughed. Feeling the stealthy running fingers, the guests smiled fearfully. The black dwarf tumbled out from beneath the table and ran over to Lacosta, trying to cut off the collar of his caftan.

Lacosta caught Kabysdokh's wrist and squeezed hard. The

shears fell to the floor. Holding their breath, the guests looked from the czar to the new jester.

"Who is this naughty boy with the unhealthy skin color?" Lacosta asked loudly. Then he bent down, and spanked the dwarf. "A serpent lives in his heart."

The czar laughed, and the guests followed suit uncertainly.

"Dancing!" Peter commanded, clapping his hands.

The guests, looking at one another in embarrassment, got up from the table.

The court musicians, specially taught by the German kapellmeister Kleinmickle, played. Setting an example, Peter opened the ball. His partner was the pink and white German wife of the ambassador from Braunschweig. The ambassador stood to one side, waving his hand to the beat with an extremely satisfied look. Servants passed around *flin*—warm beer with cognac and lemon juice. The alcohol did its work: in their shorn clothes, disheveled and drunk, the guests hopped, stomped, and whirled the squealing women. A strange merriment, with a tinge of a moan, had engulfed them all.

Divier was dancing with Anna Menshikova. The snub-nosed red-haired beauty was as sharp eyed as her brother, as well as being big bosomed and broad hipped. He had noticed her at the table and had not taken his eyes from her, and the girl's eyes had kept wandering "accidentally" to the dark, handsome stranger. She was not adept at flirting, and her unsophisticated glances singed the passionate pirate with blue gunpowder flames. He judged her with a sailor's eye and came to the conclusion that he should take her on, without delay. And he did. He methodically looked from the girl's face to her high bosom and tried to guess whose daughter she was. Then the dancing began. Divier asked Anna, who was expecting the invitation, and did not let her go.

Menshikov, wig askew, rushed over, his hand on his sword.

"Let go of her!" he cried in a high-pitched voice. "What are you holding her for! That's not for you!"

Divier saw that Peter was coming over, and he did not let go.

"What's going on here?" Peter asked, bringing his short eyebrows together. "Why aren't you dancing?"

"But this is my sister, *Min Her*!" Menshikov cried indignantly. "It's Anna! I won't let any Jew . . ."

"He's not any Jew," Peter interrupted. "He is my adviser on affairs of secret police, Anton Manuilovich Divier."

Beheading that man had been worthwhile. The thought whirled through Divier's handsome head. Here's my payment. This voluptuous girl is Menshikov's sister. Apparently, you can really live in this country.

Toward morning Peter left Lefort's palace and headed down familiar streets to the pretty little house of Anna Mons. Drunken Kabysdokh followed his master. Reeling and falling, he sang a bawdy song, and then grew silent.

"Well, where are you?" Peter turned. The dwarf could be killed by a dog, and that would be a shame.

"Here I am!" Kabysdokh called from someone's flower bed. "My stomach let me down, Your Majesty . . . Ah!" the dwarf cried. "A snake! A snake is coming out of me! Sire!"

After a moment's hesitation, the czar strode into the flowers, bent over the squatting dwarf, and reached out.

"That's no snake, you fool!" Peter said in relief; he was afraid of snakes. "Look, it's a tapeworm. Why aren't you treating your hemorrhoids? I'll cut out the lump tomorrow and teach you some anatomy at the same time: nothing but benefit. Just watch that you don't run off!"

Kabysdokh howled in terror, and the dogs on the other side of the fence replied.

V

Happy Island

1703–4

"But it's time to talk about the people!"

"What is there to say? The people are the people."

"Construction will require tens of thousands."

"Tens! Why not hundreds?"

"The country's full of strangers. They have to be found and brought here."

"Strangers! They don't know our language and they're thin in the gut."

"No one is stronger in the gut than the Russian muzhik."

"You're right, there, Excellency: the Russian muzhik is an extraordinary fool. You won't find another like him in the whole world."

"It's time, gentlemen, time to talk about the people!"

Divier sat in the corner of the room, away from the table, and smirked. What did "the people" mean? That gray mass that was being beaten to erect the fifth bastion of the fortress? The Ivashkas and Agashkas? Or that painted goose, damned Aleksashka Menshikov? There he sat, one leg over the other, with his "strong guts."

Divier didn't exactly hate Menshikov, but he was extremely wary of him. His attempt to become engaged to Anna had ended unhappily: they had set dogs and servants on him, and only the staff he carried and his fast legs had saved him from being torn to pieces. Divier knew that the master's order had been "Kill him!" He knew it and still didn't hate him. After all, could you hate a log for falling on your foot? You just chopped it up into pieces and put it to good use in your oven. . . . But he couldn't chop or stab Menshikov—the czar would have his head for that. And so he had to be as wary of Aleksashka as of a snake in the grass.

Anna had a pale round face and light blue, slightly watery eyes, always astonished by something. Her thin, silky skin stayed warm even in the worst weather on the Neva River, and that was pleasant and so arousing that it made his knees feel heavy. Her favorite word was "Oh!" "Oh, Antosha!" "Oh, my goodness!" "Oh, dear oh dear!" Antoine Divier had decided to marry her no matter what.

Sitting in the corner of the room in the czar's house on Happy Island, in the mouth of the Neva, he waited for the master to come. Peter was due any minute: he had excused his men and stayed behind at the construction site of the fortress, wandering around, pulling his feet out of the icy mud near the bastions.

His transfer six months before from Moscow to Saint Petersburg Divier took as a promotion: here he was responsible for secret police work and order and the construction of the new city. And even though that damned Aleksashka had been sent here as governor general, Divier saw a stroke of luck in that too: Anna lived in her brother's house.

"To spite the Swedes, I'll build a city and port within arm's reach," Peter said, as he explained Divier's future responsibilities to him. "Saint Petersburg will be the Russian Amsterdam . . . Do you know why I'm calling it that?"

"In honor of the holy Apostle Peter," Divier said without blinking an eye.

"You're fast, Anton," the czar chuckled. "You catch on fast."

But fast wits were not enough to get by in the city of Saint Peter, on Happy Island. Laborers adamantly refused to travel to the ends of the earth to work in the rotten swamps. The soldiers who were erecting the fortress walls turned tail and ran; they preferred serving time in Siberia with their nostrils torn out than lying in a pit here. Nothing helped: not Divier's heavy hand, not whippings, not executions. More and more Divier recalled his useful experience on the pirate island of the Holy Infant.

". . . The czar has given his orders and ours is to obey," came a voice from the table.

"You can't build a city with your own two hands. You need people."

"Where are you going to get them? Will you give up your own?"

The czar burst in, rubbing his cold, red hands. He came over to the table, picked up someone's wineglass, and gulped the contents down.

"It's bad!" he said when he had caught his breath. "Bad, gentlemen! If the sixth bastion is not begun by the end of the month, I'll have your hides! Every one of them! . . . Anton, the map."

Divier unrolled the map of the Neva's mouth as he walked.

"Here"—Peter jabbed the map with his chewed fingernail—"is the site for the Admiralty Wharf. Here—the warehouses and docks." He looked up, his heavy gaze beating down on the heads bent over the map, and his voice turned into a scream. "Where is it all? What are you staring for—this isn't the first time you've heard of this, is it? Where are the pilings? Were they stolen? Alexander!"

"*Min Her,*" Menshikov muttered, without looking up. "*Min lipste frint* . . . There he is," he said, pointing at Divier, "he's lazy and careless . . ."

"May I report, Your Majesty," Divier said, with a quick sideways glance at Menshikov, "the pilings, two hundred forty-nine of them, are in. One was burned in a bonfire because the wood was too dry. You can't see them because they are under water—the water's high." Then, bending down confidentially to the czar's ear, he said in a whisper that could still be heard by Menshikov, "Please give me fifteen minutes of your time, Majesty, for an urgent private conversation."

Peter, used to Divier's laconic manner, looked up in surprise.

"Well, all right," Peter said. "Stay on afterward. Let's have some wine—I'm frozen through. And how about something to eat."

Menshikov, who had been sitting with his head down to his knees, rushed off like a swift shadow to the kitchen. Thank God, it had passed, glory to Thee, O Lord! The best thing was that the unpleasant conversation about the pilings was over. A very unpleasant conversation, since Menshikov had sold fifty of them at a discount to a local Finn.

Peter, his boots noisy on the floor, strode to the bedroom, shut the door, and sank heavily onto the bed. His throat ached, his temples throbbed. He felt his forehead and realized he had a fever. His liver hurt too, and there was an ache and a sharp pain there after his fast walk. He picked up the silver-framed mirror, a present from Anna Mons, opened his mouth, and examined his tongue closely. The tongue was clean, and Peter felt something akin to gratitude toward it: good, loyal tongue, didn't let him down. Sighing in satisfaction, he pulled his travel apothecary toward him—a delicate chest made in England, encrusted with bronze and ornamented with an oil painting of a sloop on a canal—unlocked the central lock, and opened the lid and the hinged side walls. Clucking his tongue in thought, he passed his fingers over the caps of the silver bottles, lined in gold; there were sixteen, each in a velvet nest. He glanced into the copper mortar and pestle. Then he pulled out the red linen-lined drawers holding salves, capsules, precision scales, and surgical knives and clamps, and in the lower right, in a round depression, he found what he was after: a flat gold case, resembling a snuffbox, with a cobra depicted on the cover. Peter opened the box and flicked his finger gently in the contents—a medicinal concoction of ground wood lice and slugs. The mixture had dried a bit and was covered with a brown crust. Peter spat into the box and carefully stirred the mixture with a golden spatula. Then he dug some out and swallowed it without a grimace. The czar prepared the mix himself. His court physician, Blumenfrost, didn't want to hear of it, although he felt that it could not harm Peter's health and in certain instances could elicit a purging vomit.

Locking the case and putting the key back in his wallet, Peter got up from the bed, stretched, and then cracked his fingers. He went to the door and listened: they were speaking in low voices in the living room, and he could not make out what they were saying. He kicked the door open and came out of the bedroom. On the edge of the map on the table stood a chalice of Rhine wine and a large piece of boiled veal on a gray tin plate. Peter took one look and pushed away the glass.

"Vodka with pepper . . ." He picked up the meat with both hands and took a juicy bite, down to the bone. "Well, what have you to say for yourselves, gentlemen?"

"Seven runaways were caught and beaten, three died under the knout . . ."

"Flour, salt pork, and whitefish have been delivered to the main warehouse . . ."

"The sun sets early, the nights are long, and we light bonfires to illuminate night work . . ."

"In the last week, ninety-four soldiers died a natural death caused by bloody diarrhea . . ."

"Since last night the water rose in section three, the lowlands are flooded, people went up in trees and spent the night waiting there . . ."

"The wood fellers are working at half speed—they need more axes . . ."

"We need iron nails . . ."

Peter chewed and listened. Then he elbowed aside the plate with the gnawed bone and said, "Anton, you stay. The rest of you go now."

Stepping soundlessly, Divier slipped into the entry, shut and locked the door behind the departing men, and returned to the living room. The czar was not there.

"Come here!" Peter's voice came from the bedroom. "And bring the vodka—I have chills."

Peter lay in his narrow iron bed, a wolf-fur blanket pulled up to his chin.

"Sit at the foot of the bed or on that chair," Peter said. "What do you want?"

"We need people in order to build Saint Petersburg, Your Majesty," Divier began, sitting on the edge of the bed. "Tens, hundreds of thousands of people. The Dutch Amsterdam was built over centuries, and we will build the Russian Amsterdam in a matter of years."

"We will," Peter said, clenching his teeth to stop the chattering.

"On the island of the Holy Infant," Divier continued, "that's our pirate island, we also built a fortress and port. We brought people from all over the world and built it. It was no easier there: the heat was horrible, the humidity worse, and there were snakes in the swamps. People died, we brought in new ones, they died, we brought some more. . . . We kept them in barracks, under lock and key, fed them whatever there was. Reveille at five, lights out at nine. Whoever didn't work or worked badly did not eat, he didn't get anything. That's how we built a city."

Peter listened attentively, playing with his mustache with one hand taken out from beneath the blanket.

"It was harder for us than for you, Your Majesty," Divier went on after a pause. "Where could we get the men? Just survivors of sea battles or Negroes from Africa. But you have millions of men, and all handy. If you were to . . ."

"Well?" the czar hurried him on. "Go on!"

"Say, if you were to take a man from every tenth household and bring them here! I made an estimate: we could have the wharf foundations in by spring and the wharf finished by the end of the year. We'd make the warehouses of stone—we can quarry stone nearby, it's granite! We'll pave the streets in granite too, so there won't be any mud. We'll build bridges and palaces . . . I've made the calculations here—the construction will cost kopecks, because the material—the stone, the lumber—will be gotten by your people. And what do those people need? Plank beds, a bowl of soup, a barracks for five hundred men, and a lock for the barracks. Your Majesty, we won't be able to get hired workers here anyway, not for love or money! It's a shame, of course, every fourth one won't make it, on the average—but there's no other way: cities are built on bones."

Peter tossed off his blanket, got up, and poured himself some vodka. He drank it down, wiped his mouth on his sleeve, and asked, "How many people do you think we'll have to bring here?"

"For a start, about a hundred thousand," Divier said. "Keeping in mind that there will be deaths and escapes along the way."

"And by the end of the year, you say, we'll have a wharf?" Peter came up close and stared at the bridge of Divier's nose.

"Yes," Divier said, "and the warehouses. If we start in the spring . . ."

"Well, English freedom has no place here, it's a total waste," Peter said, his gaze unwavering. "If I put this in your hands, what will you need to start in the spring?"

"Allow me to build barracks, Your Majesty," Divier said. "Each barracks for five hundred men. Ten barracks make a camp. And then the work will get going!"

The work got going. They set up the barracks in November, the quarry in March, the wharf and warehouses in May, the markets and Governor General Menshikov's palace in June. Nine thousand men went into the ground in January, and in April, thanks to the sun, only seven and a half. Man isn't a dog, he can get used to anything. But in July, at the height of the work, swamp fever joined the dysentery, and a whole ten thousand men were dumped into pits.

Also, that July, a hundred paces from the czar's house, a log cabin was built for the jester Lacosta. Divier came and supervised the work, making sure the joints were tight and the rooms comfortable. The builders, seeing Divier, would spit furtively over their left shoulder and make the sign of the cross: "Unclean spirit! Lord, spare me!"

Lacosta and his daughter moved to Saint Petersburg at the end of the month. The very first evening, Divier called on them, under his arm a toy humpbacked horse carved in wood by the clever Zhamkin in the eighth barracks.

The girl was five now. Frail, with sad black eyes and a delicate round chin, she resembled her father.

"Hold this," Divier said, giving her the horse. "You're a nice little girl. What's your name?"

"Masha," she said.

"She used to have a different name, didn't she?" Divier asked Lacosta.

"Yes, Riva," Lacosta said with a smile. "But that name sounds strange to Russian ears, and I do not want to ruin the child's life."

"Is that a family name, 'Riva'?" Divier asked.

"Yes," Lacosta said with a shake of his head. "That was my late mother's name. . . . But what can you do?"

Candles crackled as they burned, and the girl played with her new toy. Host and guest stared at each other in silence for a long time.

"I'm so glad you're here!" Divier said at last and gently smacked Lacosta on the knee. "I'm working like an ox here from morning till night, and I'm all alone. . . . Now at least there are two of us."

"Shafirov is coming next week," Lacosta said. "He's a decent man and really one of us."

"Shafirov comes and goes," Divier said. "But he'll move here too sooner or later. They'll all move here."

"Yes, that's what the czar wants," Lacosta agreed. "You know, Antoine—he called me in recently and we spent the evening talking about God. That, as you know, is somewhat outside the parameters of my duties. And suddenly, he says, 'Anton is a fine man, things are going well in Saint Petersburg. But he's burying countless men. Is that God's way? Or does your God allow it?' . . . All of Moscow is talking about you."

"That I'm a villain," Divier said with a wry smile. "I know. But I serve Czar Peter, and Czar Peter wants to build a city. . . . So I'm building it."

"But those thousands of men," Lacosta said, raising his arms as if to ward off death. "They have families, children, maybe . . ." He quickly, anxiously looked over at his daughter.

"A hundred years from now their descendants will be praising Czar Peter for this city," Divier said. "No one will remember these thousands, no one will care. That's how this country works. And probably not only this one."

"You must really hate this country!" Lacosta whispered.

"Not at all!" Divier responded with alacrity. "Believe me! It's simply alien to me, absolutely alien, from my first day here. The people are alien, with the exception perhaps of one. I work here and that's all. If I didn't work, I'd pack up and go to another country."

"Where?" Lacosta asked.

"I don't know. There isn't a country for me where I'd be surrounded by my own people—like you, like Shafirov even. Of course, you realize that I wouldn't have settled you in a barracks for five hundred just because Czar Peter wants to build a city. . . . Actually there is one little island in the world where I felt at home among people like me, even though I was the one and only Jew there. . . . So, they curse me in Moscow?"

"They do, Antoine," Lacosta said. "And how."

"That's all right," Divier said. "That's better for the czar: they curse a foreigner, a Yid, and he is above it all. . . . And you know, I don't mind having all the pinecones fall on my head. It's, as you say, within the parameters of my duties. I get paid for that . . . And for this. I put some furniture in your house: table, beds, a place for your books."

"I'm very grateful to you," Lacosta said. "I was very lonely back in Moscow. You're right: they're alien to us somehow."

"You know, I'm going to ask you for a small favor," Divier said, frowning. "I need to talk to someone, face to face, tomorrow afternoon would be a good time. The city is tiny, and everyone sees everything. You could spend a couple of hours at my place. How about it?"

"Naturally," Lacosta said, nodding in understanding. "Man to man."

"How do you manage in that department?" Divier asked, lowering his voice.

Looking over at the child, Lacosta brought his mouth close to Divier's ear. "I go to prostitutes. It's easier, and incidentally, I never have to ask anyone for favors."

Anna came secretly, in a borrowed torn vest and with a plain kerchief over her curled and teased hair. She carried a yoke with buckets over one shoulder, as Divier had instructed: just a girl out for some water.

"Oh, Antosha!" Anna began prattling in the doorway. "If you only knew, if you only knew! I barely got away with all this masquerading! I took the vest from Froska and the buckets in the entry. Alexander Danilovich never takes his eyes from me, he's so suspicious. He went to Kotlin today, and I rushed to you."

Divier listened and took off Anna's dirty vest and handkerchief and seated her on the bed. There was no place else to sit, since he had removed the chairs to the other room. Sitting close to her, he slowly ran his thin fingers down her white, plump cheek, from the temple past her lips to her chin.

"Oh, Antosha!" Anna went on, bending her face to meet his tanned, seeking fingers. "You don't know, you don't know this at all, but Alexander Danilovich plans to marry me to Sheremetev's nephew Mitya. They say it's a brilliant match and very suitable for our family."

Her eyes suddenly filled with tears; she put her heavy arms around Divier and pressed tight against him, as tight as possible—you couldn't pull her away. "Let's go fall on our knees at the czar's feet, Antosha! He likes you, he'll give permission . . ."

"He likes your brother more," Divier said. "When did he decide this, your brother?"

"Last week," Anna sobbed. "He's already sent people to Moscow and he's planning to go himself. . . . Oh, what will we do, what will we do?"

"Don't cry." Divier licked a tear from Anna's cheek and kept caressing the nape of her neck. "Don't cry, hear me? He makes his plans, we make ours. He won't be able to swallow me whole, I'm bony. . . . Will you marry me, I'm asking you? It's important for me to know."

"Why do you ask, dear Antosha!" She let go of him and spread her hands. "Who else would I marry? Mitya Sheremetev? I'd rather go in a convent or jump in the river! He's like a toad, that Mitya Sheremetev, worse than a toad! Let's run off to the ends of the earth, Antosha!"

"We don't need to run anywhere," Divier said firmly. "We'll do everything necessary right here."

"And we'll go to church?" Anna asked, with hope, as if for a distant miracle.

"We will, we will," Divier grumbled, making a face. "Church or the devil's jaws, what's the difference! Now listen to me well: we don't have a lot of time, we must hurry. We can't run anywhere—they'll catch us and kill me. We'll lie down—here, now. Then they'll give you to me out of shame."

"Oh, Antosha, what are you saying!" Anna moved away for a second and then pressed even closer. "Alexander Danilovich will beat me! And think of the shame, the sin! How can I? It's just that you don't know our ways, you're a foreigner. Just kiss me, your silly Anna, and let's go fall at Czar Peter's feet. No, no, not there, not there, kiss me here, Antosha, darling, and your hand, your hand, move your hand higher, or I don't know what I'll do, don't, don't, Alexander Danilovich will beat me, he will, that vile Aleksashka. Kiss me, kiss me again! Oh, your hands are so cold, warm them here, on your Anna, your silly Anna. What are you doing, Antosha? Oh, I can't stand it, you're tearing my clothes, you wild man! No, Antosha, no, don't, it's a sin, how will we face people . . . No, no, let go, darling, I'm all yours anyway! Oh, it hurts, oh, oh, . . . Oh, Lord, that's so good . . ."

Of course, it's good.

VI

Tournament of Jesters · 1709

Divier fretted. That morning neither beef grease for lubrication nor chains from the free blacksmiths had been delivered to the Mytny Court. The sections of the Moika drawbridge were put together and lay in the mud along the bank like corpses, the construction held up. And Divier was late for his lesson with Lacosta. Giving punctuality primacy over the few other human merits, Divier chewed his dry lips, paced among the laborers from Barracks 17 in their enforced leisure, and kept checking the sun, which had passed its high point in the sky, and his gold pocket watch—a gift from the czar on the occasion of their victory over the Swedes at Poltava. The lackadaisical free blacksmiths drove him crazy. If they'd been living in Barracks 17, he'd have had those chains a long time ago.

Divier sent his assistant, Vasili Tuvolkov, to Anna and to Lacosta with the message that he was running late. Anna, pregnant with their second child, accepted her husband's habits and was sincerely grateful for such attentions as sending Vaska with a message. Lacosta needed to be warned. Tomorrow's tournament had been preying on his mind the entire month, and even Divier wasn't too comfortable about it. Who had ever heard of a court jester risking the knout! What barbaric tricks! They should have worked for a whole two hours today, seriously—and now these free smiths had ruined the day's schedule.

After Vaska returned—"The mistress waits! The jester waits!"—Divier gave a last look at the sun and at his watch and decided that there was no point in expecting the chains and the grease today. Vaska could stay and keep the men there: maybe it would come by evening.

Clambering up on a dry hill, Divier wiped the mud from his boots and headed for Lacosta's house. On the way he took a look into the spacious, airy pavilion built especially for tomorrow's tournament. Everything was in readiness there: a podium for the chairman of the Drunken Synod, benches and tables for the guests, and a stage for the performers. The prince-pope's podium was decorated with elder branches and the stage with fresh hay, sunflowers, and daisies. The artist Kruger had painted the backdrop with unicorns, magical birds, and forest trees. The left wall showed King Charles XII of Sweden in jester's clothes astride a goat, and the right wall Czar Peter in armor astride a steed.

Divier found Lacosta in an extremely agitated state. He paced the room, sat down suddenly, leapt up waving his arms, and sputtered, "Jewish fate—if it weren't for Riva—I'll kill him—"

"You can't kill him!" Divier explained gently, as if to a sick man. "You can wound him lightly, but better yet, just chop the knout off. . . . Well, let's start."

Lacosta opened the lid of his trunk and took out two broadswords. He handed one to Divier, who, delighted, easily lifted the heavy weapon.

"Keep your elbow bent!" Divier instructed, fighting off the advancing Lacosta. "Shoulder first, don't expose your chest!"

Lacosta, who looked as though he should be clumsy, moved with astonishing stealth; his thin body submitted to the inexorable logic of attack. Maneuvering and defending himself, Divier snorted with pleasure. The floorboards rumbled. Little Masha-Riva peered through the doorway of the next room, her fists pressed to her round chin. She watched the proceedings with interest and no fear.

"Not bad!" Divier pronounced, lowering his sword. "But you shouldn't get too carried away. . . . Let's take a rest!"

They went into the other room and sat at the table. Masha-Riva set a pitcher of gooseberry kvass before them.

"Uncle Anton," the girl said, "Papa almost killed you, I saw it myself. He'll kill that savage Russian tomorrow, won't he?"

"Shhh!" Lacosta put a finger to his lips. "We don't say 'savage Russian' even for a joke."

"But you said he was a savage!" Masha-Riva countered.

"Forget about that, little girl," Divier said. "Whether he's savage or tame, this is his country and we're just guests here. We can think whatever we want of him, but it is not good for our health to say it aloud. You have to understand that, dear girl."

"This whole idea is simply madness!" Lacosta said, wiping his brow with his thumb. "Gladiators! In our day! And what's so funny in that?"

"In our day." Divier inclined his head. "And what's the difference between our day and ancient Rome? Nothing! The same masters, the same servants. The same aims. The same weapons."

"Yes, yes," Lacosta said, squinting as he agreed. "Nothing changes. And it will be the same a hundred years from now and two hundred years. Well, there'll be a different czar, and he'll have a different Jew to be beaten."

"I think it was better in the past," Divier said softly and slowly. "People fawned the same way, and people were killed the same way—but no one went on about universal happiness and progress."

"They did, they did!" Lacosta interrupted hotly. "It's impossible that there ever was a time when they didn't go on about it! That's a hereditary disease passed from generation to generation. And every generation is convinced that it's done better than any other. And why? Only because the steel of its weapons"—he slapped the blade of his sword—"is a bit harder than that of fifty years before."

"The good old days," Divier grumbled. "The good old days . . . When people say that, their hearts feel warmer."

"Because the future is an abyss, it's nothing, and in that nothing death awaits you—tomorrow or next year. But the good old days are the past that you managed to get out of somehow to reach today."

"If you say that to the czar," Divier said, and automatically looked at the door, "he'll chop your head off. His God is Tomorrow. Well, Today too."

"But I did say that!" Lacosta exclaimed.

"And?" Divier asked with interest.

"He sighed," Lacosta said. "And huffed. He's smarter than people think. He said that the future is the past reflected in a magnifying mirror."

"He said that?" Divier squinted suspiciously. "You must have said that to him."

"Well, maybe," Lacosta conceded. "At least, he agreed with me."

"There's one thing I don't understand," Divier said. "Why does the czar need for you to go under the knout?"

"An experiment," Lacosta said with a wry laugh. "He wants to see the color of Lacosta the Jester's blood—is it red or black? . . . Yet I'm certain that he almost loves me."

"Well, come on," Divier said. He got up and picked up his broadsword. "Let's continue."

Peter appeared in the pavilion an hour before the tournament was to begin: to see, check, and correct. To the czar's pleasure, there was nothing to correct; he merely gave orders to have the hay raked into the center of the stage and personally drew a funny mustache on King Charles seated on his goat. After a lengthy explanation to the artist Kruger of why a funny mustache was needed to give a proper understanding of the picture, the czar sat down to play chess with Vytashchi. The jester and master of the knout had had an excessive amount to drink the night before and therefore, afraid of being late for the tournament, had spent the night in the hay in the pavilion. His costume was rather the worse for wear, but it still looked festive: red-striped yellow silk tights, red lace shirt with blue sleeves, and a pointy turquoise cap with an imported cowbell on top. More than anything in the world Vytashchi wanted to be having some hair of the dog that bit him instead of moving fragile figures on a checkerboard. His equine thighs jerked nervously; Vytashchi made mistake after mistake and impatiently waited to lose.

"If you try this hard in the tournament," Peter said, wrinkling his nose at the alcohol reek coming from his jester, "you'll lose your own back, not just a king." And he added in a lecturing tone, "You should drink for health and pleasure, not for the sake of being a swine."

"Why, I'll—I'll just," muttered Vytashchi, burping into his sleeve, "I'll break every rib in that Yid's body . . ."

"I forbid it!" Peter said. "The tournament is not for punishment but for laughter. For every rib of Lacosta's I'll break two of yours! . . . That's not how the knight moves, you fool!"

Vytashchi felt sick. He didn't know how to use the knout with precision, and he had to take the czar's threat seriously.

The invited guests began arriving and quietly sat down in the back rows, unwilling to disturb the czar's game. Only Prince-Pope Nikita Zotov, drunken not the first day and not the second, made noise just by arriving: the camel pulling his cart hissed and spat, and the bells on the spokes of his wheels jangled. But even Zotov did not disturb the czar: Peter won the game, pushed his fist into Vytashchi's forehead, and got up from the board.

Behind the prince-pope's musical cart came the jesters, dancing and poking one another: fat Shansky, skinny, stoop-shouldered Shakhovskoy in a deacon's brocade vestments and a cardboard golden miter, gaunt Pedrily in a brick-red Roman toga with a bunch of switches in his hand, and the snotty fool Abramka arm in arm with the female fool Glashka. Kabysdokh in the old-fashioned garb of old Russia—a long caftan, long-sleeved shirt, and tall boyar hat—kept getting under the feet of the dancing jesters, pinching and spitting, imitating the prince-pope's camel.

In accordance with the plan, Lacosta was part of the tail end of the procession, dressed in a long black coat and a yarmulke. The traditional Jewish garb, unusual in those days, caused animation and laughter in the audience. Peter laughed too, his head thrown back: this was his success as a director; he had insisted on Lacosta wearing the silly Jewish rags. Lacosta had resisted and even shed a few tears, but the czar threatened to fire him and send him back to Hamburg: he had to be firm for the tournament's success, and now, by the audience reaction, Peter could see that he had been right. And that small satisfaction was pleasing unto the czar.

The fife players blew into their fifes and the zimbalists plucked their strings. Prince-Pope Zotov climbed up on the dais, turned clumsily to the guests and, holding on for dear life, cleared his throat.

"By the authority vested in me," the prince-pope said, "higher authority, lower, and sideways, the authority to bring together and put asunder, to punish and pardon, I open the Saint Petersburg tournament of jesters. I, master of all jesters and fools, chairman of the Drunken Synod, accept this fellow"—and without turning he pointed his hand at the left side of the stage, at the foolish-looking Charles XII—"into the junior ranks of our drunken company. Ever since Poltava he's been crying and bawling, so we'll cheer him up. Glory to the victor at Poltava, our czar Peter!"

The audience joined in with unfeigned delight. Any victory is worth the sacrifices. Only the conquered weep over their dead.

Zotov listened to the hallelujahs with a severe expression and then sank into his armchair and whispered over the railing to Vytashchi. "Bring me something to rinse my throat!"

The jesters' program began.

The first ones to come onstage were the fools Abramka and Glashka. Stamping their shoes made of woven birch bark, they sang ditties.

My sweetie has
The cutest nose:

Room for nine chickens
And all their toes.

Don't go out with soldiers,
Don't let them kiss your lips,
Their bristly mustaches
Tickle worse than whips.

I wanted a drink of milk
I was surprised and how,
When I got underneath to suck,
It was a bull and not a cow!

When Glashka finished that verse, she winked at Abramka, to make it clear that he was the bull she was singing about. Then, without another word, she pushed up her sleeves and attacked her partner. To uproarious laughter they rolled on the floor, punching and kicking each other. Kabysdokh jumped up on the stage and circled them, trying to pull up the girl's skirt. She squealed and kicked.

Lacosta watched the fools with great indifference. He considered himself a jester against his will and regarded his position in Peter's court with an ironic smile: a job's a job. He had spent a long time studying the czar's tastes and never had figured them out—Peter could be wild and boisterous or quiet, thoughtful, and meek—and now Lacosta wanted only one thing: to be left alone by his colleagues, especially Kabysdokh. Watching the tussle onstage, he thought how he would behave when it was his turn: what he would say, what he would do. He thought about that to avoid thinking about his battle with Vytashchi.

The fools were followed by Shakhovskoy and Pedrily. Lacosta did not listen to what Shakhovskoy was saying but merely watched his face, his grimaces, the haughty look in his intelligent, mean eyes, the movements of his snakelike lips above the infantile bare gums. Heavy Pedrily with his switches looked like a jolly old uncle next to Shakhovskoy's elderly child.

"The saddest jester from the jester group," the prince-pope announced from his dais and shook his leather rattle filled with dried peas. "The Hamburg Yid Lacosta!"

Holding on to the skirts of his coat, Lacosta slowly climbed onstage and looked at the audience. One hundred and fifty people sat before him, happy smiles on their faces, expecting pratfalls or bawdy songs. One hundred and fifty blurred white faces. One huge white face from wall to wall, a smile slapped on. The best thing would be to sing something—just because his singing would be terrible. And that was just what that frozen, meaty face expected from him—a jester had to sing badly—and then the cheeks would shake, the chin move, and the eyes fill with red and blue tears of pleasure.

"Many many years ago," Lacosta said, swaying as if in prayer, "in the desert country of Maror flowed the black Sambation River. Nothing grew along the banks of this river: not a shrub, not a tree; and no one came near the black water: not snakes, not men, and only doves flew over the waves. And there were two lovers here, separated by the watery expanse: Abramka and Glashka."

The face moved its eyes over the two fools. The idea of the two love-starved fools sitting on rocks and separated by a river seemed incongruous, and so the pavilion rocked with laughter, and the Face, in anticipation of further nonsense, moved and scraped benches across the floor. Lacosta listened with satisfaction: he was hearing the rumble of rocks rolling along the stony bottom of the black Sambation River.

"Six days of the week," Lacosta continued, "the Sambation roiled wildly, tossing out rocks like cannonballs. There could be no question of getting across, on foot or by swimming, and the river was so noisy, Abramka and Glashka could not even exchange a word of love. They could only look at each other over the river, and there was honey in their eyes. They waited for the Sabbath, the holy day, when everything on earth had to rest, when the Sambation would rest and its waves would smooth out and its rocks fall to the bottom. And then they would be able to get across."

Lacosta stopped and waited. The Face watched curiously: what would happen to the fools?

"On Saturday the river calmed, and its surface shone like skin, like glass. And Abramka on his side and Glashka on hers approached the water with blissful smiles—only to remember that it was forbidden to work on Saturday, that they could not disturb the river's Sabbath rest. Then they wanted to send a message with a dove—but even doves don't fly on Saturday."

"And why is that?" Prince-Pope Zotov asked from the dais grumpily and suspiciously. He wanted to hear about Abramka swimming across the river, embracing Glashka, and the rest of what they would do.

"That's our Jewish law," Lacosta explained.

"Today's Saturday," Zotov countered, "and you stomped through puddles to come and do your work here."

"I'm the czar's fool," Lacosta said, turning to Peter, and bowed. "And the law is not written for the czar's fool."

Peter beckoned, pulled him close by the ears, and gave him three smacking kisses on the cheeks.

"An edifying story," Peter said. "Every man must realize what forbidden means. That would bring great benefit to the sovereign and to the country."

Divier, stirring in the last row, watched the stage and the hall. He saw the czar kiss Lacosta, and suddenly he thought that Peter would give up the meaningless and cruel battle with Vytashchi, would free his sad jester from that bloody joke. Lacosta sat on the czar's left and seemed to be waiting for his liberating word. Onstage, Kabysdokh was imitating members of the animal kingdom: a donkey with an enormous penis, a cat, and Peter's favorite dog, Lizavetka. After the dwarf came wrestlers: the fool Abramka, a sturdy man, fought with Pedrily, dressed in a bearskin. Next on the program were Lacosta and Vytashchi.

"And now," Zotov said, shaking his rattle, "let's see if Jewish wits can withstand Russian strength and shrewdness."

It strained the imagination to call square-shaped Vytashchi in his striped pants shrewd. Holding the knout over his right shoulder, he stalked the stage and stared grimly at his colleague. Lacosta stood on the left, with Charles XII looking over his shoulder. In expectation of someone else's pain and blood, the crowd grew hushed.

In one smooth, swift move, Lacosta took off his baggy coat, and Peter raised his eyebrows in surprise: this was not part of the plan. Lacosta was wearing a severe German outfit of gray cloth that fit him well. He held a straight broadsword in his hands. Vytashchi's grimness was replaced by a thoughtful look and then by rage.

"Choice of weapons, Your Majesty," Lacosta said in a high-pitched voice. "The knout doesn't suit my hand. And I, your servant, can't take the knout on my back either." Lacosta spun on his heels, and the audience gasped: Czar Peter was painted on the back of Lacosta's jacket.

Peter blinked and frowned. Then he shook his head and roared with laughter. The Face on the benches supported him uncertainly.

"That's clever!" Peter said. "No wonder you were born a Yid in this world. . . . Eh, Vytashchi?"

With his habitual hop, Vytashchi crossed the stage and took a look at Lacosta's back—and was dumbfounded. What was that! Hit a Yid and land on the czar! He'd get skinned alive for that! And aiming for the head was no good—he could miss; a head's much smaller and faster than a back! Vytashchi was unpleasantly troubled, and he wheezed.

The prince-pope gave the signal to start. Lacosta raised the broadsword, and Vytashchi hopped back to his place without any spring in his step. He swung the knout over his head with a whistle. Lacosta paled noticeably.

Running straight legged, Vytashchi released a deep-breathed "Eh-ye-ah!", threw out his arm, and cracked the whip. Lacosta struck but missed. The strap flashed past the blade, and the knout's tail wrapped itself around Lacosta's neck and chin. Blood dripped from his lips. The audience murmured in satisfaction as it awaited the second blow.

Seeing the blood, Vytashchi relaxed. What was so hard about that? So, he'd hit him on the head and face! One good hit and the Jew would fall down.

Cutting through the air, the knout whistled more confidently, more fiercely. Its black leather body became an extension of the torturer's hand. Squinting with his right eye, Vytashchi drew his hand up behind his back and then sent it forward and down sharply, bending at the waist.

When the whip came over Lacosta's head, reaching toward his face and eyes, he leapt at Vytashchi like a released spring. The heavy broadsword cut the knout right at its handle, which was decorated with blackened silver nails. The body of the whip changed direction, arcing slowly in the air, and landed in the audience. Prince-Pope Zotov, mouth agape, watched its flight from his podium.

Lacosta, brandishing his sword wildly, attacked Vytashchi. The audience froze. Divier, leaping over benches and legs, ran toward the stage. Lacosta lifted the sword with both hands and brought it down flat on his opponent's head. The blade knocked off the cap with the cowbell, then glanced off the head and cut Vytashchi's brow. Vytashchi shook his head, and large drops of blood scattered far into the audience. Lacosta, with a crazed, bloody face and swollen lips, was taking aim again, this time planning to strike with the sword's edge, to the bone, to the death. Divier reached him, grabbed him from behind, and forced him to drop the sword.

"What did I do?" Vytashchi repeated, his white lips moving thickly. "What did I do? What's the matter with him?"

"Jewish cleverness wins!" Zotov declared, and Divier felt Lacosta strain, trying to escape. But Divier held him tight.

Peter rose from his seat and went up on the stage in silence.

"The wound is not dangerous," the czar said, examining Vytashchi's forehead knowledgeably while the jester's face contorted in pain. "It's a joke scratch; it'll do him good. Russians are always beaten because of their stupidity: strong but stupid. We must learn military cleverness, even from Yids. Let go of him," he said to Divier. "Why are you holding the victor?"

Lacosta went over to stand next to the czar. The blood had not returned to his face.

"Well, well!" Peter continued in a good-natured grumble. "On the occasion of the victory at Poltava and today's battle"—the czar spoke in a solemn, raised voice—"I bestow upon my jester Lacosta the title of king of Samoedsky, with a salary increase, and the uninhabited island of Sommera in perpetuity. . . . And you, Vytashchi, get fifty for vodka—here! And drink it up with the victor, so that you bear no grudge."

• • •

The tavern smelled of sour cabbage soup, onions, and vodka. Lacosta and Vytashchi sat on opposite sides of a table, bent low over their mugs, their heads meeting occasionally; Vytashchi's head was wrapped in a canvas bandage, and a yarmulke sat lopsided on Lacosta's. They had drunk a lot; both were inebriated and in a warm and friendly mood.

"What am I?" Vytashchi repeated for the umpteenth time, gazing fondly at Lacosta's head. "I do what they tell me. Do you think I personally wanted to torture you? Not on your life!"

"Well, yes," Lacosta mumbled, resting his chin on his hand. "That's what I say . . . What they tell you . . . If I have a daughter . . ."

"That's a cross to bear! Not on your life!" Vytashchi went on talking, looking deep into Lacosta's eyes. "And here's what else I'll say: You may be a Yid, but you're a good fellow. Let's drink to friendship! And let's have a kiss!"

Vytashchi was a lonely man.

VII

Confusion on the Prut River • 1711

Compared with Poltava, the coming Turkish campaign seemed like a picnic to Peter. His Germanized divisions would knock the stuffing out of the Turkish hordes, the Tatar horse thieves. Riffraff, the hated sleepy Asians. Trample them, destroy them! Now that he had access to the North Sea, he would create a permanent stronghold in the South! And a short while after that they'd tear down the Muslim minarets from the Cathedral of Saint Sophia in Tsargrad.

It would all have to come to pass with dignity, European-style. And merrily. Field Marshal Sheremetev was dependable but slow; they had to reach the Danube before the Turks, not give them a chance to reassemble. Cantemir from Vologda and Brancovo from Multyana were birds in the hand; they wouldn't escape. There was little military benefit from those princelings, but their example was good and useful; their brother Slavs would follow suit—the Bulgarians and Serbs, they would rise against the Turks, draw away the enemy's strength, and the Greeks would lift their heads too. The prospects were brilliant, astonishing. The entire European south would go with Russia, to Russia. That would lead to inevitable riots in the Turkish army, rebellion against the injudicious sultan, reclining on his cushions. And the frightened sultan would betray the damned Swede Charles, who had dropped his litter near Poltava and slipped out of the Russian fist like a snake. Bringing the captured Charles XII into Saint Petersburg could be made a beautiful spectacle.

It was all so colorful and marvelous! And Peter's spirits rose and rejoiced, lifted toward such joyful horizons! Germans and Dutch are naturally more diligent and hardworking than Russians. But only Russians are capable of taking such pleasure in tomorrow's events. It's only for the boundless Russian dreamer that two birds in the bush are better than one in the hand. And that is the mystery of the Russian soul, so impenetrable to the Germans.

In the last few days before leaving for the active army, Peter was almost always out of breath, and he accomplished much. He replaced the bulky and obsolete boyar Duma with a compact and obedient Senate, established a tax and fiscal department with extreme powers. The savage Asians had to be conquered by a modern, well-ordered state—and it would set a good example for his descendants. The encounter fifteen years ago between Russia and Turkey was like a struggle between two steppe wolves, tearing at each other's throats. This time, everything would be different: the Russian army, trained and equipped in the latest manner, armed with cannon, fusils, and a secret wonder weapon—projectile, three-sided knives—would crush the foe in accordance with all the rules of advanced military science. There would be so many pleasant things to do after the victory, so many cheerful tasks: the formation of the Pan-Slavic alliance, with Russia at its head, the annexation of new southern properties, the strengthening of the Black Sea Coast, and the construction of a fleet. . . . On the day of his departure, March 6, the marriage of Peter and Catherine was announced. The wedding would be celebrated when they returned from their victorious expedition.

The maiden Marta, who entered Russian history under the name Empress Catherine I, had led a life of brilliant and daring circumstances, as typical of the "fledglings of Peter's nest" as the lives of Menshikov and Shafirov. The servant of a Pastor Gluck in Marienburg, in 1702 she became a living spoil of war for a Russian noncommissioned officer, from whom she was taken, because of her good looks and pleasant personality, by Field Marshal Sheremetev. All-powerful Menshikov took her away from the elderly field marshal not without resistance; and it was not without resistance—there was something about her that took tight hold of a man's heart!—that he ceded her to Czar Peter. The former laundress became Peter's civil wife, bearing him two daughters, Anna and Elizabeth, before their marriage was announced. The czar's marriage to a former prisoner of war, who had risen from the cart of a noncommissioned officer to the czar's carriage, was a horrible blow to the adherents of the old Russia of blue-blooded state marriages. But by the beginnning of the second decade of the eighteenth century, they had apparently come to accept their sovereign's decisions and actions as uncontrollable elemental catastrophes. If there was any criticism of the outrageous misalliance, it was voiced in a furtive whisper, and only in the dark.

Catherine, who was blessed with excellent health and an evenly merry disposition, lacked only breeding and virginity for the marriage bed. But Peter—the first and last straight-thinking Russian czar—was not worried by those flaws.

Leaving the government to Menshikov and the Senate, Peter set out with his wife to the south, to the army. On the way, the czar stopped in Polish Yaroslav, where King Augustus and his senators were waiting for him. All attempts to bring the Poles to joint action against the Turks were fruitless. The senators voted to adhere strictly to the terms of the Treaty of Karlowitz and not to get involved in this new war under any circumstances. Accompanied by the small cavalry corps of General Ronne, the czar left Polish Yaroslav without special annoyance; he had not counted too much on the Poles, who were totally absorbed by their own misery. Without their agreement, Peter was in effect freed of any great responsibility for them in this war. Hapless Augustus he pitied as a chum: the pleasant burden of glorious victory would miss his shoulders yet again. And the formal side of the business had been concluded decently: the Polish allies declared themselves ready for anything, and the great Lithuanian hetman Potsei took charge of their troops just in case.

On the road to Yavorov and farther toward the Vologda border Peter was brought pleasant, hopeful news. Prince Golitsyn had smashed the Kiev military leader, a traitor who had attacked Russia. Five thousand rebels were killed, the rest scattered or taken prisoner. Hospodar Dmitri Cantemir sent his ambassador, the Greek Polikola, to ask to become a subject of the czar, which he was allowed to do: the suppliant was sent a seventeen-point diploma and a locket of Czar Peter set in gold with fine quality diamonds. With Cantemir came the resolution of their problem of food: the hospodar would provide the Russian army with everything it needed. And even though the expedition would be a short one, Peter ordered more provisions to be stocked from the Budzhak Horde for another magazine, a reserve.

The czar's retinue was put together sensibly: there wasn't one extra person, just the most necessary. Even the dwarf Kabysdokh had been left in Saint Petersburg. This wasn't Poltava, however, and some thought was given to pleasant pastimes; so the jester Lacosta and the witty Feofan Prokopovich came along, even though the latter developed bloody diarrhea as soon as they entered Walachia. As for Catherine's circle, it was to consist of her favorite ladies and maidens and the generals' wives and companions, who had set out to war with their mates.

On June 12, Peter, Catherine, the ministers, the treasury and treasurers, and the Preobrazhensky and Semyonovsky Guards regiments triumphantly arrived on the shore of the Dnestr River and joined the infantry units of Weide, Allart, and Prince Repnin. A day later, after a well-organized general parade, the czar called a large military council.

The council revealed an unfortunate situation, and the opinions of the participants were unpleasantly divided. Despite the czar's strict instructions on collecting supplies and the special commissaries who had gone to Hungary for bulls and to the Ukraine for sheep and flour, the Russian army was without food. They did not have enough to last a week. On that basis Generals Baron Allart and Baron Densberg and Lieutenant Generals Baron Osten and Berkholtz counseled the czar to halt the advance and remain on the bank of the Dnestr until the intentions of the enemy were clarified—there had been no sign of them—and to give the troops a rest. Furthermore, the Dnestr was a convenient route for bringing in supplies, if they could be found. The most dangerous undertaking, in their opinion, would be to penetrate deeper into the hostile steppe near the Danube. According to local residents, that grim expanse would not have water or bread, and crossing it would take at least five days. And even on the other side the army would not find food.

Grand Chancellor Count Golovkin, Baron Shafirov, and Privy Councillor Sava Raguzinsky disagreed, as did Generals Ronne, Weide and Bruce, and Princes Dolgoruky and Repnin. They did not want to limit their marvelous troops merely to defending the river. If they got down to the last crumb, they could always obtain food by force of arms, and the victors would get the spoils of the conquered Turks. The Greek regions would rebel once Russian troops entered Turkish domains. General Field Marshal Sheremetev had reported from Jassy that one could manage to eat in the steppes. And finally, the Turkish forces would be half destroyed just from seeing the victorious army of His Majesty on their soil.

Listening to his ministers and generals, Peter laughed bitterly and deeply regretted that his beloved friend Lefort, the merriest and most selfless victor over the Turks at Azov, had not lived to see this day, and that daring Aleksashka was back in Saint Petersburg. Still, it was better to seek nourishment in battle than in an empty field. The hope for a rich plunder would satisfy a soldier better than a bowl of meat soup.

Everything seemed clear, and yet a pale cold worm was sucking the blood from his heart. Where were the damned Turks? Where was the Crimean khan? Where, finally, was Charles with his remaining troops? Peter suggested for the second time—though not very forcefully—that Catherine, seven months pregnant, should leave the army and head with her ladies to Poland. Hearing her gentle, implacable, and desired no, Peter was calmed; his heart grew warmer. He sent for young General Sharikov, known for his panache and fearlessness, questioned him a long time about hawk hunting in Tambov, and drank with him.

The next day at dawn, the Allart and Densberg divisions moved out into the steppe. A day later the czar and his ministers, their retinue, and the guards regiments followed. They marched without stopping until they were in the army's spearhead. The steppe, usually green at this time of year, looked ugly. Clouds of locusts had eaten the grasses down to the roots. The few Budzhak locals had run off, leaving the ancient burial mounds, like black markers, in the hot, wild haze. The oppressive heat and lack of water did not make the troops any livelier.

When they finally reached the Prut River, the czar ordered barrels of water carried on the horses of his retinue to the soldiers dying of thirst and singing hoarsely in the steppe. Delighted crowds formed around the barrels, and many soldiers were crushed by their comrades; others died from drinking too much water too fast.

The unification of the divisions of Allart and Densberg, exhausted by their crossing, with Sheremetev's corps took place in the field marshal's camp not far from Yassy. Weide arrived too with his division, followed by Lieutenant General Bruce's artillery and Brigadier Moreau de Brasse's cavalry. The deathly weary men jumped into the river with a war whoop and then flopped in the aromatic grass and slept long and deep. They cried out and grimaced in their sleep. Perhaps they dreamed of the arid steppe, or perhaps of bread and soup.

The abundant shedding of soldiers' blood was unthinkable without abundant generals' feasts. As they waited for lights out, the generals traded battle stories and edifying experiences over friendly drink. While the Russians had vodka and wine, the Turks most probably had milky rice porridge—but the contents of the military leaders' plates and glasses did not determine the contents of their conversation, which were equally of blood. The soldiers on both sides were totally indifferent to braggadocio and got a lot of sleep before death.

The excuse for the noisy festivities in the Russian camp was the second anniversary of the victory over the Swedes at Poltava. Behind the staff tents was set up a very long table, on each side of which the curious eye would have found one hundred and ten place settings. Peter and his ministers, generals, and honored guests sat down after a solemn mass and a display of artillery fire. On the czar's right was a place for Hospodar Dmitri Cantemir, and on his left, as agreed, sat Chancellor Count Golovkin and Baron Shafirov. Catherine played hostess to the army wives, who had left their children in the care of nannies. On the czaritza's right sat the noble wife of General Allart, on the left the thin, loud wife of Major General Ginter. The table groaned under the weight of meats and fish, a gentle breeze wafting the aromas to the sensitive nostrils of the soldiers. There was a wine steward for every six guests—a captain from the Preobrazhensky or Semyonovsky Guards. Each of them had three husky, handsome soldiers to replace glasses and bottles.

The czar alternated between morose gloom and sudden animation. Watching his guests eat and drink, he struck the table with his hand to obtain respectful silence, only to say, "Drunk but smart—he has two good traits." By the end of the meal, which dragged on until eleven, the guests were logy. Shortly before it was finished, Prince Repnin's aide galloped up with good news: the prince had obtained four thousand bulls, eight thousand sheep, and three hundred small Polish wagonloads of rye flour. Peter immediately distributed the provisions among the regiments and divisions.

The next day the participants in the feast lay around in shady spots with headaches, treating their hangovers with pickle soup and whispering the sad story of the duke of Courland, a charming young man. The duke had married the czar's niece that spring, had much too much to drink at the wedding feast at Menshikov's palace, and not treating his illness soon enough, died in the arms of his inconsolable and highly attractive young bride. A sad but rather amusing story for a badly hung over man: "He died, and I didn't."

The morning after that there was another party—to celebrate the day of Saint Peter, the czar's saint. The czar was tense, his cheek and head twitching, and he berated Mehmed, the Turkish grand vizier, for his cowardice and unwillingness to show himself. Then he left his guests and went with the jester Lacosta into his tent. The guests stayed another half hour and then quietly dispersed.

By then the foe revealed himself. Twenty thousand Tatars on horseback attacked the Russian advance picket—six hundred cavalry led by Lieutenant Colonel Rop—and tore it to shreds before the eyes of Brigadier Schnevishchev, who was stunned by the unexpected attack and did not make the slightest attempt to aid the Russians. Rop was captured.

This incident was not taken seriously, however; things like that happen. It wasn't even the Turks yet, just the Tatars. And they had lost only six hundred men. "The loss of the picket will merely fire our men to action!" said Commander in Chief Sheremetev. It was decided to cross the Prut in order to deceive and pass the Turks. But they were not deceived and appeared on both sides of the river, harassing the outside flanks of the Russian army with arrows and wild cries. Scouts brought conflicting information: either the Turks were nearby or they were faraway; either they numbered one hundred thousand or they numbered two hundred thousand. In any case the Russians had not quite eighty thousand men, if counted on the day they had set out. Regimental commanders reported that there had been significant losses to disease and hunger, if not to the frequent, lightning-fast attacks by the enemy. Before conquering the treacherous Turks they had had to conquer hunger, and Peter, annoyed by the delays in the expeditions, had sent General Ronne with fifteen thousand men into Central Walachia to find food. A final inspection before the decisive battle brought a new upset, which there was no time to think about: they didn't have even forty-seven thousand men now. Soldiers lay in pits in the steppe, and in lazarettos in the rear and at the front. They had to retreat quickly or to attack immediately. Because the attack route was unclear, some generals leaned toward speedy retreat. Peter hesitated, grew angry, and blustered; finally, retreat became impossible: the Turks descended like a snowfall.

The blow struck General Yanus's cavalry corps, sent by the czar to destroy the Turkish bridges over the Prut. According to the Russian scouts, the bridges were just beginning to go up eight miles from the Russian camp; but Yanus came across two completed bridges, with an avalanche of horsemen crossing them, just two and a half miles away. The crossing had obviously begun much earlier. The Turks were building fortifications near the bridge, and their white-turbaned infantry thickly covered the plain. By the time they were discovered, more than fifty thousand Turks had crossed the river.

Yanus gave the rear guard and flanks the order to retreat. The Turks, without ceasing their crossing, surrounded the Russians with a whirling circle of their cavalry. Under fire and arrows, losing men and horses, Yanus retreated. In eight hours his corps, hedged in on all sides, had traveled only seven hundred yards. At ten that night the Turks eased the pressure, and the Russians accelerated. But it was only at dawn, near five o'clock, that General Densberg's grenadiers arrived to cover Yanus's retreat. The retreating troops had brought almost the entire Turkish army to the gates of their camp. The guards regiments, raised by the alarm, took the first wave of the attack. Without ceasing fire or giving the Russians a chance to relocate, the Turkish army continued to group around the Russian camp, preparing for either a siege or a storm. The Russians took advantage of a break in the back and attempted to retreat—going from the frying pan into the fire: the Turks extended their left flank to complete a three-sided circle that pushed the czar's men against the river, which served as a natural rear. Beyond the river, shooting rifles and bows, Budzhak Tatars and Poles of the Kiev palatine galloped along the hills. A few hours later they were joined by the Swedes.

More than two hundred thousand armed men, with one hundred sixty artillery guns, stood on both sides of the river, ready to revenge themselves on the Russians. The Russians could either surrender or die. The Turks also had two choices: attack with all their strength or wait for hunger to turn the Russian camp into a graveyard. Even if the Russians managed to escape their grasp, with the Tatars at their heels they would be unable to survive the five days without water through the steppe between the Prut and Dnestr rivers.

Peter decided to die in combat. He ordered his generals to prepare for an attack the next day, closed himself up in his tent, and said no one was to be allowed in.

Catherine did not wish death for herself or for Peter. On her own initiative she called a military council in her tent, not far from the czar's. She invited the most trusted generals, headed by the experienced Sheremetev, and the ministers: Count Golovkin and Baron Shafirov, a sly fox. Instead of losing the czar and the army, the czaritza, a woman of lowly birth and practical mind, intended to offer the Turks peace on any terms. It wasn't shame that was important to avoid now, but death: state shame could be washed away, like dirt from underwear, so long as there was a washerwoman who knew her work. With a dead hand, you couldn't even flick a piece of lint from your sleeve.

They went to Catherine, passing Peter's tent as if it were an empty space. The czar no longer existed. The czaritza was the czar now, calm and steady, sure of herself, of her fate. And there was nothing else to be sure of here in the thunder of cannons, the moments of silence broken by the cries of the ever-advancing enemy.

Shafirov was the first to arrive, in a neatly cleaned German suit and tall wig. Catherine indicated that he should sit down, and he glumly sank into a chair halfway between the entrance and her chair.

"Sit closer!" Catherine said, watching this fat Jew with interest, examining his large face with its brazen, intelligent eyes.

With a brief sigh and pursed lips, Shafirov moved closer.

"You are a diplomat, Baron," Catherine said with her light German accent. "Our best Russian diplomat. Who, if not you, should negotiate an immediate peace with the Turks?" She came closer and put her soft white hand on his shoulder, leaned even closer, and added barely audibly: "Save the czar, Baron! Save Russia!"

"It is you who are the excellent diplomat, Your Highness!" Shafirov said, looking sideways at the czaritza's hand and gently shaking his head. "Otherwise you would value my modest abilities as they deserve. . . . The grand vizier will demand God knows what in return for peace." He finally pulled his eyes from the czaritza's hand and looked up questioningly at her face.

"Naturally, naturally," Catherine said, lowering her eyelids slowly. "We will accept anything but capitulation. They would hardly want Moscow, don't you agree?"

"Charles is the sultan's ally," Shafirov said, pursed his lips, and paused. "They won't ask for Moscow, but they might demand Saint Petersburg, to say nothing of the southern acquisitions. . . . But maybe I'll be able to bargain a few things back."

"Who can sanction such concessions?" Catherine asked in a businesslike manner. "Commander in Chief Sheremetev?"

"Only His Majesty," Shefirov said, shaking his head.

"His Majesty is not well," the czaritza said and folded her hands on her protruding belly. "As you know, he does not wish to see anyone."

Shafirov shrugged lightly and said nothing.

"He might have listened to Menshikov, but Alexander is far away," Catherine continued. "You must try, Baron."

"His Majesty will not listen to me!" Shafirov raised his hands as if to ward off the very idea. "You need either a military figure or . . . or someone who could soothe the czar in a human way, bring him out of his gloomy thoughts, I would say."

"If you mean me, Baron, then your plan won't work," the czaritza said, looking straight at Shafirov. "Peter Alexeyevich has forbidden me to visit him. And if Sheremetev shows up, he'll probably kill him. His Majesty is not in control of himself."

"I know who!" Shafirov exclaimed and stood up in agitation. "Lacosta!"

"The jester?" Catherine asked in surprise.

"He is a rather sad jester," Shafirov said, pacing the carpet. "Who else should the czar talk to at a moment like this if not a sad jester? A priest?"

"But he . . ." Catherine smiled uncertainly. "He . . ."

"I will explain to Your Majesty, if you have no objection!" Shafirov was speaking heatedly now. "Believe me, it's a good idea."

General Allart entered the tent. His wounded arm was in a sling, and his shaved cheeks had a clayey cast.

"Prince Repnin placed the main column under attack," Allart said in a dull voice. "Twenty-five hundred carts, wagons, and carriages were taken by the enemy. We are without food or gunpowder. Rop's wife and three children were killed."

"How horrible!" Catherine's round shoulders shivered. "And the children . . . What about your wife, General?"

"I don't take my wife in the column," Allart said dryly. "Madame Allart is here, in my carriage."

Pushing back the carpet that served as a door, Sheremetev entered with a bitter sigh, and the angular Yanus squeezed in behind him.

"Yes, yes," Sheremetev said, his pure, elderly eyes gazing with pity at Catherine, "bad news. Our cannons will stop in three hours. But, Majesty, we had time to pass out a new wonder weapon to our men—metal knives, eight hundred to each regiment." Seeing Yanus's skeptical glance, the field marshal smiled wryly and stepped into the shadows.

"If you gentlemen don't have the courage to talk about immediate and urgent peace as the only possible way of saving the army," Catherine said with a brief, pointed look at Sheremetev, "then you force me to speak of it to you. Baron Shafirov is going to the vizier for negotiations."

"On what terms?" Sheremetev said hoarsely.

"On terms that His Majesty will sanction." Catherine cut him off. "These terms will be kept totally secret until the peace is signed. . . . If you gentlemen can offer me a military solution, I ask you to do so now."

The generals were silent and avoided looking at one another. Count Golovkin, who had come in last, tiptoed past the military men and sat down behind Shafirov.

"As I understand it," Golovkin said, "the decision for negotiations comes from the czar."

"You are excused, gentlemen," Catherine said, avoiding an answer. "Baron Shafirov, stay."

When the flap closed after the last man, the czaritza sank weakly into her armchair, leaned against the tall back, and dropped her arms on the rests. Shafirov sat opposite her without speaking or moving.

"Difficult," Catherine said. "So difficult . . ."

"You carried yourself exceptionally, Your Majesty," Shafirov said in a homey tone. "I was amazed."

"It's only the beginning," Catherine said, without moving. "Go, Baron, find your jester."

Rising noiselessly, Shafirov kissed the czaritza's hand and left.

Peter lay with his face to the wall on his narrow iron cot—the royal toy of almost every European sovereign: it was unseemly for a crowned soldier to lie around on eiderdowns. He did not turn when he heard careful steps but asked in a hollow, weak voice, "Katya?"

"No, Your Majesty," came the respectful reply. "It's Lacosta, the jester."

Peter did not turn, did not express displeasure or happiness—nothing. Resting his hand on the table, Lacosta sadly looked at the czar's round head and matted hair. Near the jester's hand lay a piece of paper on which the czar had written in his clumsy hand:

> Gentlemen of the Senate! With this I inform you that I am, with my army, through no fault or sin of our own, but only because of false information received, surrounded by an army four times stronger, and all paths for supplies and provisions are cut off; and that without special intercession from God I cannot foresee anything except total defeat or being taken prisoner by the Turks.

> If the latter occurs, you must not consider me your sovereign and must obey nothing that I order, even if it comes from me, until I appear among you in the flesh. If I should die, and you receive trustworthy information about my death, then you shall select from among you the most worthy to be my successor.

Some time passed before Peter spoke again, without moving. "Are you still here? Well, speak or go!"

"Long long ago," Lacosta said, absentmindedly moving the czar's will around on the table, "a thousand years ago, maybe two thousand, this happened in a nomad camp. The people of the camp—men and women—took their flock to a big bazaar in the nearest town, a yellow stone town that lay in the foothills of a sun-baked mountain. It was an hour and a half's walk there, down a dusty road that wasn't wide enough for two wagons.

"Everyone went. There was no one in the camp except an infant and the harmless local fool, who was left to watch the baby, to keep him from crying and screaming while the parents were at the bazaar. The fool was a kind fool, and he was always ready to do anyone a service. No sooner had the shepherds disappeared from view than he took up his work with fervor. He sang lullabies, tossed the baby in the air and caught it, ran around the tent carrying it. The tent was like this one." Lacosta looked around the czar's tent, and then at the back of Peter's head. Peter was listening.

"The fool tried hard, but no matter what he did, the baby screamed and cried and would not stop. Then the fool sat down cross-legged on the owner's pillow, pressed the child close to him, and patted his head. The harder he caressed, the quieter and stiller was the baby. Discovering this amazing circumstance, the fool pressed with his whole hand and his fingers. Soon the child grew still, and the fool sat without moving, so as not to disturb him. When the shepherds returned from the bazaar, they found the blissfully smiling fool with the dead baby in his hands. He had pushed through the fontanel with his clumsy fingers."

"You're the fool," Peter said angrily, sitting up abruptly and lowering his feet to the floor. "You don't understand anything! He was doing research, he was blind and went to the end, as any researcher and experimenter would, and the infant had been given to him accidentally. Would you have him stop halfway?"

"But I feel sorry for the child," Lacosta managed to say. "He could have done it some other way . . ."

"Someone else would have done it another way, but not this man!" Peter rested his elbows on his knees and his chin in his hands. "You can't understand that, and you're not alone. Only one man in the whole nation understands that. And he is paying for that understanding."

"What about the nation?" Lacosta asked quietly. "Isn't the nation paying too?"

"The nation is an instrument," Peter said with a tired, bitter laugh. "Only the master is responsible before God."

"But if the instrument breaks," Lacosta said, trying not to look at the czar's eyes, round and horrible, "the master can't go on."

"Only God is higher than the master," Peter said sternly. "As He wills it, so be it."

"What does He want?" Lacosta cried bitterly, and Peter looked at him in puzzlement. "I don't want the Turks to put me on a stake, I don't want to be a eunuch in the aga's service! Who said that the God of Israel demands the soul of the Russian czar! Who?"

"Just take a look outside," Peter suggested ironically, lying down again. "Don't you hear them?"

Beyond the tent walls came the explosions of artillery bombs and the roar of the besiegers.

"Give them what they want, Czar," Lacosta said with chattering teeth. He came over to the bed and sank to his knees, as if it were a throne. "Let them choke on it. You'll gather strength and take it all back! You won't stop halfway! Breaking the instrument with your own hands is arrogance and pride!"

"Why give it?" Peter said, staring indifferently at the ceiling. "They'll take it anyway."

"Arrogance!" Lacosta repeated in a frenzy, as if mouthing a curse. "We Jews know what that is. . . . You are doing a terrible thing, sire. Make them an offer, instead of just . . ." He wanted to say "lying there" but checked himself and went on. "Send Shafirov, let him negotiate, let him—"

"Do you think I'm thinking of myself?" Peter interrupted softly, imperiously. "I've stopped thinking about myself; it's as if I no longer exist. Well, another hour or two . . . But it will all end with me, and they're just waiting for that in Moscow, and my son is waiting for that more than anyone else! I've worked for twenty years, and today we'll go back not twenty years, but two hundred. Do you understand that, Jester?"

"Send Shafirov," Lacosta insisted. "He'll crawl on his belly, not you. He's good at it, you know that. Maybe he'll get something."

"They'll knock everything down, burn everything," Peter said. "The Turks are horrible—but our own people are a hundred times worse. After me there'll be a new Time of Troubles, the great Asiatic troubles. And the Poles will come to pick at Russian bones, and so will the Lithuanians and the Crimeans."

Peter made a fist and struck himself on the head once, and then once more. "Here I am in the same situation that my brother Charles was at Poltava."

"Sire, Your Majesty," Lacosta whispered in fear, fidgeting on his knees. "There's still hope—Shafirov—"

"Lousy hope." Peter shut his eyes tight, and suddenly he saw the Polish Rows in Moscow, and his dear friend Lefort, and the panting Shafirov, tangling with the beggar Aleksashka over a stolen hat. "That's glorious: Shafirov, the last hope of Russia. . . . Let him go. Tell him: I will accept any terms except capitulation. I need to preserve my army and Moscow."

"And Saint Petersburg . . ." Lacosta breathed, almost not believing his own ears.

"Cede it last, if there is no other way out," Peter said, sitting up once more and looking down at the kneeling jester. "Charles will tear at the north, the Turks at the south. But cannons decide the fate of cities, not negotiations! That's why I won't leave here without the army, though only a madman would let me out of here. . . . If only Shafirov could make a deal!"

Leaping up from the bed, Peter paced the tent as if it were his camp pushed against the river, surrounded, blocked on all sides. He stopped for an instant by the table, glanced at his will, carefully passed his hand over it as if it were alive, and then started pacing again. He walked around Lacosta as if he were a piece of furniture.

"Shafirov will go now," Lacosta said, getting up.

Peter did not hear and did not respond.

Standing before Grand Vizier Mehmed, Shafirov took pleasure in sipping the dark, bitter coffee from a tiny cup of white Chinese porcelain. From inside the cup, a dragon with gold flecks for eyes looked at him. The coffee, brought after two hours of standing, was undoubtedly a good sign. And it was good that the Turk had sent away his bodyguards and especially Counselor Poniatowski: the Pole, naturally, represented Charles's interests and moreover had a quick mind, very quick. Now Shafirov was ready to sit right on the floor—his legs could barely hold him.

Mehmed sat on a red carpet with severe black designs, resting his elbows on a brightly patterned silk cushion. Curiosity showed beneath his mask of polite indifference and feigned weariness: this fat Russian with darting eyes came certainly not just to announce the obvious: tomorrow at dawn the czar's army would be destroyed. Then why was he here?

For two hours the conversation had wandered and meandered, and sometimes stopped completely for long periods; the silence was painful only for the standing Shafirov. The Turk mocked him and asked about the health of the czar and of Czarevich Alexis and whether the domes of the Kremlin churches were covered with pure gold. Insultingly, the conversation never touched on the war or the coming day. Just once, in response to a hint from Shafirov on concessions, the vizier delicately waved his hand and noted in passing, "Tomorrow we'll get everything without your concessions."

It was only after Shafirov said, with a gentle look, that he had something extraordinary to tell the vizier, person to person, that Mehmed grew more animated, sent his men away, and ordered coffee. But he had not yet suggested that the czar's emissary sit down.

The coffee was drunk in a silence violated only by the drinkers' smacking lips.

"A wonderful drink," Shafirov said, looking at the golden-eyed dragon one last time, and the vizier bowed his head slightly in acceptance of the compliment.

"You are right, *monsieur le ministre*," he said in guttural French. "But you, I believe, wanted to speak of fire."

"Yes and no," Shafirov countered quickly, shifting from one foot to the other. He had trouble believing that this courteous Turk, who spoke French and had the manners of an Englishman, could have him placed on the stake. "Fire flares up quickly and quickly goes out, like military glory. There are things much more lasting."

"For example?" The vizier's brow went up.

"Gold," said Shafirov confidently, urgingly. "We were just about to pay the officers' salaries, and our treasury glitters with gold."

"You are an experienced man, *monsieur le ministre*," the vizier said, making a tent of his fingertips. "You must realize that tomorrow or the day after, gold will be brought to my tent, right here." And with an easy gesture Mehmed pointed to the spot—a large carpet in the middle of the room. "What else did you wish to tell me?"

"The czaritza's jewels are worth twice, maybe three times the payroll," Shafirov muttered. "The tiara alone . . ."

"I will receive it along with the head of Her Majesty," the grand vizier said gently, almost cheerfully.

"With the dead head," Shafirov corrected.

"What do you mean by that?" Mehmed's eyebrows rose again.

"Almost nothing," Shafirov said. "The czaritza's neck is incredibly white and lovely, and for a moment I pictured her head severed from her body."

"Ah yes," the vizier said distractedly. "I have heard much about your czaritza. They say she is a beautiful woman."

"She is an extraordinary woman," Shafirov whispered, leaning forward, but not moving from his spot. "That's why Czar Peter made her his czaritza."

"Is that so?" The vizier's geriatric blue lips smiled, and he leaned toward Shafirov, as if in expectation of details that are not customarily spoken out loud. "What makes her extraordinary? And why, really, did your czar marry a prisoner?"

Why, really, did he? Shafirov thought angrily, and said, lowering his eyes, "There isn't another like her in the whole world. Those arms, those divine arms! Those lips—full and slightly parted!" He sneaked a glance at the Turk and saw that he was listening closely. "And her breasts, her breasts! Like two hills with a valley of paradise between them."

Shafirov stopped and sought the right words. "I swear to you that there isn't a man whose blood is not excited by the sight of the czaritza."

"And you?" the Turk asked. "You too?"

"Me too," Shafirov said truthfully. "But for me"—and he stressed the *me* bitterly—"there's no point of even dreaming about it."

"Is that so?" The vizier spoke either with sympathy or with irony. "Sit down, sit right here."

Shafirov sank to the carpet and tucked in his feet with difficulty. His heart was thumping, his mouth was as dry as a blazing oven. If the Turk didn't have him put on a stake, Peter would chop off his head personally for this kind of talk. *"Shatkhen,"* came the almost forgotten Hebrew word. "Filthy, dirty *shatkhen*!"

"A woman is worth more than gold, more than glory," Shafirov said, smiling pathetically and sweetly. "A woman like that."

"But what is she like?" the vizier asked with greedy curiosity.

"You are a soldier, my lord," Shafirov said solemnly. "And I will tell you man to man: Czaritza Catherine could raise a dead man from his grave. But only a live Catherine!"

"Is she big?" the vizier demanded. "And white?"

"She's big and white," Shafirov confirmed. "Many heroes

would give their lives for a night with her. And you, my lord, will save the lives of thousands of your men, taste a man's pleasure that is incomparable to anything in the world, and also receive the czaritza's jewels. And the payroll!" Shafirov added the last when he saw the vizier's sarcastic smile.

"And Azov, and Taganrog, and a few other things that we will discuss," the vizier said still smiling and running his fingers through his small gray beard. "So you say . . ."

"Yes, yes. You've covered yourself with glory in battle, but you can conquer the Russian czaritza only with her consent."

"You will bring her here?" the vizier asked, biting his lips. "When?"

"To save the honor of her homeland she will sacrifice her own honor," Shafirov said painfully. His face was covered with shiny beads of sweat. He took out a large white handkerchief and patted his forehead.

"But when?" the vizier demanded impatiently.

"Tonight," Shafirov said. "That, naturally, will be a secret paragraph in our agreement."

"Secrets are kept in metal trunks," the vizier said. "But even metal cannot withstand time, *monsieur le ministre*."

"Military glory dulls with age and turns into a historical anecdote," Shafirov countered. "But a victory over a woman, at the right time, can change the course of history. And tonight, my lord, you will enter history much more permanently than you could tomorrow morning to the thunder of cannons."

They fell silent, looking off in different directions. Shafirov was stunned and thought that if the Turk or Catherine did not agree, tomorrow would bring an end to Peter, and Russian history would turn onto a different path and, most likely, fall topsy-turvy once again. Mehmed, smoking a water pipe, thought that the fat Russian minister probably considered him a barbarian and an Oriental fool—when actually he was an old man who simply wanted to sleep with the extraordinary Czaritza Catherine.

"Coffee!" the grand vizier called and clapped his hands.

The rumble of the Turkish cannon suddenly stopped, as if chopped off with an ax. A distant gun barked once or twice and then fell silent too. The deep silence of the night fell over the Russian camp, and that unexpected silence astonished Field Marshal Sheremetev.

Unable to influence anything—neither the course of the Turkish attack nor Shafirov's negotiations—the field marshal sat in his tent drinking tea. An experienced military man, he knew that their cause was hopelessly lost and that only a miracle could save the czar, the remainder of his army, and Sheremetev himself. But he did not believe in miracles. And anyway, should a miracle come down from the starry southern sky on silken wings, what would he want? Imprisonment rather than death? But Sheremetev was an old man who had lived a blindingly brilliant life, and he was tired of that brilliance; he had an almost comradely feeling for death. Sitting in the dark of his tent, he sensed the coming peace with gratitude to God—and he smiled. Being a prisoner of the Turks with all the adjustments, the anxiety, and quite possibly the physical discomforts did not suit him in the least. Prison when you're twenty, well, even thirty, isn't so bad, it's good experience, but for an old sick man death is much more preferable. And in the end, who if not a field marshal should die in battle, accompanied by artillery fire? Sipping his tea and thinking these thoughts, Sheremetev came to terms with approaching death.

That was why the sudden silence, destroying his plans, came as such a surprise. Stretching his neck, he listened closely; the silence was total. Tens of thousands in Peter's camp and in the Turks' camp and beyond the river all listened suspiciously with the Russian commander to the unexpected quiet.

Rising quickly from the table, Sheremetev pulled on his wig and walked outside. Catherine's tent was a stone's throw away, but he did not go in. With creaking bones, he sat down in the cool grass under an old elm tree nearby, and leaned against the dependable, friendly trunk. What had caused the cease-fire? The question bothered him, like a toothache. Whichever way he looked at it, he came to only one conclusion: capitulation. But the Jew Shafirov wouldn't possibly dare accept that on his own! Nor could the czaritza. Well, actually, she could . . . she was a woman, and a German one at that. . . . Sheremetev recalled the victory at Marienburg, remembered Pastor Gluck's servant girl taken prisoner—an accommodating girl, Marta, and he wanted to smile but couldn't. Who would have thought then that nine years later that girl, hauled out by the field marshal from under the noncom's wagon, would be deciding the fate of Russia? Shaking his head in its uncombed wig, he looked first at Catherine's tent and then at Peter's, as dark and silent as a headstone.

Count Golovkin came up quietly. Turning, Sheremetev met the questioning look of the chief of the diplomatic department and shrugged.

"I don't know, Count," Sheremetev said, his hand describing a semicircle, as if caressing the silence. "I simply can't imagine . . ."

"But it is Shafirov?" Golovkin said, in a half statement, half question.

"Who else!" Sheremetev replied. "It's he . . ."

"What did he give in return?" Golovkin asked, no longer addressing the field marshal but the silence. "What could he have given them?"

Sheremetev shrugged once more and stared at the ground.

"We'll soon find out, Count," he said after a silence. "He has to go past us."

And so they waited with almost no conversation. Neither could say with any certainty how long they sat there under the tree. When Shafirov finally appeared, they came out of the shadows and barred his path.

His head thrown back on his short neck, Shafirov gave them a challenging, almost scornful look.

"Well?" Golovkin asked impatiently. "Why have they stopped shooting?"

Shafirov pursed his lips, huffed and puffed, sighed, and threw his head back even further. "Gentlemen, I ask you to remember this night," Shafirov said solemnly. "Tonight I saved Russia! I did!"

Sheremetev smiled skeptically and looked away. That Shafirov, that Jew! Maybe he really did . . . But why huff and puff, why use such language? Only the czar had that privilege—not some Jew. And he was supposed to be a diplomat! His chief, Golovkin, wouldn't forget those words for the rest of his life!

"Explain," Golovkin said dryly.

"I will report on the negotiations to Her Majesty," Shafirov said and started for her tent.

"Stop fooling around!" Golovkin said angrily. "I am ordering you: speak! Did you hear me?"

"You insist?" Shafirov asked. His protruding eyes glistened triumphantly in the dark.

"Absolutely!" Golovkin said, trying not to look at his deputy.

"We are returning Azov, and sacrificing the Taganrog fortifications," Shafirov said. "Shall I continue?"

"Now that you've started, finish up!" Sheremetev whispered, harshly. "What else?"

"Her Majesty must confirm the agreement," Shafirov said, his head cocked musingly. "All the points."

"You're out of your mind," Golovkin said, chewing his lip. "What does Her Majesty have to do with it? The czar will sign the agreement if he wants to. What's the matter with you, Shafirov?"

Shafirov was digging his toe into the ground. His lips were pursed.

"That is the demand of the grand vizier," Shafirov said. "Czaritza Catherine must immediately come to his headquarters. Or the attack will begin in three hours." And he added with vengefully narrowed eyes, "You ordered me to tell you and I have. But the grand vizier did not insist that this demand be brought to your attention."

"How could you say such things without chopping off your tongue!" Sheremetev moaned, stepping back and crossing himself. "Her Majesty! Under a Turk!"

"She can lie under a muzhik!" Shafirov hissed through clenched teeth. "She can lie under you! But not under a Turk!"

"How will your tongue move to tell her?" Sheremetev went on, groaning.

"A Russian tongue couldn't, but a Jewish one will," Golovkin said coldly and clearly, as if taking each word apart. "Go, Shafirov. Her Majesty must be waiting for you."

Shafirov's relief was like having a mountain fall from his shoulders: the monstrous, idiotic, and terrible secret was no longer his alone; he did not have to drag it around like a loaded bomb. On the trip back from the Turkish camp, the secret had winked its wanton eye at him familiarly and brazenly: "Your hour has come, diplomat Shafirov! Your place in history is assured—if not as a wise bookman and political organizer, then as a successful pimp. And generations will wonder why the grand vizier let Peter's throat slip out of his soft fingers at the last moment." Walking along with the aga who had been sent to accompany him, Shafirov fought the desire to go to the first horse or bush he saw, bring his lips close to whatever part came handy, and whisper in total delight and amazement, "The real price of this peace is a pound of the czaritza's sweet flesh!" The secret was astonishing and at the same time extremely simple.

The secret had its roots in the cool, magnificent past, and that made it seem more alive and fragrant: master and mistress, peasant and wife. And all this metal nonsense, the latest guns, long-distance fusils, and secret metal knives, were nothing, an empty sound compared with what the grand vizier would be doing with the czaritza at dawn. That was the price of peace, the price of tens of thousands of men and of the future of Russia: a Jewish head and a German pussy. And all the talk about unprecedented progress and beneficial changes in human nature was nothing more than exercises on drums; here was the perfect example.

The secret bubbled in Shafirov like water in a samovar. He had to share the secret with someone or something, a horse even; he had to open his tightly shut mouth soon—to relieve some of the pressure that was about to make him burst. Exchanging a few words with Golovkin and Sheremetev let off excess steam, but with relief came fear: that most important and monstrous conversation with the czaritza was yet to come.

Catherine was waiting for Shafirov, sitting in the same armchair as when he had left; she must not have gone to bed. The steady light of two candles on the table and from the *chandelle* standing on a tall bronze pedestal in the corner illuminated the czaritza's round, white face and her voluptuous shoulders, resting against the chair back. When she saw the ambassador, she tilted her gently rounded chin as a signal to sit in a chair near hers. Shafirov sat down and leaned forward—he was small before this woman, pregnant and bloated yet belonging to another, special breed of people, in a heavy dress ornamented with pearls at the hem and with elbow-length sleeves. And he felt pity and remorse—the old Turkish vizier seemed so impotent next to this perfect child-bearing machine, who according to Shafirov's plan would now have to go to the old man and diligently embrace him, like a bought washerwoman, warm his balding head with its taut dry skin on those two mighty globes filled with hot milky power.

Shafirov bent even lower, crawled down on the floor, and knelt before her.

"We are saved, Your Majesty," Shafirov said, head down. "Perhaps, we are saved . . ."

"Saint Petersburg?" Catherine asked quickly.

"God forbid," Shafirov said, "not at all! But the vizier demands a greater sacrifice. Believe me, Your Majesty, it would be much easier to part with Saint Petersburg, than . . ."

"Than what?" Catherine's fingers drummed on the arm of her chair.

"You can win back a city or build another one," Shafirov whispered. "But . . ."

"Will you speak up!" Catherine slapped the armrest.

"My tongue won't move to say it, Your Majesty," Shafirov mumbled, remembering Sheremetev's words. "The vizier demands a sacrifice from you, from you!"

Her eyebrows lifted high. Catherine reached over and ruffled Shafirov's cheek.

"The damned Turk wants you to come to him secretly," Shafirov whispered.

"When?"

"Now."

"And then?"

"He'll let us out of here with our banners and weapons," Shafirov said. "Your visit is his condition."

Clasping her hands on her round belly, Catherine sat back in the chair and, looking down at the back of Shafirov's bent head, laughed. Was he mad, that Turk? Must be some old bugger. . . . That Shafirov was a sly one. "It's easier to part with Saint Petersburg." Of course! The Turk didn't even want Saint Petersburg, he wanted her, Marta; that is, Catherine. All men were the same, that was for sure! Hugo, and that noncom, and old Sheremetev, and Menshikov, and Peter, and . . . Hugo was probably the best, God rest his soul—a real man. As he used to say gently, practically singing the words, "Now, Marta, once we beat Czar Peter, we'll buy a cow, and we'll have a dairy business!" He had large warm hands, and the hairs on them were white and soft. And if she didn't go to the old Turk now, Czar Peter would be beaten, dead like Hugo. But that wouldn't help Hugo or anyone else. And she'd have to climb under some Muhammad's wagon again, start all over at twenty-seven—she wasn't a girl anymore. And who else but his own wife should be saving her husband?

"The Turk won't trick us?" Catherine asked in concern.

"I don't think so, Your Majesty," Shafirov said and shook his head. "We will receive the appropriate guarantees."

Pushing Shafirov away lightly, Catherine swiftly rose, picked up a candle from the table, and went over to the mirror.

"You should utter a historic phrase now, Your Majesty," Shafirov noted, keeping down a bitter laugh.

"Well, think of one, Shafirov!" Catherine said, regarding herself closely in the silvery depths of the Venetian glass:

slightly parted plump lips, round dimpled cheeks. "I've let my maid go to bed. Hand me the rouge from that case."

"Here, Your Majesty!" Shafirov said, passing it over quickly. "And your powder! This one? And, if you will allow me, I'll bring you an officer's greatcoat."

"Will we walk?" Catherine asked in surprise. "It's far, isn't it?"

"Of course not! We'll take my carriage, I'll give the orders."

"Is this dress nice?" Catherine asked. "Or should I wear the purple?"

"The purple is better," Shafirov said and grimaced painfully, as if someone had stuck a poisonous thorn in his heart and twisted it.

As they passed Peter's tent, the czaritza slowed for a moment; she had the feeling that her husband was looking at her imperiously and encouragingly from behind the slightly parted curtain, that he had recognized her as the clumsy, fat-bellied officer.

Releasing the curtain, Peter sat down at the table, filled his clay pipe with black Dutch tobacco, and, sucking in the malleable flame of the candle, exhaled the strong, aromatic smoke.

A little more than twenty-four hours later, at dawn, the Russian troops, with their banners, cannons, and drums, crossed the Prut River and headed home.

Peter and Catherine went to the resort at Karlsbad to rest.

Grand Vizier Mehmed was made to sit on a stake by the sultan. Shafirov, who was left as hostage until the Russians fulfilled their obligations of the peace treaty, felt a surge of unpleasant emotions.

VIII

The Appearance of Elijah the Prophet

1714

The food wasn't food: spicy, bloody, with pieces of singed, fiery pepper. Chewing carefully, Shafirov remembered the delicate soups and dumplings of home and smiled sadly. The joy of victory over Mehmed, with which he had been bursting that night on the Prut, had long since withered and weakened. Now, three years later, something else brought him joy: his term as hostage was over, and he was going home—to his wife and daughters, his books, his soup. And, mentally returning against his will to the banks of the Prut, he felt guilty about being the cause of the Turkish vizier's death. The Turk hadn't been a bad man, and he'd been a cultured one at that. And the fact that if he hadn't been put on a stake innumerable catastrophes would have befallen Russia did nothing to alleviate Shafirov's sense of guilt.

Three years ago it had all looked different. Then, he had

been ready to chop the vizier into kebabs single-handedly—anything to get out of their dead end, to save himself, save Peter, Catherine, Russia. Now the triumph that awaited him in Saint Petersburg did not take his breath away. Well, maybe they would build an allegorical arch based on the czar's sketches. What would it depict? he wondered.

The thought that Peter knew about that night was an unpleasant one, and it frightened him. He was a hero, of course, he had saved them—but that hadn't happened yesterday or the day before. Today the czar had other concerns, and other people were entrusted with resolving them. Had Sheremetev and Golovkin said too much? If they had—and that was most likely—and a rumor had started, then the czar's gratitude would turn to disaster for Shafirov. The rumor would slither like a snake, crawl up silently, and bite. End of story.

Shafirov did not dwell on unhappy thoughts. It was nicer blocking them, even with his hand, and thinking about his home and family. He planned to return to Saint Petersburg by spring, by Passover, the only Jewish holiday he celebrated, even in captivity. Mumbling the prayers quickly and murmuring the songs, he had asked God to lead him out of Turkey as He had once led the Jews out of Egypt with His strong hand. . . . And the day had come at last—Shafirov was going home.

He had felt this captivity. The attitude of the sultan's people toward him, sometimes as overly sweet as halvah, more often hostile and menacing, let him know that he was not far from the stake himself. If it ever occurred to the czar to delay paying his obligations to the sultan or to refuse them, a perfectly sound idea, the stake would cease to be a heart-chilling threat and turn into a real one with a sharpened end, black with blood and feces. . . . Such thoughts and visions, for all their horror, gradually led Shafirov to come to terms with the icy eternity on the other side of death. The turquoise blue mornings of Turkey seemed like a gift from God, and as he looked at the calm, distant horizon through the window of his closely guarded house, he thought, with damp eyes, that success and career were hollow, that chasing after money was bad for the soul, and that only books, golden mounds of books could bring relief and peace.

All these meditations ceased and were forgotten as soon as his day of liberation came around. Fear for his future, fear of the czar remained. And the weariness, which he would probably never lose.

In a flash, Saint Petersburg seemed close, as if there were less than a day's ride left. And he pictured the most unpleasant scenes vividly: squabbles in the Senate, the envy of enemies and friends, and his failure of a brother, who had to be set up in some job that would look important and support him. His younger brother's fate worried Shafirov: it was neither right nor suitable for relatives of the vice-chancellor to be shivering in poverty. Not right, and unfair. He would have to find his brother something decent in the post office: profitable and respectable. And it was time to think seriously about a proper match for his oldest daughter: young Volkonsky was a suitor, and so was Tolstoy. He could give the income from the salmon business on the White Sea as dowry; for money like that people of the noblest Viking lineage would shut their eyes to the ancestry of Shafirov's father, Pincus. They wouldn't come to Passover seder, naturally, but that wasn't necessary: it was enough that Shafirov would come to exchange the traditional three kisses with them on Russian Easter. His guests for Passover would be Divier and Lacosta. If they didn't have a *minyan*, it wasn't so terrible; Saint Petersburg wasn't Smolensk; you could count the Jews on one hand. And the goyim didn't need to know about a seder in the home of the Russian Vice-Chancellor Shafirov. They would serve stuffed pike and bouillon with dumplings . . .

Remembering the dumplings, Shafirov poked the pieces of peppery meat before him with his two-pronged fork and grimaced. He'd be home soon! And life would resume at a gallop, like a bump-cart hitched to a stallion from the royal stables. So what if you're tossed in the ruts and your soul gets shaken out! At least you're traveling forward, into the distance filled with diamonds, medals, and titles, reeking of wine and gunpowder, saturated with viscous blood and tears of joy and delight! Forward, to the horizon of home, stuck on the spire of the Peter and Paul Fortress, so different from this damned Asian sky, which resembled a silk belt thrown around the earth's hips that lazily slipped down to her pudenda. Away from here, from this miserable place, so miserable that he hadn't even wanted to study Turkish and had to take up Italian instead. Enough! How much farther along the southern route to Saint Petersburg, kind gentlemen?

Borokh Leibov was headed for Saint Petersburg along a different route, the western road. His journey wasn't short and it wasn't long from his hometown of Zveryatichi, near Smolensk. Leibov was a man of medium age and medium height, broad shouldered and strong, with dark eyes that had a stormy, penetrating look. His large, white face with its straight, narrow-bridged nose was covered by a broad, bushy beard, silver threads among the black. Sitting in his *britchky,* Leibov huddled in a sheepskin coat, which he wore over a jacket, and stared indifferently at the infrequent villages and wet forests on both sides of the road. He did not like to travel, most of all because he begrudged the loss of time moving from one place to another. This wasted time, stolen from a rational life that demanded meaningful activity, this time spent in a *britchky,* cart, or carriage, could not be restored. And it could have been spent in a way useful for the soul or for commerce: studying the Talmud and the commentaries or arguing with the tavern keepers, whose profits Leibov, a tavern buyer, watched closely.

It was not commercial business that was taking Leibov to Saint Petersburg. He had decided to found a Jewish primary school in Zveryatichi and was going to Saint Petersburg and Moscow for help and support from Jews, open and secret. To the latter group he definitely assigned the powerful Shafirov, who was coming back from Turkey, according to rumor, by Passover. To Leibov a baptized Jew was as repulsive as a snake or rat, but the prospect of opening a heder in Zveryatichi overcame his disgust. Shafirov was probably the only one whose help could bring about a positive decision smoothly and quickly. It was worth the trouble of dealing with that filthy *meshummad,* so that the children of Zveryatichi could have their own school and study the holy wisdom of the sacred books with the rabbi. Leibov had even found the right spot for the school—directly opposite Saint Nicholas the Miracle Worker, across the square. That was where they had to begin fearless battle with Father Amvrosi—tempter and catcher of weak souls. You couldn't resort to half measures in a business like this, because God, without any question, was on the side of Borokh Leibov.

Father Amvrosi, however, was of the contrary opinion: he was convinced that God was wholly on his side. Besides which, on Amvrosi's side was the Smolensk bishop, Filofei, which was also important. An old enmity tied Leibov and Father Amvrosi, and that enmity was stronger than some friendships. Their mutual hatred and scorn would die only when one of them went to his grave. And each planned, with God's help, to outlive the other.

Doubts were strangers to their hardened souls. Convinced of their holy righteousness and of God's support, they saw in each other the personification of the devil's evil and were prepared for bloodshed. They mocked and insulted each other, and whenever they bumped into each other, by accident or on purpose, they exploded like bundles of kindling. Leibov would make horns over his head with his hands and hop around, bleating like a goat, while Amvrosi jumped up and down and crowed like a rooster. The language of humans would have been their common tongue, but they did not wish to have anything in common, and so to stress their insurmountable differences, one clucked and crowed and the other bleated. And each felt himself a defender of God and a hero.

In that holy struggle, calumny and denunciations were suitable weapons. "Borokh Leibov and his wife," Amvrosi reported, "took the peasant girl Matryona Emelyanova, who was working for them on the Sabbath against God's law, and bound her hand and foot and suspended her from the ceiling beam from evening to the morning bells, covered her head, and used pins and needles to release blood from her." Called upon to testify, Matryona denied it and nothing happened. However the fame and authority of Borokh Leibov and Father Amvrosi grew significantly among their brethren. Both came to be seen as truly righteous men and heroes in Zveryatichi, and their followers patiently awaited the outcome of the lengthy duel.

Opening the heder opposite the church of Saint Nicholas the Miracle Worker was planned as a daring counterattack. God knew whose side was right and reasonable, but the might was on the side of Father Amvrosi. And might can conquer right.

Recalling the rooster cackles and crowing with disgust, Leibov stared glumly at the road. The school in Zveryatichi would eventually become like the one in Yavne, a bulwark against the unclean goyim, a torch for the faithful and thunder for the weak of heart who violate the laws and testaments. For a Jew who violates the testaments is worse than a goy. . . . Seeing an inn, the last one before Saint Petersburg, beyond the turn and the black firs, Leibov pulled out a sack with his kosher food for the road: matzo, onions, and meat fried in oil.

Anna Danilovna was completely happy. Divier had turned out to be a family man, a loving husband and father. Every evening in front of their large stone house on Mytnaya Embankment stood carriages and coaches that had brought important guests: people sought if not the friendship then at least the disposition of the powerful and terrible Anton Manuilovich Divier. And sturdy Anton was unflagging in his work and in his pleasure, and remained as willing in his connubial labors as in years past; Anna, if not pregnant, was always sleepy and smiling languorously.

Alexander Danilovich Menshikov never showed his face on Mytnaya. He did not miss Anna, or if he did, he did not show it. When he met Divier on the czar's business, he was haughty and cold, as if a stranger; but sharp-eyed Divier often caught the squinty, vengeful looks from his brother-in-law. Those looks, however, neither frightened the former pirate nor worried him: as wary and cunning as a forest animal, he had achieved what he wanted. His position with the czar was exceptionally secure, because he was not only hardworking but honest; having ample opportunity to do so, he never stole, or almost never, and the czar, thanks to Divier's efforts, was made aware of that. Besides, through his service and his innate curiosity, Divier knew many interesting details about life at court, including Menshikov's. And he kept most of those fascinating details close to his vest, for a rainy day. Appearing everywhere, expected or not, his fiery black eyes darting beneath his thin, immobile eyebrows, noting things that might seem insignificant to others, Divier never allowed anyone to become a close friend. Friendship would have confined him and held him back. Today's friend could accidentally harm him tomorrow, or betray him on purpose or under torture. The carefree friendship of the days on the island of the Holy Infant were gone forever, and Divier did not regret it, as he never regretted anything he had done and left behind. The absence of close friends was the best protection against intrigue, the best guarantee of personal safety—and so the Grosse Kommandant of the growing Saint Petersburg and the czar's Councillor on Secret Police Matters had no friends. The exception that proved the rule was the jester Lacosta.

The day after Shafirov returned from Ottoman captivity, Lacosta went to see Divier at his house. It was almost warm. By the end of the day under the yellow light of the spring sun the mud would be dry, and by morning it would be covered by a thin layer of ice. Skirting puddles, Lacosta slowly made his way along the embankment. Some pedestrians recognized the czar's jester and bowed without mockery: Lacosta the Jew was in Peter's good graces. Others merely gawked at his severely cut German suit, all black; he looked like a pharmacist.

Divier had not returned from work yet, and Lacosta and Anna had coffee in the small parlor. On the wall hung paintings in glowing gilt frames: a portrait of Peter—a royal gift—and colorful naval battles. Above the French mahogany buffet hung an engraving done by the court engraver, Zubov: Anna Danilovna, bare shouldered, high breasted, with a mysterious and weary half smile on her lips. In the corner, in a silver cage, sat a large parrot with a blue breast and pink comb.

"Antosha taught him to whistle like a pirate," Anna said, moving the sugar bowl closer to Lacosta. "It's so alarming! Come on, Fedya, whistle, do!"

The parrot opened his beak wide, moved his square tongue, popped his eyes, and whistled deafeningly.

"Pretty, isn't it?" Anna said in a delighted whisper. "Isn't Antosha marvelous!"

Tilting his head to one side, Lacosta agreed, yes, the parrot did whistle very loudly. "A good bird," Lacosta said. "Does she lay eggs?"

"I have no idea," Anna said in surprise. "She must be old . . . Why?"

"I'd like to get a bird like that for Masha," Lacosta said, giving the bird a friendly look. "So that the child will be amused. I see that she gets bored sometimes."

"But she's a bride by now!" Anna exclaimed. "She shouldn't be thinking about birdies! . . . How old is she?"

"She'll be seventeen this summer," Lacosta said. "But she's just a child! Believe me, no one would call her more than fourteen or fifteen, at most."

"You have to bring her out into society, Yan Semyonovich," Anna said, wrinkling her high brow. "Society. Then she won't be bored."

"But I'll be bored and lonely," Lacosta said, drumming his fingers on the table. "A jester's daughter at a society ball . . ."

"You're no jester, Yan Semyonovich!" Anna dismissed the idea. "It's just a title! No one even at court takes you for a jester."

"What do they take me for then?" Lacosta asked curiously and stopped his drumming.

"Well"—Anna thought a bit—"just a pleasant man."

"A pleasant man at court, that's a dangerous occupation," Lacosta said. "Far more dangerous than royal jester."

"Will you have some liqueur?" she asked. "Cherry?"

"Why not." Lacosta accepted.

"You must let your daughter go out. You must!" Anna chided as she poured the liqueur. "At least to our house; we have young cavaliers here, military and civilian. You can't do anything worse than keep a potential bride under lock and key! She'll break the lock and run off somewhere." As she looked at the crystal decanter glittering with cheery reflections, Anna smiled happily, insouciantly.

"God forbid," Lacosta said with a shudder.

Divier came in noiselessly and quickly. Recognizing Lacosta's back, he ran up to the table.

"Yan! I'm glad you came . . . Anya, are we alone tonight? Then let's have a family meal. Have them serve, my dear; I'm as hungry as the devil." He patted Lacosta's shoulder and looked him in the eye. "As a thousand devils!"

"The Naryshkins are coming for second supper," Anna said, getting up. "And Gleb Gagarin promised to come."

"I won't stay that late," Lacosta said, shaking his head. "Let's just sit and chat for a half hour, Antoine."

"As you like," Divier said. "But let's have a snack!" He looked at his wife.

"Sit down, sit down," Anna said, leaving the room. "They'll serve in a minute."

"You have excellent liqueur!" Lacosta said. "What a fine color . . ." He poured himself some more and a glass for his host. "Have you seen Shafirov yet?"

"Yes, of course," Divier said. "He sent his regards to you. He's lost a little weight, but just a little."

"Will there be any official celebration?" Lacosta asked, rolling the glass between the palms of his hands.

"No," Divier said. "Nothing. But the czar will probably reward him: villages and a medal."

"Nothing at all!" Lacosta was surprised. "But—"

"Prut was no Poltava." Divier shrugged. "Prut has to be buried, so it won't stick in the memory. Three years ago, there might have been a celebration, but now . . . As they say here, an egg is good at Easter."

"Hard to forget," Lacosta said after a pause. "My Masha would be an orphan now if not for Shafirov. He pulled us all out of the grave, I'm telling you, Antoine."

"But you talked to His Majesty too, didn't you, Yan?" Divier said in a whisper, leaning close.

"Shafirov sent me!" Lacosta replied in a whisper. "And now God has brought him out of there. . . . I want to give a Passover seder and invite Shafirov. And you too, of course!"

"Where?" Divier asked, sitting up in his chair.

"At my place," Lacosta said. "And, if you mean . . ."

"Who else will you invite?" Divier went on. "You see, it would be unfortunate, very unfortunate, if rumors of our seder went around the city. More than very unfortunate."

"I understand that," Lacosta said, spreading his hands. "We won't get a minyan: you, me, Shafirov, and one more Jew."

"Who?" Divier asked, looking up.

"His name is Borokh Leibov," Lacosta explained. "He came to me to ask for money to open a Jewish school somewhere near Smolensk. A little strange, you know, rather intolerant. . . . But he's all alone here, and inviting a lonely Jew to seder is a holy deed, Antoine."

"Well, you can't help it," Divier said, bending his handsome head, which had not a single gray hair. "You have to invite him. But I'll check out this Borokh Leibov. You say he's strange?"

"A bit," Lacosta elaborated. "He treated me as if I was his debtor and had robbed him to boot. You know, there are Jews like that . . ."

"Yes," Divier said. "He must know how to have a seder? I sometimes get mixed up, just between us, when to sing and when to drink. So do you, Yan."

"He knows, he does! You don't have to worry on that score. And Shafirov knows too!"

"That's true," Divier agreed. "You and I have forgotten."

"Not completely!" Lacosta argued hotly. "And that's not the main thing, when to drink and when to sing."

"What is?" Divier regarded Lacosta closely, demandingly.

"The main thing is that we feel like ordinary people only when we're among our own, be it Shafirov or even that Borokh Leibov. We Jews are here and the goyim are there."

"I guess once a year we can permit ourselves that luxury," Divier muttered.

Anna came in. The men grew silent and then spoke of something else.

Shafirov decided to celebrate Passover at his house.

It came to him when he learned that there would be no fireworks, no allegorical arch. Well, fine then! That was his reward for loyal service—for his Jewish head, his Jewish tongue, for three years of sitting near the stake, practically on the stake! If there was nothing to thank God's anointed Peter for, then he would thank God for His mercy at His seder . . .

The idea of having a secret seder at Lacosta's house, behind locked doors, dropped away. Come what may, Passover should be celebrated fearlessly and openly, in Shafirov's palace, in the formal dining hall. And let all Petersburg talk about the Russian vice-chancellor Peter Shafirov praising his Jewish God for bringing him out of the Ottoman grip.

After some thought Shafirov decided to move the celebration from the formal dining hall to the cellar which was as comfortable and almost luxurious. Having miraculously escaped one mortal danger, he could see no point in risking another: openly mocking the Holy Synod, who were suspicious of Shafirov as it was. And Lacosta probably wouldn't have wanted to eat matzo and sing Jewish prayers in front of the whole world, and Divier certainly wouldn't. It didn't really matter on what story they celebrated Passover—the first floor or the cellar. Anyway, Shafirov's cellar was much safer than Lacosta's hut, which any curious person could enter without invitation. He would have the servants bring the formal dining table to the cellar and hang the walls with carpets. And a velvet armchair for the Prophet Elijah. That was always so touching: waiting all evening for the door to open, for Elijah to come in and sit down in the chair. Knowing that Elijah wouldn't come but waiting nevertheless. There was something childlike and unspoiled about it. The light blue velvet chair for Elijah.

Since there would have been no point in inviting Anna Menshikova to the underground seder, Shafirov decided to make do without his family too: they wouldn't have understood anyway. Therefore, it was a male group: the host, Divier, Lacosta, and that Borokh Leibov from Zveryatichi. Well, let there be a Borokh! What was a better time for a mitzvah than Passover? Especially since, according to Divier, Leibov was a smart man and wouldn't gab about spending Passover in his cellar.

The table was brought downstairs, the carpets hung, the

velvet armchair set up. Walking in his spacious cellar, Shafirov thought about where his path, starting in Egypt in times immemorial, had brought him. And this was the place: the Polish Rows in Moscow's Kitai-Gorod; that's where it had all started, with the fight with Aleksashka. And as Joseph lived under the pharaoh, so Shafirov lived under Peter.

The windowless cellar hung with carpets resembled a mysterious cave, and it was sweet and joyful to compare himself with Joseph—a foreign Jew, who thanks to his wits and cleverness had risen high and saved the czar and Russia. Who needed fireworks and arches—Joseph was probably still a Yid as far as his envious Egyptian enemies were concerned, and he prayed to his God in secret, perhaps in the cellar of his palace. And as to whether he had taken the pharaoh's wife anywhere, that question remained open; if it had been necessary, he would have. Just because there's no mention of it in the Bible—that's understandable: no one would be writing books about that night on the Prut either. "The czaritza sacrificed her jewels for the sake of Russia" sounded much more noble and bookish. Shafirov knew what she had sacrificed; too bad he wasn't the only one. As the late Mehmed had said then, "Secrets are kept in metal trunks, but even metal cannot withstand time." . . . The pharaoh's wife must have been a beauty, no worse than Catherine but in an exotic way.

On that mischievous thought, Shafirov shook his head in its bulky curled wig. Thoughts like that, and on this night once a year with his own people, without all those Egyptians. Well, twice a year—but no more. A candy is sweet when you don't have it often.

Divier was the first to arrive. He looked around attentively and smiled in satisfaction. Instead of a greeting, he said, "You've arranged everything wonderfully, Peter Pavlovich. And most important, no one will ever guess . . ."

"Except the Prophet Elijah!" Shafirov said happily. "There's his chair."

"He's welcome!" Divier chuckled. "But if my relative Alexander Danilovich gets wind of this, there'll be no end of unpleasantness."

"There's an envious man!" Shafirov shook his head in dismay. "If his envy were fire, all the people close to the sovereign would have long ago turned to ashes. Menshikov is like a beetle devouring the tree he lives in! I've said that to his face."

"A mistake," Divier replied laconically.

"No, it's not!" Shafirov said with a frown, pursing his lips. "I know for a fact that in many battles he looked on from afar like Neptune through his glass at the Battle of Troy."

"You said that to him too?" Divier asked.

"Yes!" Shafirov raised his voice. "That too! To his face!"

"A double mistake," Divier said and narrowed his eyes.

"I know it was," Shafirov admitted with a sigh. "But it's too late now; I said it, he heard it. . . . But what pleasure it was to look at his obnoxious face! He turned as red as a lobster."

"Well, in that case," Divier said, inclining his head, "that must have been pleasant."

"You'll see, he'll be his own ruination!" Shafirov said, rubbing his hands together. "Envious lout! Bastard!"

"People like that you must get rid of at once," Divier said in a steady voice, "or don't bother them at all, even if it is to your disadvantage. Prince Menshikov holds a grudge a long time, Peter Pavlovich."

"I know, I know!" Shafirov waved the thought away. "But we'll fight it out yet! Truth will find a way!"

"Truth?" Divier said in surprise, and his eyebrows moved up on his forehead. "Are you serious?"

"Why not?" Shafirov shrugged. "If I'm lucky . . ."

"Well yes," Divier said, and as if to return his disobedient eyebrows to their place, ran his small, dark hands down his face. "Luck works both ways. I prefer not to trust to luck, and I haven't been wrong once."

"But in individual, happy instances . . ." Shafirov tried to defend himself wanly.

"I'm not talking about my department here," Divier said, trying to put an end to this useless conversation. "Let's talk about yours—diplomacy. What is diplomacy?" And he answered, as if with a swift sword stroke: "The art of lying!"

"Yes, yes," Shafirov agreed distractedly. "A great art." And he stopped talking, to Divier's immense satisfaction.

"And you, Peter Pavlovich, are a great master of that great art," Divier continued in a softer tone. "Your position does not permit you to remain in the shadows, nor do you want that. . . . But truth—what is truth? Here the beginning and the end of truth is Czar Peter, and that's right: if there were no royal truth, everything would creep and slip, as if on runny clay: states, ideas, logs. And you and I"—Divier raised his voice to counter his host's disagreeing gesture—"and you and I would be the first to be bruised by those logs."

"You must know better," Shafirov said sadly.

"Perhaps!" Divier agreed readily. "I say let's not lie at least one day a year, this day. . . . Truth! The truth is a matter for God, while we make up our own truth out of either calculation or not knowing better."

"What about the czar?"

"The czar, fortunately, doesn't even think about it," Divier replied. "What he does is the sole truth for him, heavenly truth. And then we pull it apart, dragging pieces to our own corners, like jackals. After all, you're not going to start convincing me that what you do is your own, heavenly truth."

"Let's assume not." Shafirov avoided a direct answer. "But you say that the czar—"

"The czar has changed since Prut." Divier interrupted with a snap of his fingers. "He's wary and suspicious. But to tell you the truth, that suits me. Spiritual candor is not conducive to great deeds, especially with helpers like his. You have to keep a very close watch on things, believe me!"

"Why ever since Prut?" Shafirov asked and gave Divier a sharp look.

"He's come of age," Divier said with a barely perceptible laugh. "Maturity. New truth. . . . But that shouldn't affect us."

"You think not?"

"I'm sure of it, as long as we keep on serving him faithfully for the money the czar pays us. We must do whatever we are told. And say as little as possible about our new homeland—no one believes us anyway. We were Jews, foreigners, for everyone, and we still are. Your homeland, after all, isn't a spoon you have to drag all over the world with you. Russia is home for Russians, Peter Pavlovich. And Russians are headstrong; the higher up the more they want to change things their way, even if it's only an inch. To make things better for themselves. And it's not just money—we're talking about government structure!

"As for us, that's another story. We're hired help, passers through. Serene Prince Alexander Danilovich, my brother-in-law, is a scoundrel—worse than all of us put together—but he's one of them; he's allowed to, and we're not. The czar trusts us as long as we keep our noses out of higher politics. Our job, Peter Pavlovich, is not to rock the boat!"

Lacosta entered the cellar, pushing back the carpet draping the entrance. Behind him, holding the skirts of his black holiday coat and bending his head with its pointy black hat, came Borokh Leibov. He was carrying a small canvas sack. He examined the decorations in the cellar and, shaking his head more in condemnation than in delight, moved toward the host.

"Peace to us and your home, Reb Shapir!" he said loudly.

Shafirov winced, as if his tooth suddenly hurt. "Reb Shapir": was that a way to address the Russian vice-chancellor, privy councillor, chief of the embassy department, chevalier of the Orders of the Polish White Eagle and the Prussian Magnanimity, Baron Shafirov? That was too much, even for a Passover seder! But the host's pained reaction did not bother Borokh Leibov in the least; on the contrary, it pleased him. He shut his eyes and smiled in satisfaction.

"To the table, gentlemen!" Shafirov exclaimed, trying to get over the embarrassing moment. "Otherwise we'll miss the Great Exodus from Egypt." He took a gold watch from his pocket, a watch the size of a snuffbox, with his baronial crest outlined in diamonds and rubies. "Five minutes to nine . . . That's for Elijah!" Shafirov said, so that Leibov would not sit in the wrong chair.

The guests were seated—but Leibov remained standing behind his chair. Shafirov watched him warily.

"So," Leibov said, giving them a stern look. "The wigs have to go."

Lacosta and Divier obediently pulled off their wigs, but Shafirov hesitated, as if called upon to take off his pants.

"Only married Jewish women wear wigs," Leibov explained to his host in irritation, as if talking to an obtuse child. "Jewish men wear yarmulkes." He dug deep in his sack and pulled out three of black silk.

With a small sigh, Shafirov took off his wig and put a yarmulke on his balding, round head. Leibov watched him carefully. Under the guest's seething eye, there was almost nothing left of the vice-chancellor and chevalier in Shafirov: he suddenly resembled an elderly and not very healthy Jew, a merchant or tavern keeper. He felt no hostility toward Borokh Leibov, only confusion and fear, as if facing an uncontrollable and highly agitated man capable of anything, screaming or attacking at any moment.

But Leibov was praying at high speed, his upper body swaying sharply.

When he was done, he sat down, looked over the abundantly set table, and asked, "Is the food kosher?"

"There's no pork today," Shafirov babbled in self-justification. "But, you realize, I can't vouch completely for—"

Divier watched the interplay between Shafirov and Leibov and smiled. He wasn't afraid of the demanding guest. Lacosta looked serious and rather glum.

"Is there leavened dough in the house?" Leibov interrupted impatiently. "Bread? Beer?"

"There is," Shafirov said. He sighed and shrugged guiltily.

"And you call yourselves Jews!" Leibov rebuked. *"Reboine sheloilem,* Reb Shapir . . . So!" He decisively pushed away the table setting, lifted up the tablecloth, dug deep in his sack once more, and brought out his food: gefilte fish, a piece of meat, a jar of horseradish, salt, jam, a glass bottle, and a pack of matzoth. Spreading it out before him on the bare polished wood, he squinted challengingly at his host.

"I have matzo," Shafirov said in embarrassment, looking at Leibov's miserable repast. "Wonderful matzo . . . Here!"

He pointed to a silver platter covered by a white silk cloth embroidered in gold with a Star of David and lions.

"You eat your wonderful matzo and I'll eat my own wonderful matzo," Leibov said stubbornly. "A Jew must eat matzo for Passover, even if it's not kosher. It's better than nothing."

He reached out and flicked his fingernail against the edge of the silver platter and listened closely to the tender ringing. "Pure silver. A good piece. It belongs in a synagogue or on the table of the zaddik."

Shafirov felt embarrassed. There, I'm embarrassed, he thought, touched. Who would have imagined it? Some psychopath, a fanatic, has put me in my place. My grandfather Shafir must have been like him, also from near Smolensk. . . . I'll have to donate that platter to a synagogue, anonymously, of course.

Divier was sick of Borokh Leibov. He leaned back in his chair, narrowed his eyes, and quietly started the Passover song about the little white kid:

Eckhad gadya, chad gadya,
Eckhad gadya!

"Stop!" shouted Leibov, waving his arms. "Don't you know the order? I'll tell you when to sing."

Shafirov and Lacosta gave Divier a reproachful look. Divier, to his own surprise, stopped in midsong, and, not knowing what to do, stared at the wine bottle Leibov had brought.

"That's Passover wine," Leibov said, lifting the bottle in both hands. "We'll all drink it. At Passover, a Jew must drink this. Where would Reb Shapir ever get Passover wine? It is said: if the leavened dough is not swept out of the house before Passover, avoid that house. Well then: you are bad Jews, but you are still Jews. A bad Jew is better than a good goy. And I came to do a mitzvah and have a seder with you."

Shafirov, reclining on his elbow on the table, huffed. He had been certain that he was the one performing a mitzvah by inviting a poor Jew from Zveryatichi to his seder, and he was not planning to be disabused of that pleasant certainty.

"Now repeat after me," Leibov continued, "and then, when I tell you, repeat one by one . . ." He got a worn book from the sack, opened it, and almost without referring to the text, began. "So. We were slaves in the land of Egypt and the Lord, our God, brought us forth with his strong hand."

He read for a long time, occasionally taking a pinch of salt, a bit of horseradish, a drop of jam. When he finished, he set the book aside and said, "Now we can have a sip."

The Passover drink was very strong, and this gave rise to pleasant hopes in the hungry Divier. Shafirov also grew more animated as he drank, and he reached for a bite of food to follow it, but Leibov leaned over the table and slapped his hand.

"The time for food has not come!" Leibov frowned as if he had swallowed something bitter. "Be patient! A Jew must be patient and then he will understand that he is a real Jew."

"Yes, we must be patient," Lacosta echoed and adjusted his yarmulke. "You can't do anything about it . . ."

"Those who rebel against patience are like sheep and goats," Leibov said in confirmation and made horns at his head with a habitual gesture. "You can rebel only against the persecutors of our faith, and that is a *mitzvah*."

"And you rebel?" Divier asked curiously.

"I rebel with God's help," Leibov said, giving Divier a hostile look. "For the glory of God I will start a heder in Zveryatichi, and Jews"—he looked beseechingly at Shafirov—"all Jews must help me!"

"Of course, of course!" Shafirov exclaimed in relief, receiving a request at last from his guest and feeling on firmer footing. "We'll help you with money—anonymously, of course—and you can open a heder in your place near Smolensk."

Leibov, however, did not warm up to him at all, and his voice was still hard and dry.

"It is said: a nameless contributor is more pleasing unto God than one who gives his name. . . . So: repeat after me, Reb Shapir. And the Lord, our God, sent a plague on the Egyptians, the children of the pharaoh . . ."

Approaching steps resounded in the corridor leading to the cellar.

"Who's that?" Divier asked quickly.

"The Prophet Elijah," Shafirov joked anxiously, turning his head.

The carpet door flew back. On the doorstep, rubbing his forehead, which he had struck on the low doorway, stood Peter. He looked from beneath his fist at the men who jumped up from the table in horror, and laughed at the effect his visit had made. Then, stepping heavily on the rugs, he approached the blue velvet armchair, sat deep in it, and spread his long legs comfortably.

Shafirov, mouth agape, stared dumbly at the czar. Divier chewed his thin lips, his sinews dancing. Lacosta and Leibov looked away and muttered prayers.

"How can this be? You're having a party, celebrating your Yid Easter, and you didn't invite me!" Peter said with mock reproach. "I'm quite curious to take a look at your Easter, and it's even beneficial for my general knowledge." Peter pointed at the bottle. "Baron, pour me some of that!"

With unsteady hand, Shafirov poured the Passover drink into a silver chalice and handed it to Peter. Peter sighed, crossed himself, and swallowed the wine in one long draft.

"It's good!" Peter said with a splutter and, looking around, grabbed the piece of meat lying in front of Leibov. He bit in and chewed. "Why have you stopped? Go on!"

Slowly, Leibov rummaged in his canvas sack, fished out a black yarmulke, and silently offered it to the czar. Shafirov turned white and felt there was no air to breathe. Still chewing, Peter twirled the headgear in his hand with interest, looked inside it, and finding nothing except grease and dandruff, put it on.

"There," Leibov said, watching the czar warily, "whoever wants may repeat after me: And the Lord, our God, sent the plague on the Egyptians, the children of the pharaoh . . ."

More than anything, Shafirov wanted Borokh Leibov not to call him Reb Shapir.

IX

Masha-Riva

1715

The Spruce Lodge, or as it was simply called, the Lodge, stood outside Saint Petersburg on the Moscow road, in the woods to one side. The farm consisted of a roomy cabin behind a sturdy log fence, resembling a fort fence with pointed timbers, and several outbuildings: a shed, partitioned by thin walls into many rooms, stables, and a steam bath. They say that there once was a real spruce lodge in the middle of the yard, and a lovely Gypsy woman used to greet travelers with a ladle of vodka—but the Gypsy woman either died or was taken away by a handsome traveler, and the lodge was dismantled before the heavy autumn rains and never put back, either because people were too lazy or because it wasn't needed. But legend never told when it happened—ten years ago or the year before last.

This autumn came early and was windy. The wind blew

fallen leaves into the farmyard; it drove dreary rain at the walls and windows. Inside the warm cabin, however, the rain seemed rather nice, perhaps because for the men who had entered and seated themselves comfortably the watery mess was no longer a problem. And over a glass of wine they took tender, slightly mocking pity on those who were traveling under the "nice rain" to get to the lodge.

The travelers were the young, still mustacheless Prince Vasily Gagarin, Tulyakov, and Chevalier René Lemort. The rest were already there: the robust wastrel Rastopchin, Golovin, and Krivoshein. Fyodor Rastopchin was the only one over thirty; his face, covered with scars and wrinkles, with high Tatar cheekbones, was the color of tea, and his flat black mustache was bristly. Rastopchin was prized by his circle for his experienced willingness to party.

Waiting for their friends, Rastopchin, Golovin, and Nikita Krivoshein drank Romany wine and looked out the gray windows impatiently. The host, Semyon, did not come near his guests but kept sticking his wide-browed, bald head out the kitchen door and checking the table: what to bring, what to clear. Everything necessary and appropriate was already there, and Semyon's round, darting eyes regarded the dark bottles, the plump roast chickens with stuffed rear ends, and the pots of sauerkraut with the same steady and kindly expression as they did the faces of the guests, also long familiar.

Sharp-eyed Semyon was the only one to know the true story of the Lodge. He told it to his guests, willingly and colorfully, and always differently. Sometimes the farm stood on the site of an ancient pagan temple, and on this stone, every Thursday at six in the morning, the chief priest Chymyn offered a sacrifice to the god Karyga—he would slit the belly of a black-eyed maiden from there up to her breastbone.

Sometimes Chymyn didn't kill a maiden with his bone knife—instead she waited in the lodge, which stood right where the hay shed was now, and at six in the morning every Thursday special strongmen of the Chukhon tribe came to her, one hundred and one of them, and they raped her until the black-eyed beauty, weeping tears of joy, gave up her soul to the god Karyga. To hear Semyon tell it, the fate of the Gypsy was varied too: sometimes, after sleeping with the one hundred and one strong men, she died in childbirth, or sometimes, with the permission and blessing of Semyon himself, she went off to Gypsy lands and ruled there but would certainly come back, because she was a woman, and where could she derive more womanly pleasure than at the Lodge—not in Gypsy lands, where the men eat nothing but cherries! You could expect her back maybe next week!

His audience, starting with robust Rastopchin, was most touched by the story of Black Eyes in the lodge; every man imagined himself in those heroic and exciting times, not like theirs, and naturally he was the one, with his strength and finesse, who brought those final happy tears to her eyes. As for the lovely Gypsy, they waited for her patiently and habitually, asking Semyon each time if she had come back and comparing unfavorably with her indisputable but imaginary qualities the heavyset charms of the inhabitants of the partitioned cells in the hay shed.

These pretty inhabitants, hiding their boredom, listened day in and day out to the guests' wise conversation on lofty topics: the great state restructuring and the damage to morals, which at first glance seemed unfortunate but on closer inspection was actually progressive and useful. The inevitable example was always the Lodge, with its Mankas, Katyas, Lubkas, and especially Marfutka, who thanks to Semyon's efforts was believed to be either the sister or the niece of the lovely Gypsy and therefore so popular that people waited in line for her favors. The friendly rivalry among the young men never turned to ugly jealousy; there were few fistfights.

"Hey, Semyon!" Rastopchin cried and clapped his hands as he turned away from the window. The owner of the Lodge appeared instantly from the kitchen, almost on the run. "Why don't you call the girls! It's boring here: just rain and more rain."

Readily accepting responsibility for the rains that fell from the heavens, Semyon nodded his bald head and went into the entry. His guests watched him make his way through the mud to the hay shed, where the girls came out in response to his call, covering themselves with kerchiefs as they ran squealing through the rain. The pleasant cries made Rastopchin squint and smile dreamily. His smile was tender, almost childlike.

The girls, five of them, sat down near the wall and came over one at a time to the table when called. They were broad shouldered, strong girls, with short legs, like those of workhorses, and pleasantly stupid faces. They filled the room not so much with their voices (they were whispering, covering their mouths with their hands, as if they were picking their teeth) as with the flash of their voluminous and colorful clothes, which made the men alert. Their eyes lost their insouciant, sleepy expression and filled with the sparkle of sharpened steel dipped in oil.

"Where's Marfutka?" demanded Rastopchin.

"Be right here," Semyon promised. "You know her, captain sir, she'll stay in bed when she's not supposed to and can't be found when she *is*." And he added proudly, "A wonderful girl."

Nodding in agreement, Rastopchin said nothing, then, leaning over the back of his chair, called "Katya!" And then, "Manka!"

The girls came over quickly and sat down on the edges of the chairs on either side of Rastopchin.

"Let's drink!" Rastopchin said. "I'm bored. All that rain. It's depressing."

"You too, my beauties, you too!" Krivoshein invited the other women. "We'll all drink. The rain is for everyone and so is the wine. . . . No, no, my dear, you sit over there, and leave this chair for the marvelous Marfutka."

Rastopchin narrowed his eyes over his wineglass and looked with dismay at the place reserved by the far-thinking Krivoshein.

"Gentlemen, I ask you to take note!" Golovin said, his arm tracing an arc and coming to rest on Lubka's shoulders. "A simple hut, crude food, morally healthy maidens—this is true unity with our wonderful and long-suffering people. And this, if you will, is a mark of the times: that in this horrible weather we drag ourselves to the sticks to immerse ourselves in the people."

"You'll immerse yourself, Count, I promise," Rastopchin said. "Eh, Lubka?"

"What's the rush, is there a fire?" Lubka asked reasonably. "It's still light out. There's time."

"I'm completely serious, gentlemen!" Golovin continued. "We're living in historic times. The old feeble world is broken, the new one has begun. And it's not just that we've caught up with the haughty West and are now producing excellent cloth and even needles. We have made a moral revolution! Why, just take our little Lodge—this would have been unthinkable just twenty years ago, to sit casually and talk with Lubka or Marfutka . . ."

"The marvelous Marfutka," Krivoshein added.

". . . and nobly feel part of the people," Golovin finished. "The people are our support!"

"Isn't that right, Lubka?" Krivoshein had had a lot of Romany wine and had turned red.

"As you say, master!" Lubka shrugged her powerful shoulders. The gesture made Golovin's hand fall from her shoulder and land on the bench with an unpleasant smack.

"You're always like that!" Golovin's brow furrowed. "But all of us"—and his injured hand encompassed all of them, his comrades, the girls, and Semyon—"are the Russian people, and that's what's so wonderful. We are one flesh, one blood, and one soul."

"What's flesh?" Manka whispered, her lips touching Rastopchin's ear.

"Meat," Rastopchin explained, slapping Manka's heavy behind. "Meat, yes, but don't mix the soul in here, Golovin. Where would you say Semyon's soul is? In his pocket. And Manka's?" He patted the girl again. "We know where."

"But you're wrong!" Golovin persisted. "Of course your soul and mine are higher than Semyon's or Lubka's . . ."

"Leave the marvelous Marfutka out of this," Krivoshein insisted, unstoppable. "She is definitely of royal blood, albeit Gypsy. And you, Golovin, you find all this so near and dear and interesting, because you recently rose up from the people. . . . How old *is* your nobility? While we Krivosheins, for us the people are just that. A collection of people."

"I mean . . ." Golovin couldn't come up with a response. "I mean . . ."

"But our times really are progressive," Krivoshein continued unflappably. "We used to have girls brought in from the villages and kept in some garret, but now we come to this lovely hole. But why I like sitting in this hovel, at a filthy table, is beyond me."

"That is the temper of the times," Rastopchin said, glad that the conversation had moved away from the question of nobility, which he found unpleasant. "As for the people, you're right, Krivoshein; after a glass of wine we start carrying on every which way about it."

"At least it's after wine!" Krivoshein added. "Pretty soon all it will take is a cup of tea."

"While the people have some vodka, wipe their mouth with their hand, and without any talk, go to bed," Rastopchin summed up and looked at the door. "But where is that Marfutka? Is she coming or what?"

But instead of Marfutka, the chevalier René Lemort, huddled in his wet cloak, entered the cabin.

"This damned Russian weather!" Lemort said, irritated but with a sweet smile on his pure white, glasslike face. "But how good that I am here. Gagarin and Tulyakov will be here soon; I passed them."

Chevalier Lemort, the grandnephew of the French ambassador, was distinguished by a delicate figure and a merry disposition. Not a wealthy man and given to what Krivoshein termed pathological thriftiness, Lemort lived in constant and sincere awe and delight of his Russian friends' spendthrift generosity. He was happy to spend all his time visiting, drinking, or conversing. His charming smile, which seemed a bit dumb when joined with his bulging and darting eyes, had become the talk of the town among those high-society youth of Saint Petersburg given to sprees and pranks. "Grinning like René" meant being a swell fellow without any special qualities (which only held you back in the sparkling gay life) and being irreplaceable for festive parties that turned into drunken brawls and gluttony. All attempts by the French ambassador to find his grandnephew dignified work had met with failure. Without denying the benefits of work, the chevalier nevertheless placed greater hopes in a successful union with a rich and beautiful heiress, but thanks to his easygoing manner he was in no rush for that either.

"You may have passed Gagarin and Tulyakov, friend René, but you have to catch up with us. Sit down!" Rastopchin poured wine into a low glass. "Or would you prefer vodka?"

"I would," Lemort said with a nod. "I got chilled."

"We'll warm you up!" Rastopchin said with certainty. He was glad to see Lemort and happy that they could end the conversation that had been boring him and give their all to good fun. "Hey, Semyon, damn your eyes! What about the music?"

"Coming!" Semyon nodded his heavy head. "It's ready!"

And at a sign from the host, a sleepy, black-haired man with a flat, broken nose came out of the kitchen, not quite sober. He raised a violin to his bearded chin, crossed his eyes in concentration, and brought the bow sliding across the strings. Semyon had picked up a balalaika from the corner; he held it to his chest and plucked the strings with his rough, square fingernail. The girls got up from the table to dance. Arms on hips and shoulders moving, they floated lazily around the room, like ducks on a pond, stretching their necks and their smooth heads with heavy braids.

"Make it livelier!" demanded Rastopchin and clapped his hands.

But the girls didn't need urging. They were getting into the swing of things on their own, clicking their heels on the floor, turning in place with short little cries, their wide skirts flaring. The original lack of expression on their faces was replaced with pleased smiles. Their lips parted, their nostrils flared, touching beads of sweat formed on their pure round foreheads. Semyon and the dark muzhik played louder and sprightlier. Watching the girls closely, the guests quietly stamped their feet in time to the music.

No one noticed the front door open to let in the Gypsy-slim Marfutka. Behind her, treading softly, came a strong young woman with a sweet round face. A black dog the size of a sheared sheep followed the women inside, its toenails clicking on the floorboards. Baring its teeth, the dog leapt into the middle of the room, and the dancers scattered clumsily in various directions. The men jumped up from the table. The dark musician sighed and put down his fiddle and bow.

Shouldering aside Marfutka, the tall woman strode over, freed her hand from beneath her purple shawl, grabbed the dog by the scruff of its neck as if it were a cat, and easily lifted it off the floor. Raising her arm, bare to the elbow, filled with white marble strength, she tossed the scrambling dog at the door, which flew open from the jolt.

The men laughed in release, observing the strong woman. The muzhik, sensing Semyon's sharp look, picked up his instrument and began playing. Tapping and turning as they went, the girls slowly came from their corners.

"Now that's all right!" Golovin muttered in amazement, holding his glass. "New girl! What's your name!"

"Agashka!" the girl announced in a low velvety voice, and, crossing her arms under her heavy, trembling breasts, she floated into the circle like a swan into a herd of ducks.

"She should be wrestling bears, not dancing!" Krivoshein noted, whether critically or ecstatically, it was not clear. "She's very . . . very . . . ! But still my preference remains with the marvelous Marfutka; my concepts of beauty and charm are unshakable!"

"Krivoshein, you're a reactionary!" Golovin said, never taking his eyes from Agashka. "Just take a good look at her!"

The criticism seemed to please Krivoshein. He smiled.

"Reactionary, reactionary," he said, rolling the *r*'s expansively. "Why not? It sounds good. And then, somebody's got to be a reactionary! Who better than me?"

"You keep joking, Krivoshein . . ." said Golovin, getting up from the table.

"She really is unique, that Agashka," Rastopchin noted.

"To the highest degree!" Krivoshein agreed readily. "And if an organ grew out of her forehead she'd be even more unique . . . Really, gentlemen! In the old days the crowd, or as we now call them, the people, made idols of the noble and rich. Anyone who stuck a pearl the size of a child's fist in his hat became an idol. Everyone talked about him. Nowadays nobility is useless and even harmful sometimes. Today's idol is Menshikov. And tomorrow some dancer with an organ on her forehead will be on everyone's lips . . . Hey, Marfutka, everyone's forgotten you, poor thing! Come on, come here!"

"And what do you have to say for yourself, Semyon?" Rastopchin asked, turning to their host. "To have such a surprise for us!"

"We don't care if it's a dog, as long as it lays eggs," Semyon said clearly.

Golovin danced, panting, his arms around Agashka, as tall and round as a tree trunk.

Settled on Krivoshein's lap, a handful of sugar nuts in her dusky, slender palm, Marfutka watched the strong woman with envy. Lemort watched with a kindly and somewhat ironic smile. Gagarin and Tulyakov, who had just arrived, watched in astonishment from the doorway.

Agashka rose above the circle of dancers like a wild, inaccessible cliff above the hills. She tempted and enflamed the men. That wild inaccessibility and her total accessibility.

They calmed down only after Golovin, looking doomed and solemn, as if at a public execution, led Agashka to the hay shed. And the conversation started leaping from stone to stone again.

"I think she's a bit too big," Gagarin said, chewing on a stewed prune. "And that angelic face . . ."

"Right on the button!" Rastopchin exclaimed. "That's it exactly. It's not a demonic face, but an angelic one!"

"Poor Golovin!" said Krivoshein, moving Marfutka from his tired left knee to his right. "Though maybe right now he's happy in the embrace of the people."

"You know, gentlemen," Tulyakov announced, "an object no less amazing has appeared in Saint Petersburg."

"Who? Who?" voices cried.

"Masha Lacosta," Tulyakov said.

"The jester's daughter?" Rastopchin asked, pleased that he knew all. "The Jewess! I know her. I know—"

"Lovely Jewess!" Krivoshein corrected. "René and I saw her at Divier's. She's very pretty. Right, René?"

At the mention of Divier's name, Semyon came closer and pricked up his ears.

"Yes," Lemort said and nodded. "But she's the daughter of a jester. It's rather . . . off-putting."

"So what!" Rastopchin said. "Look at Agashka! Golovin didn't ask her what her father did, whether he sells fish or tends a garden."

"What garden?" Lemort asked.

"What difference does it make?" Rastopchin waved him away. "What I mean is that it doesn't matter who her father is or her mother—just as long as she's pretty. It's only if you're married that it matters."

"I can't marry her," Lemort said with a shake of the head. "The jester is impoverished. I checked. He has nothing except his salary and some stupid uninhabited island. Of course, he is a friend of Divier . . ."

Semyon grew tense.

"Don't get involved with Divier," Gagarin said.

"But Masha isn't Divier's daughter, she's the jester's!" explained Tulyakov. "And just because they're friends, does that mean you can't court her? That's ridiculous, gentlemen. We're living in the eighteenth century, after all!"

"If he weren't a jester, I would probably marry her," Lemort mused. "But being a jester's son-in-law—that's unseemly for a nobleman."

"Mutual attraction is the only reason to wed," said Krivoshein. "Now marvelous Marfutka and I are mutually attracted and we're going off to get married."

"Well, there's no problem about that!" Lemort exclaimed. "The little Jewess adores me."

"What makes you say that?" Rastopchin asked with a suspicious squint.

"I know women," Lemort said, tilting his head. "I can tell from a single glance."

"I'll bet you a dozen bottles of champagne that you won't get anywhere with her!" Tulyakov cried out, turning red.

"I think you failed in that sweet endeavor, Tulyakov, isn't that so?" Krivoshein said, laughing over Marfutka's shoulder. "I'll add another dozen bottles to the bet."

Rastopchin thought and added a half dozen.

"I don't like this," Gagarin said. "After all, she's not a dog, a horse, or a serf girl. She's almost one of our circle. And the Jew Lacosta is not Vytashchi or Kabysdokh, even though he is a jester."

"But it's only a joke!" Lemort smiled gently. "And then we'll all drink the champagne here, at the Lodge. The day after tomorrow, all right? In the evening?"

"Well, we'll see about that," Tulyakov hissed.

The appearance of wildly smiling Golovin and enormous Agashka—round-faced and reddened—put an end to the argument.

The guests stayed until after three in the morning.

Sharp-eyed Semyon came to report to Divier at eight-thirty.

Divier found Lacosta at six in the evening.

But an hour before that, a covered coach drove away from Lacosta's hut. In the coach, side by side, sat René Lemort and Masha. At their feet was a small trunk with Masha's things for the first few days. Lemort took nothing.

"There," said Lemort when the coach passed the round-sided barracks on the outskirts of the city and entered the heavy darkness of the forest road, slippery and rain soaked. "And now we're almost happy, as I promised. It's dark, we're cozy, and you and I are strangers in this barbaric land and that's why we're so close to each other. La belle France awaits us!"

Masha sniffed and managed to keep from crying. France awaited! The ancestral château of noble chevalier René Lemort, his kind parents, who would never know that she was a jester's daughter! And she burned with shame before her father, the jester Lacosta.

And Lemort suddenly, with a sweet catch in his throat, began to believe that someone was waiting for him somewhere, that in the nonexistent château the nonexistent servants were preparing the bridal suite for the young master returning from barbaric Russia. He wanted so badly to believe it, and he did! They would spend the night at the vile way station, and then head for la belle France, with so many marvelous châteaus and so many loyal servants.

"We'll get married as soon as we get to France!" Lemort

said with total sincerity. "You'll see, my parents will love you. In the summer we'll live in the château, in the winter in Paris, at our palace."

"You can't imagine how horrible it is to be the daughter of a jester," Masha said gratefully. "Everyone laughs and whispers behind your back, as if you were the daughter of an executioner."

"Forget about that as soon as possible!" Lemort proposed with determination, and it seemed to him that he really could shield Masha from the venomous whispers—and that he really would do so. "Now you are Madame Lemort and I will shield you . . . Almost Madame Lemort," he corrected himself gently and significantly, and taking the girl's hand, kissed her fingers and then her wrist—as high up as the unfortunately narrow sleeve permitted.

Stopping at the sleeve barrier, Lemort changed topics according to the circumstances, and spoke of sleeves, décolleté, laces and hems, men's and women's. Masha listened attentively: there was much to learn before appearing at the French château.

"My father is pedantic about etiquette; he changes three times a day, even if there are no guests and he is alone in the whole château," Lemort said, chasing away memories of how his father had been arrested many years ago for his debts and had died of jaundice in prison.

"I'll learn," Masha promised hotly. "I'll learn everything, you'll see!" She was engulfed with gratitude to René Lemort, almost as if he were God—because he was taking her away to France, he was marrying her, a jester's daughter. She was prepared to do anything for him—be it embarrassing, shameful, or painful. She had already betrayed her father for his sake—René had begged her on his knees not to say a word to him about their secret departure for France, and she had obeyed. She would tell her father later, when they had arrived at the château and everything was behind them. And even though her father would cry and tear his hair out, René was right: here in Russia, the chevalier Lemort could not marry a jester's daughter. And if anyone was at fault, for what happened and what would happen, it was her father; why did he have to be the czar's jester, why did he make his daughter a miserable outcast? Of course, it was all his fault!

They reached the way station in total darkness. A sleepy host answered their knock, scratching his unkempt head. You can get lice here, Lemort worried to himself. As if my own weren't enough . . .

They followed the host, who carried the trunk into a cramped room with plank walls that did not reach the ceiling. There was no one else in the station. The host, swaying from either sleepiness or drink, dumped the trunk by the wide bed covered with a faded patchwork quilt.

"Double rates," the host said.

"All right, all right!" Lemort shouted. "Get out with you!"

There wasn't any bench in the room, and Masha sat on the edge of the bed. She wanted to be already in the château, not in this repulsive way station! But she did not dare mention this to René.

Lemort started hurrying, bustling. He did not talk of lakes or châteaus anymore.

"It's stuffy in here," he said. "And it stinks. . . . We'll get up with the dawn tomorrow and travel on. You go to bed now, go to bed, I'll turn away."

He ran over to the lamp, bent down, and spat on it. The light hissed and went out.

In the dark, Masha turned back the quilt and crawled along the wide bed to the log wall.

"Take off your clothes!" Lemort ordered coldly, a different man.

Masha listened and obeyed. She did not feel shame—it was dark after all—nor fear, nor curiosity. Pulling off her dress, she thought with a brief, suppressed sigh that she should have told her father about France—and then, surely this filthy hut would not have seemed quite so filthy and disgusting to her. Then the bed creaked, as if a log had fallen from the sky, and René's unpleasantly cold hands roved over Masha's body; squeezing, scratching, separating.

Masha was awakened by the rattle of dishes and the sound of voices coming from the main room next door. Gray light flickered in the window, covered with a dull bull's bladder.

Masha was alone in the bed, alone in the room. She pulled the quilt up to her chin and peered into the dusky corners.

"René!" she called.

The door opened and the host's unkempt head appeared in the doorway.

"Your Renny's gone," he said boldly and mockingly. "Get up, young lady, pay up and get out."

"What do you mean he's gone? Where?"

"He didn't tell me!" The man laughed, showing wolf fangs through his beard. "He took the coach and left. . . . You do have money to pay, don't you?"

"Just a minute," Masha said. "Just one minute . . ."

She wasn't about to drown herself or hang herself. She wanted only one thing: to go back home to the jester Lacosta, her father. And impatiently she watched the host rummage through her trunk, selecting clothes to pay for her night's lodgings.

She got back home to Saint Petersburg after noon. Lacosta,

red eyed and frazzled, embraced his daughter silently and, hiding his face from her, squeezed his eyes tight, painfully tight, several times.

"It's all right," Lacosta said. "All right . . ." His hands fluttered from his daughter's head to her shoulders, back to her head, her cheeks. Masha recalled René's wandering hands and wept.

"It's all right, it's all right," Lacosta kept saying. "I'll take care of everything. I'll do it all."

"He promised," Masha said, her chin trembling. "And I . . . And now . . ."

He had his Riva back again, she was alive. Now he knew exactly what he had to do.

"Don't talk about it," he said. "Go to your room, get some sleep. And, you know—have a good cry."

He walked his daughter to her room, shut the door behind her, listened to the double fall of tossed-off shoes—and was transformed. His movements became stealthy and swift. He slipped over to the large oval mirror in a gilt frame and looked closely as he smoothed his hair, gently poked the bags under his eyes, and rubbed hard at his face, as if forcing the features ravaged by tears and no sleep into a new shape. Then, lightly tossing back the lid of the trunk, he looked greedily at the broadsword, from hilt to tip—a present from Divier. The silvery sword, like a dangerous fish of prey, lay on a wavy piece of deep blue Utrecht velvet. It was beautiful: Lacosta noted the fact coldly.

He shut the trunk and paced the room, smiling and muttering to himself. A huge spring seemed to be unwinding within him, and his movements were ruled by that inexorable spring force: from his daughter's door, past the mirror, past the trunk, the walk across the room, and only God knew how many more trips were left in the spring. Lacosta threw on his cape with a flourish, turned on his heel, and went outside.

Divier, a true friend, had helped the day before with everything that was in his power; he named the chevalier René Lemort, drew a map to his house. He rolled the map up neatly, handed it to Lacosta, and said softly but firmly, "Duels are banned by the czar under punishment of death for both sides. Besides which, Lemort wields the weapon better than you; he's studied and you haven't. . . . A good way would be to drown him in the river with all the loose ends and clues."

"I'll try," Lacosta said hoarsely. "But, Antoine, how do I lure him out of the house to the river?"

"That's just one way," Divier said patiently. "Another is to wait for him outside the spruce lodge, on the Moscow road. Use a cudgel or stick with an iron ball on a chain, like an ordinary robber. The wolves will do the rest."

Lacosta did not intend to ask Divier for anything more than friendly advice. Holding down his cloak, which was flapping in the damp wind, he went to see Vytashchi.

Vytashchi lived on the edge of Kulikov Swamp, in a large, clean house. In the icon corner, beneath the steady votive light, hung a tuft of aromatic dried herbs. Staring at his uninvited guest in consternation, Vytashchi smoothed his hair and then politely scratched his chest.

"You might as well come in, I guess," Vytashchi said, finally moving aside. "Sit here."

"I came on business," Lacosta said, without sitting down. "Can you help me? Can you?"

"Help?" Vytashchi, towering over his guest, repeated the question. No one had ever asked him to help, and he was confused and pleasantly excited. "Well, why not? . . . Help how?"

"It's like this," Lacosta explained briefly. "Right now we're going to call on a man, and you say to him: 'The jester Lacosta challenges you to a duel.' Can you remember that? A duel."

"You want to fight with him?" Vytashchi's visage lightened. "You just tell me who, and I'll tear his head off! I'll help you!"

"No! I have to do it myself. Thank you."

"What did he do?" Vytashchi asked. "Insult you or hurt you?" In that clean house his voice was concerned and anxious.

Lacosta went over to the table, sat down, and chewed his lip. "He . . . ruined . . . my daughter," Lacosta said.

"What are you sitting around for? Let's go!"

Lacosta, huddled tensely and staring out the window at the leaden waters of the Neva, waited in a damp corner of the tavern, five minutes' walk from the house where Chevalier René Lemort lived. He did not have a long wait: Vytashchi flung open the door and barged in.

"Hey, you! A bottle of vodka!" Vytashchi demanded once he'd found Lacosta in the corner.

Lacosta was twiddling his thumbs, and he gave Vytashchi a questioning look. The knout master sat down on the groaning bench.

"He says," Vytashchi reported, "that a nobleman can't duel with a jester. Impossible."

"What else?" Lacosta untwined his fingers and touched Vytashchi's back. "Think, man!"

"I remember. He said, 'A jester has to be taught a lesson with a stick, not a sword.' "

"Good," Lacosta said, chewing his lip in satisfaction. "That's what I thought . . ."

"Let's have a drink," Vytashchi said and poured. "Does he mean me too, with a stick? Why, sticks would break on me!"

"That's what I thought," Lacosta repeated with a smile. "A jester gets a stick, but a noble chevalier can be taught with a broadsword."

"The knout rips into everyone the same way!" Vytashchi noted with expertise. "The important thing is to keep the tail from getting soaked."

"A jester isn't human," Lacosta went on. "A jester is a toad, a gnat. Use a stick on a jester! And his child is a special treat, a spicy one, for a sweet tooth. . . . Now you—your name is Stepan, right?"

"They called me Stepan Medved," Vytashchi confirmed solemnly.

"Stepan, do you have a family? Children?"

"God didn't grant me that," Vytashchi explained simply. "A floor washer comes to me, a clean woman."

They drank and munched on hunks of green onion.

"Have some bread!" Vytashchi suggested. "Sprinkle it with salt and eat it."

"I came to you, to ask you," Lacosta said, biting off a piece of bread, "because we are, essentially, equally miserable. Well, to add to my misfortune, I'm also a Jew. But you're the knout master. First of all, though, we're both jesters."

"Why, are things better for a jester in Jewish lands or any other?" Vytashchi asked hopefully. "I thought that it was the same everywhere; it's that kind of work."

"What does *jester* mean?" Lacosta went on, without listening. "At work you're a jester, but at home? I've been to your house; are you a jester in your own home? Or are we only half jesters, Stepan? Or does everyone despise us, every hour, every minute, and laugh not at our jokes but at us!"

"They do," Vytashchi said. "But I don't give a damn." He spat juicily on the floor and then rubbed the spot out with his enormous foot.

"Pour me a drink!" Lacosta said. "Now tell me, tell me, Stepan, have you ever felt that people were looking at you as if you were an animal or something? How does that make you feel—uncomfortable, disgusted?"

"No one talks to me," Vytashchi said, swallowing the vodka and looking at Lacosta trustingly. "Just the floor washer."

"Our whole tribe is damned," Lacosta said, leaning over the table and swaying. "Damned! We've got the plague and so do our children. We shouldn't have children! You don't have any, Stepan, and it's easier for you than for me."

"The floor washer doesn't want any," Vytashchi said with a sigh. "I've begged her in Christ's name, and beaten her, and everything. . . . It's nice to have a little babe, even a wolf knows that. And we may be jesters, but we're like people too."

"You put it correctly—'like people'!" Lacosta cried bitterly. " 'Like' means you can spit at us, beat us with a stick."

"Well, you can do that to anyone," Vytashchi said. "It's very simple."

"Then we're even worse off," Lacosta said. "There's only one thing left for us: to run away. And so Riva wanted to run away with the first person who asked, no matter where. . . . That's easy to understand, Stepan!"

"Wait a minute! Where can you run to? I was born here, my place is here. Run away! Why coddle my misery in a foreign land? I'm better off home!"

"Your place," Lacosta said. "I don't have one. Just as I stopped off here in passing, I'll move on."

"Don't say that!" Vytashchi countered hotly. "Where are

you going? Why if anyone lifts a finger against you, I'll tear his skin off—just say the word! I swear by the cross . . ."

"Thank you, Stepan," Lacosta said and embraced his rock-hard shoulders.

Sharp-eyed Semyon was more intense that evening than usual. A lot of champagne had been ordered, and the owner of the Lodge was expecting unusually boisterous merrymaking, leading to fights and more. Tulyakov had been waving his fists around for the last hour, shouting, and not letting anyone else speak.

"And I tell you that he didn't get anywhere! The Jewess locked herself up! The jester complained to the czar!"

Krivoshein tried to argue reasonably. "Well, if he didn't get anywhere now, maybe he will later. The marvelous Marfutka agrees with me."

"I'll ask you not to argue!" Tulyakov took it as a personal offense. "I know better! The Jewess would rather hang herself!"

Agashka could have quieted Tulyakov—but she had over-indulged in *pelmeni* at lunch; she had stomach cramps and refused to come to the guests. The news of her gas did not make Semyon any happier. Of course, it wasn't his fault that that wan Frenchman had promised to sleep with the daughter of that damned jester here at Spruce Lodge and not someplace else—but when Divier got Semyon's report, he wagged a threatening finger at him. He wagged his finger! And every dog in Saint Petersburg knew what that meant: the next time he would stamp his foot and the treasury would take away his establishment, and Semyon would go out begging from house to house for a crust of bread. Or they'd send him off to the Urals, to the mines, in chains.

Time passed, the guests talked and drank, Agashka farted

in the hay shed, but René Lemort still did not come. Tulyakov got tired of yelling and sat in grumpy silence. The girls were bored without work, sitting in the corners and listening to the men's talk as if it were distant music, Chinese or Persian.

"This idolatry is a dangerous business," Rastopchin said, smacking his lips after a drink. "I mean, take that Jewess: she's slender, dusky, with coral lips, we all speak positively of her, and Tulyakov's prepared to risk his head for her. . . . But the years will pass and she'll grow gray and wrinkled, her breasts will dry up and sag, her teeth fall out, her braid grow thin, and a hairy wart will grow on her chin—and no one will be interested in her, no one will need her, everyone will want to spit in her tracks. 'Get along, old woman, go your own way!' . . . And that, gentlemen, is what I imagine every time I think about getting married—that is, obtaining a full-time idol—I picture a disgusting old woman, 'Get going, Granny! Scat!' And I don't get married."

"Well, you can't do anything about that!" Gagarin said, opening his palms. "The years have taken their toll on us too."

"New times have come," said Krivoshein, shifting Marfutka from one knee to the other. "And even newer times are on the way. And tomorrow some old man with a stick will come, impoverished and weak-kneed, but clever and a good talker, and he'll say, 'I know how to give every hungry man a piece of meat and every miserable man a bag of happiness.' And everyone will limp off after him, and whoever stays behind will be drowned in the river. And that thin old man will be an idol!"

"You've been drinking gloom, Krivoshein!" Rastopchin said with a grimace and smacked his sturdy round knees with his hands.

"René, René is here!" Gagarin called, turning to the creaking door.

Tulyakov got ready to fight, staring drunkenly at the door.

The black-haired peasant came through the door, holding the violin under his arm.

"Damn it!" Gagarin cursed. "Where the hell is he? . . . Let's have another drink, I guess!"

"I want oats!" Tulyakov said. "Give me oats!"

Semyon, showing no surprise, hurried to the shed and came back with a tin bowl of oats.

Tulyakov picked up a handful and sprinkled it over his head.

Bitterly he said, "I'm a horse!"

René Lemort's horse was plodding through the mud along the side of the road next to the black, wet pines. It was twilight, and the damp evening light mixed with heavy fog lay low over the woods. Lemort was in the saddle, leaning to the left. A little farther—and after the last turn to the Lodge he could let his mare, worn out by the vile road, canter.

At the very exit from the woods, a horseman dressed like a pharmacist in black, came out like a wood spirit and blocked the road right in front of Lemort's horse. The mare stopped indifferently and hung her head. The black horseman bent forward and struck Lemort in the side with the handle of his broadsword, knocking him from his saddle. He leapt down into the mud and helped the Frenchman to his feet.

"I don't have anything!" Lemort said, pressing his hands to his injured side. "I'm a poor foreigner!"

"You have a sword, young man," Lacosta said. "Or do you prefer to teach a jester with a stick? Then take a stick!"

"But I've told you that I don't want to fight with you,"

Lemort said, holding the sword away from him and backing up. "I can't! It's ridiculous! I'm a nobleman . . ."

"And I'm a jester," Lacosta said, waving his broadsword. "Defend yourself, or I'll cut you down like an ordinary peasant."

"I'll marry her!" exclaimed Lemort, grimacing at the whistling over his head.

"It's too early for her," Lacosta grumbled and took a swing. "It's too late for you."

Lemort attacked, and the point of his sword scratched Lacosta's upper arm. At that instant Lacosta's sword descended on his neck.

Peter was carving an ivory box to hold English capsules for kidney colic. His head bent to his shoulder, squinting, he listened closely to the steady hum of his lathe, set up beneath the large window in the shop. He liked this room in the palace attic, not too large but not cramped, airy and cozy. And today, having returned from the funeral of his son's wife—Princess Charlotte, who'd died of puerperal fever—he went right up. It had been unbearably stuffy at the funeral, the shimmering half light in the church had made him dizzy, and the whispering crowd had irritated him. The formal condolences sounded insincere. In the third day of his drinking spree, the widower Czarevitch Alexis did not hide his relief over the coffin. The marriage to the princess four years earlier at Peter's command had been an unhappy one, and Alexis had felt burdened by his wife. It was a lucky thing that he had not brought his mistress, the low-born Efrosinya, to the church: one could expect almost anything from the czarevitch.

After the service, Peter developed a headache and the usual

pain on the right side, below the ribs. Looking over the crowd distractedly, the czar thought with irritation about how to refuse his son, who wanted to marry the heavyset Efrosinya. After all, the boy's stepmother, Catherine, hadn't been born on a throne either. Czarevitch Alexis was stubborn and willful but not very bright—he took after his mother, Eudoxia Lopukhina. Silly pup, how dare he compare his slut with the czar's wife?

Rubbing the box lid on his sleeve, Peter reached for a new blade on the side table. There were cubbyholes along the walls and trunks holding carpenter's, joiner's, and turner's tools, brought from Holland, Germany, and the British Isles, sent from all over the world by monarchs who knew the czar's tastes. To the left of the window, near the corner, stood a divan covered with a Persian rug, and next to it a stand with nests for a half dozen cudgels of various sizes. The smallest, in the far left nest, looked more like a graceful walking stick; the largest, awesome in the far right nest, could easily stun a cow or horse.

At the door, blinking sleepily, the czar's favorite dog, Lizavetka, lay on a worn silk blanket. At the head of the divan and to the side, in a wooden crate with tall sides, Kabysdokh puttered. The dwarf had grown old and fallen into a second childhood. The gray-haired little man sang a sad lullaby about a gray wolf and then rattled his crate angrily and cursed.

Not many of the czar's entourage had access to this room. To come in was an honor, to walk out on your own feet—good luck.

The lathe sang; Kabysdokh sang in his crate. Looking down to check the drawing by the engraver Zubov, Peter cut out a snake over the cup on the lid. On a soft white cloth on his worktable, two Madagascar emeralds burned with green fire—eyes for the snake.

Swaying on her bowed legs, Lizavetka got up and walked to the door, growling. There was a knock.

"Jester Lacosta, Your Majesty!" the duty officer reported.

Peter continued carving and nodded.

Lizavetka sniffed Lacosta's shoes and headed back to her blanket.

"Permit me, Your Majesty"—the jester's soft voice spoke—"to congratulate you upon the birth of your grandson. And to offer my condolences on the demise of Princess Charlotte of Wolfenbüttel."

"Did you kill the Frenchman?" Peter asked, without turning around.

"I did, Your Majesty," Lacosta said, staring at the back of the czar's head.

"Do you know what you should get for that?" Peter finally set the box aside, turned, and stared at the jester without blinking. The bags under the czar's eyes were gray.

"I do, Your Majesty," Lacosta said and sighed. "But he seduced my daughter."

"So what, you fool!" Peter shouted, his head jerking. "Is she better than the rest?"

"Worse, Your Majesty," Lacosta said quietly.

The czar looked his skinny jester over from head to foot and bounded over to the cudgel stand. He picked one from the middle, hefted it, and returned it: too heavy. The second one from the left, with gold wire on the handle and black leather on the head, was commensurate with the jester's weight and body type.

"Turn around!" the czar ordered. He took a swing and struck Lacosta on the back. Lacosta crouched and covered his head with his arms. The czar's cudgel played on his shoulders, sides, and arms: Peter beat him without choosing a site.

"You're a Jew, almost a German, but you're more savage

than the lowliest peasant," Peter said when he was finished, wiping his brow with his sleeve and then with his large linen handkerchief. "You killed a man of your own will! . . . Sit there on the divan."

"Every day people are killed in the squares," Lacosta said, sitting down with difficulty. "Is that anything new?"

"That's done by my will," Peter said sternly but not angrily. "To rule means to teach, and I teach my people: some with kindness, others with punishment. People answer to me, and I answer to God."

"But they're people, not animals!" Lacosta countered piteously. "Every man thinks his own way . . ."

"Yes, they're people," Peter said, sitting down next to Lacosta. "But they're my people, like my fingers, my nails, my hair. It's hard for you to understand, Jester. And not only for you."

"I understand it well, Your Majesty," Lacosta muttered quickly.

"Inside every man is either a thief or an indolent oaf," Peter continued. "People don't steal only because they are too lazy or because they have evil intentions. You must be twice as wary of those who do not steal!"

"Man is evil!" Lacosta said with conviction, amazed to discover that he harbored no feelings of injury or anger toward the czar for the beating—no more than he did toward the cudgel that had been used. "In childhood he tears wings off butterflies, twists off dragonflies' heads, and hangs cats—childish cruelty, blood interest. And when he grows up he kills those like him: developed, mature evil. And nothing can stop him from that except power, rule, the czar's hand."

"Then you do understand!" Peter nodded in satisfaction. "Yet you killed the Frenchman! If you had told me, I'd have made him marry her!"

Lacosta stubbornly said nothing, staring at the quiet Kabysdokh.

"If the czar's hand allows itself to weaken," Peter said, jumping up from the divan, "not only the little people but the entire epoch will turn savage! You were right: it begins with bugs and cats and will end with a horrible extermination of men. . . . In Holland they can use laws, but here we have to run people with the stick."

"Once upon a time they used the stick in Holland too," Lacosta said without looking up.

Peter came over, raised Lacosta's head by the ears, and looked into his eyes.

"If I could live three lives, maybe I would teach our Russians to live by reasonable laws. But I am given only one lifetime, and that one is coming to an end because of the likes of you!"

He let go of Lacosta, went over to his lathe, and touched the wheel.

"Go away, Jester," he said, looking out the window. "I don't want to talk to you. You're smart, but you're not one of us. . . . Ha, Dutch laws! Who would believe them here, when I myself no longer believe in them?"

When he heard the soft closing of the door behind Lacosta, Peter went over to Kabysdokh's crate, crouched, and started poking the napping dwarf with a sharp stick.

X

The Czarevitch 1717–18

Typically Eastern European foul weather came to Vienna, dipping its wing and unleashing vile rain. The Austrian capital, faced with the wild steppe guest, looked frightened and even pathetic. The gusts of wind carried the hoarse breath of Asia. It seemed that the thick, churned-up darkness was hiding hordes of slant-eyed horsemen who would gallop in from all directions toward the imperial palace, the cathedral, the Grabenstrasse.

Hail poured onto the Grabenstrasse, the icy pellets brazenly knocking at the windows of the home of the Russian resident, Abraham Veselovsky. Veselovsky had just returned from Vice-Chancellor Schönborn's, and, chilled, he was warming his rump at the fireplace in the oval hall, holding a letter in his hand. The letter was from Saint Petersburg, from his cousin's father, Peter Pavlovich Shafirov.

"Dear Abraham," Shafirov wrote,

the czarevitch's flight continues to worry the Sovereign beyond all measure. In that evil event he sees a connection with the plans of his surviving enemies and therefore attributes primary importance to the affair. Anyone who is in the least involved in this crime is under tight surveillance—and you, naturally, are a prime suspect. Captain of the Guards Alexander Rumyantsev, sent to help you, reports your every step. If you manage to obtain the release of the czarevitch to the czar, or to kidnap him, or, in an extreme case, to get rid of him without a trace—a rich reward and a brilliant career await you. If the opposite occurs, and there is an unfortunate turn of events, you will place yourself and your brothers, Isaac and Fyodor, in mortal danger; Yasha is the only one who is a favorite of Prince Menshikov, and he is in no danger. . . . My position, as you know, is secure enough, but even I could fall into harsh disgrace.

Having read about the imminent disgrace, Veselovsky moved an armchair closer to the fire, sat down, lit his pipe, and chuckled. His uncle Peter Pavlovich had every right to worry, every right! He must not be the only one in Saint Petersburg worrying, and that was proof in itself that Czarevitch Alexis had a chance of winning. Not only did he have friends in Russia, but the Austrian Crown was hiding him, the Swedish King Charles and maybe even the Turks would support him. Russia was tired of reforms, Russia's tongue was hanging out, panting. Not just Czarevitch Alexis but any pretender, any passerby had a chance to get the throne. Whoever gets in his way will lose his head. And whoever helps, even covertly, will be raised higher. Just not interfering would be help! And then things would be good for everyone: Isaac, and Fyodor, and even Yasha, not to mention such an experienced and irreplaceable man as Uncle Peter Pavlovich. The issue wasn't whether Alexis would let Russians wear beards again and dress the soldiers in the Streltsy uniform; the issue was the future of Russia, and consequently, the future of Sweden, Turkey, and Poland. Once he became czar, the czarevitch would probably return the northern and southern sea gates to their old owners. Or he might not: czars differed from czarevitches. But, really, what difference did it make to the Veselovsky brothers who sat on the Russian throne? Whoever was better disposed to them should sit on the throne, God willing. And Alexis would probably give them more than his father. At least he wasn't stingy with promises.

"Intimate," Veselovsky continued to read, "to my colleague Vice-Chancellor Schönborn, that further secret support for Czarevitch Alexis in Austrian holdings could lead to a Russo-Austrian war, so undesirable for all of Europe. The Sovereign is sending Peter Tolstoy to Vienna for secret negotiations, and if his mission fails, war will be inevitable. . . . Destroy this letter without delay upon reading it."

Veselovsky reread a few phrases, then neatly tore the page in four and tossed the pieces in the fireplace. He stirred the fire with a poker and then reached for the bellpull. The door opened in response to the bell, and a servant entered.

"Who brought this letter?" Veselovsky asked.

"A foreigner by the looks of him," the lackey reported, standing at attention. "He is warming up in the kitchen."

"Call him!" Veselovsky said.

Shafirov's emissary turned out to be an old Jew in a black coat and pointy black hat, with gray forelocks.

"Are you from Saint Petersburg?" Veselovsky asked with doubt in his voice. "Did you get the letter there?"

"No, with your permission," the Jew replied, his old red eyes blinking rapidly. "I sell glue in Warsaw. The letter was given to me by a Jew from Smolensk. . . . You don't have to worry: our Jewish mail works even better than the royal mails in England!"

"Do you know who the letter is from?" Veselovsky asked.

"I told you," the old man said, shrugging his shoulders and looking down. "From a Jew in Smolensk. He sells kosher meat."

"So, this kosher butcher sent me a letter?" Veselovsky was getting to enjoy the game.

"Exactly so, Reb Abraham," the old man said and blinked. "You know, his name is Ruvim. He sells kosher meat and fowl."

"Oh, yes," Veselovsky said. "Of course." He suddenly recalled the family legend about how Peter Pavlovich Shafirov used to sell clothes in the Polish Rows and got into a fight over a stolen hat with the future Prince Menshikov. "So, it's Ruvim?"

The old man spread his hands, palms up, and smiled.

"So let it be Ruvim!"

"You may spend the night here," Veselovsky offered.

"No, with your permission," the old man replied. "I have a few more errands to do for Ruvim."

Veselovsky watched the old man go out and then rang for the servant.

"Have them prepare my carriage," Veselovsky said. "I'm going to the palace."

But he didn't go to the palace; he went to the house of Vice-Chancellor Schönborn. Rumyantsev, informed by the lackey, headed for the palace and looked for Resident Veselovsky's carriage nearby but did not find it.

Schönborn was a tall, pink old man with long hands and big feet. He was distinguished by enviable good health and exemplary sangfroid, which had become proverbial. He truly was pleased with everything: his digestion, his wife and his mistress, his work, and the Austrian Empire's international position. He expressed himself, both at work and in his family circle, in beautiful, elegant speech; his oratorical gifts were held up as a model, and that pleased him. He used the word *fairness* as often as *air* or *bread.* Nevertheless, Vice-Chancellor Schönborn did not take the concept of fairness seriously in the least.

Veselovsky's late visit initially disturbed him. The Russian resident had chosen the wrong time to come. Schönborn was involved in a responsible and delicate business. Wearing a warm cap and a worn house robe, which were not in the least commensurate with his official function, the vice-chancellor was attending the labor of his luxurious Persian cat, Fatima. The father was the blue-eyed Sultan, a gift of the Persian shah to Austrian Emperor Charles VI.

It had cost Schönborn much effort and diplomacy to get the emperor's consent to a brief union between Sultan and Fatima. Charles, who was intriguing secretly in the East, valued the shah's gift, and among those who wished to have Sultan's stud services besides the vice-chancellor were three ministers, including the minister of war, and one prince. Each was flattered to become related to the emperor even this obliquely; each hoped to be able to say casually to guests, "Incredibly beautiful kittens, aren't they? They're the offspring of Sultan; yes, yes, naturally, the emperor's . . ." But Charles was quite serious about his relations. He chose thoughtfully and did not scatter his cat unwisely. Schönborn had pleaded for a month and a half. His final argument was "I am old, Your Majesty, and that sad day is not far off when I will have to ask Your Majesty's permission to retire. . . . Granting my lowly request I will take as a sign of your kind disposition, a reward that will significantly reinforce my strength in Your Majesty's service."

And when the resistance was overcome at last, Sultan was delivered to Schönborn in the palace carriage, accompanied by an officer of the palace guard and two lackeys. Pregnancy was the result of the visit, and now the day of delivery had come. This had naturally turned into a major event, in its way extraordinary. And it was just on that day and at that hour that Veselovsky came, unbidden.

But curiosity soon took the upper hand, especially since Fatima delivered successfully, while Veselovsky cooled his heels. What unexpected news had brought the czar's resident at this late hour? Schönborn did not doubt for a minute that the reason was the czarevitch, but just today he had spent an hour discussing that very topic with Veselovsky, and he could add nothing new.

"Come in, my friend, come in!" Schönborn said, straightening the light blue velvet eiderdown covered with vile slime. "Aren't these incredibly beautiful kittens? They're the offspring of Sultan; yes, yes, naturally, the emperor's . . ."

"Truly, charm itself," Veselovsky agreed readily, his eyes narrowing at the sight of the hairless, blind lumps.

"Forgive me for my homey attire," Schönborn said, wrapping his robe tighter. "Please God, don't take it for lack of respect!"

"Of course not!" Veselovsky replied, a broad smile on his thin, energetic face. "I'm the one who burst in on you in the middle of the night. . . . Believe me, extraordinary circumstances brought me to you at this hour, in this weather."

"I believe you, I believe you!" the host said, waving his hand good-naturedly to show that the nocturnal visit had not disturbed him in the least.

"I received an urgent letter from Saint Petersburg, after our meeting today," Veselovsky said and patted his pockets as if looking for the letter. Schönborn, frowning, his lips a tight line, watched him. The last courier had come from Russia three days ago; the contents of his pouch were known to the vice-chancellor. Who had brought this letter? Did it exist at all?

"I've forgotten it!" the guest exclaimed, and the host nodded in understanding. "I locked it in my desk and forgot it at the last minute. . . . But I remember it by heart—those parts, at least, that I feel it necessary to share with you, as a friend."

The host moved his heavy leather armchair closer, set his forearms on the armrests, and leaned forward. His eyes, under their bushy red eyebrows, grew attentive.

"I am talking about a person known to you," Veselovsky said, almost in a whisper, but firmly and clearly. "His continued secret stay in the Ehrenberg Fortress, in the Tyrol, will lead to swift and inevitable war between our countries. Believe me, it pains me to tell you this; I am speaking as a friend."

"But, my dear man," Schönborn replied, "I see the visit of that nice young man in the Tyrol as a profoundly private undertaking! You astonish me with your news. War! Now! What for?"

"Precisely," Veselovsky said. "For what?"

"But any decision, naturally, must come from the young traveler himself," Schönborn continued. "We do not have the right to detain him or force a travel route upon him. But if, say, after the songs of the Tyrol he would want to listen to the arias of Naples . . ."

"Naturally," Veselovsky said and nodded once more. "In the long run, no matter how circumstances develop, it would be much pleasanter to be in Naples in this weather than in the Tyrol. Believe me, I wish your guest the best . . ."

"I know that," Schönborn interrupted and stared shamelessly at the Russian resident with his large blue eyes.

"Yes, yes," Veselovsky said, embarrassed and confused. "And I ask you to allow me to meet with our voyager for the common good. I am prepared to ride to Ehrenberg this minute if necessary."

Schönborn leaned against the armrest and rose from the chair easily. He chuckled and paced the room.

"They really are marvelous, those kittens," he said, leaning over the dirtied eiderdown. "But your Mr. Rumyantsev is not fast, not fast at all!" Schönborn came over to his guest, peered into his face, and smiled, showing his round, yellow teeth. "How could he not tell you that the traveling person, tired of mountain tranquillity, has been in Vienna for two days! Give your captain of the guards a dressing down, you must; he's being paid a salary for nothing."

"So there's no need to travel to the Tyrol," Veselovsky said, meeting the other's stare. "As for Rumyantsev, I agree with you completely."

"War!" Schönborn took to pacing the room again and seemed to be talking to himself. "Such a war would bring nothing to any of us except medals. What about fairness! A war started at the wrong time cannot be considered fair, while no one could doubt the fairness of a war begun at the right time. And how can we forget the fair interests of that miserable wanderer, that sweet young man, who has suffered so terribly! And at whose hand? His own father's! Such an example could destroy the monarchical harmony of all of Europe . . . What did you say?"

"War would shake European harmony to a greater degree than that," Veselovsky said, having had no intention of interrupting the vice-chancellor; on the contrary, he listened closely, afraid to miss a single word.

"War!" Schönborn said insouciantly. "Well, it's not hard to avoid."

"So," Veselovsky said, watching his host pace. "Where and when can I meet with the czarevitch?"

"Here," Schönborn said, stopping abruptly. "Now. . . . If, of course, my guest is not asleep. And I ask you, my dear man, not to tire him with political talk: in that area our young friend is not yet very strong, unfortunately."

"The wise counsel of Your Grace would enrich even a beggar," Veselovsky muttered, following his host from the room.

Czarevitch Alexis stood by the tall arched window of his room on the second floor of Schönborn's house and looked out on the street beyond the thin white silk curtain. The darkness in front of the house was penetrable: modern oil lanterns burned with a steady yellow-gold color. Remembering the deep darkness of Moscow's crooked streets, the czarevitch sighed, released the curtain, and returned to the low carved table that held a tubby bottle of port, a fine crystal glass, and a silver vase of granulated sugar.

It would be wonderful to set up street lamps, curtains, and glasses like this in Moscow. But Moscow wouldn't get anything; his father took the best of everything to Saint Petersburg—and Moscow could sit in a puddle and wash in mud for all he cared. His father hated Moscow, hated it! And he hated his son, and he hated Alexis's mother, Eudoxia Lopukhina, and all the Lopukhins. But then, whom didn't he hate, whom did he love? Why did he send his mother to the convent in Suzdal? Traded her in for that German wench of his, Katya the washerwoman. He only loved Germans, those yesmen, and if anyone stood up for things Russian—off with his head. . . . And the Russian people hated him: he sat like a scarecrow in his Paradise, trying to deprive his own son of power, God's anointed—it wouldn't work, it wouldn't! And he wouldn't be able to turn Russia into a German suburb, either! His grandfather Alexis the Quiet hadn't sailed on the seas like a whale, and hadn't tried to fight the Swedes and

Turks—and Russia had been peaceful and rich, would that God grant it to her now . . . Street lamps! He'd be happy to be in total darkness as long as it was in Moscow, in the Kremlin, on the golden throne, and next to him his mother, the poor martyr, the Suzdal nun. First he stuck his wife in the convent, and now he wanted to cut off his own son's head! But God would help the righteous—we'll get Mother out, we'll save her, and the people will kiss our feet for that: the people like those who were humiliated and punished wrongly. And Apraxin and Streshnev and the Jew Shafirov will come with us. They're all sick and gassy from Menshikov's pies. And we'll shut down Saint Petersburg, raze it. That wasn't the capital; his father didn't sit on the holy throne there but on a folding Dutch stool.

To think of it! To send your own son, the legal heir, to a monastery. That Kikin was a true friend; he was right when he said, "So what if it is a monastery, the cassock isn't nailed on." Truth would come out into the light from a monastery, from a prison—but it needed help. And we have helpers, helpers who are ready to work for a righteous cause and for a rich reward. Truth and reward—they had to go hand in hand.

The oily, spicy wine was noticeably diminishing in the bottle. The czarevitch drank eagerly and with pleasure. After the third glass, the doubts that had been troubling his soul dissipated: would Sheremetev support him with his military strength? Which way would Chancellor Golovkin go? Only one thing was left, immutable: animal fear of his father, of his wild gaze.

There was a quiet, loving knock at the door.

"A guest for you, Your Majesty!" Schönborn's voice was lilting and cheery, the way it always was when he spoke to the czarevitch. "You're not asleep yet, are you?"

"Come in!" Alexis replied. That creepy Schönborn! Why does he sing to me all the time, as if I were an idiot? "Order some more wine, the same, another bottle."

As he let Veselovsky in, Schönborn arched his eyebrows expressively. The young voyager drank a lot; he had a wooden leg.

"With your permission, I'll leave you alone," Schönborn said, not releasing the doorknob. "When I master Russian, we'll have a nice long talk. . . . The wine will be up in a minute."

Stepping softly, he ran down the stairs and shook awake his peacefully sleeping secretary for Russian affairs, Wilhelm Kreuze. This man had been settled in the house as a visiting nephew the day before yesterday—just as soon as they'd learned of the czarevitch's return from Ehrenberg.

"Run upstairs," Schönborn whispered, "to the room next to Alexis's. Listen and write things down. Bring me your record as soon as the guest leaves. . . . Well, hurry it up!"

The wall between Alexis's room and the next had a secret peephole, hidden by a painting of Diana surrounded by wild beasts. On the other side of the wall stood a desk with writing equipment. Running down the sound-muffling carpet in the hallway, young Kreuze, known by the code name Water Carrier in Antoine Divier's intelligence service, sat down at the desk.

"Sit down, Avraam, there's no truth in feet," Alexis said, indicating the chair opposite his. "Do you know my uncle, Lopukhin? His name is also Avraam, like yours."

"I've never met him, Your Highness, but I've heard of him," Veselovsky said, carefully lowering himself onto the edge of the seat.

"Sit comfortably!" Alexis said. "When the time comes I may put you on my right," he said, lowered his eyes, and smiled briefly. "As I will Shafirov! . . . I hear you're also a Jew?"

"Baptized, Your Highness. My grandfather was baptized a Russian Orthodox Christian, may he rest in peace."

"Well then," Alexis said indifferently. "Even if you were a Jew—what can you do? It's not your fault. And there are many fine people among you: merchants, physicians, or take you, for instance."

"The physicians are marvelous!" Veselovsky grew animated. "If fifty or sixty Jewish physicians were invited to Russia, so that they could open a medical school—"

"Do they treat teeth too?" Alexei interrupted.

"Teeth too, Your Highness. For if a man is healthy he can do better work, and you can expect more of him, and that is beneficial for the sovereign." He looked up suspiciously at the czarevitch, seeking understanding and interest in his face.

"Why not?" Alexis said. "Let's invite them. And a special medical department can be established to oversee diseases. . . . I could give such a department to you."

"I thank you, Your Highness!"

"Why not?" Alexis continued. "Now you talk about physicians. My mother, Czaritza Eudoxia, has been suffering from stomach pains all these years. Could your physicians cure her?"

"I'll find the most experienced ones"—Veselovsky spoke rapidly—"the most famous! And in the meanwhile, Your Highness, if I could learn more details about the state of health of Her Majesty, I could get an opinion and send medicine."

"How will you send medicine to Suzdal?" Alexis sighed.

"I'll find a way!" Veselovsky exclaimed. "I have tradespeople who can get anywhere!"

"I love my mother," Alexis said, stressing each word and putting his bony hands on the table. "The poor woman has no one in the world except me. If you do a good deed for her, Avraam, I won't forget you for it, as God is my witness!" He glanced over to the corner out of habit, seeking an icon; not finding one, he turned back to Veselovsky. His face was agitated and grim.

"I'll do it, Your Highness, I'll take care of it!" Veselovsky muttered, looking with sudden fear into the angry round eyes, just like Peter's, filled with stubborn hatred.

A servant in a neat wig entered, carrying a small tray. Bending his strong, white-stockinged legs, he set a bottle of wine and another glass on the table between the two men.

"I could have some vodka with you now, in our manner, Russian style," Alexis said, pouring the wine, "but I don't want to ask my host; he'll say I'm a drunkard. . . . What are you here for?"

"Take care of yourself, Your Highness!" Veselovsky moved his chair closer and lowered his voice. Wilhelm Kreuze, on the other side of the wall, stood up and moved closer to the hole. "Don't travel outside Ehrenberg without bodyguards; don't see strangers! And don't come back to Russia before it's time . . ."

"I know my father wants to destroy me," Alexis said dully, without fear or anger. "But he's not the only one with power. . . . Thank you, Veselovsky: you've probably told me a state secret, eh?"

"I received this information through my own channels, not state ones," Veselovsky said, stressing the *own.* "And those are the channels to bring medicine to Suzdal."

"Who warned you?" Alexis prodded. "I know my enemies, I want to know my friends."

Diplomat Veselovsky did not hesitate a second with his reply. "A small man, Your Highness—a palace servant. Servants often know as much as their masters. . . . Peter Tolstoy is coming here from Saint Petersburg: beware of him. He has orders to bring you back to your father."

"I won't go!" The czarevitch leaned back in his chair and cried out as if Tolstoy were already there demanding his return.

"Allow me to give you some advice, Your Highness," Veselovsky said after a pause. "It is dangerous for you to remain in Ehrenberg. If Schönborn suggests moving elsewhere, far from here—agree."

"Suggests!" The czarevitch snorted like an insulted child. "Do you think he suggests! He dictates! . . . When will you send your man to Suzdal?"

"I'll take care of it tomorrow morning, Your Highness," Veselovsky said and got up.

On the way home to the Grabenstrasse, Veselovsky thought how Peter would chop off his head if he learned the details of his conversation with his son: he had secretly entered into a conspiracy with a rebel, revealed Peter Tolstoy's visit, and called the exile Eudoxia Lopukhina czaritza.

The question Why? had long ago stopped tormenting the nun Elena—the former Czaritza Eudoxia Lopukhina, mother of Alexis, the successor to the throne. During the first of nineteen years of exile in Suzdal, the young woman had sought the answer to that eternal naive question of the abandoned, and then solid hatred for her husband-tormentor had pushed aside her tentative assumptions and shameful guesses. Sweet memories no longer disturbed her. Not finding fault with herself in what happened—and she had looked closely, going over every day, every night of all nine years of their marriage!—she laid all the blame on Peter. And now she desired and waited for only one thing: the death of her husband, the accession of her son.

Her son, in defiance of his father's orders, sometimes sent

his mother tender letters and presents. When Alexis sat on the throne, he would wreak just revenge on many, and first of all on Romodanovsky, who had insulted her. He had tormented her, the monster: "The czar does not want you anymore. Go into a convent, cut your hair from your head—or else you'll lose your head with its hair!" Czaritza Eudoxia had not agreed, had not yielded to threats or promises. And they had taken her off to Suzdal by force, like a prisoner.

Peter, once rid of his wife, totally forgot about her—as if she had never existed, as if his heir, Czarevitch Alexis, had been found under a cabbage leaf or brought by the stork. Semyon Yazykov had brought the czaritza to the convent in Suzdal, examined her cell, seemed pleased, and ridden back to Moscow. No new instructions concerning the czaritza came from the capital, and the authorities of the convent soon left her completely alone. She changed the pathetic nun's habit for worldly clothes, sat in her cell, and ate the food sent to her by family and friends. In short, Eudoxia, in refusing a lifetime of service to the Lord, became a lifelong privileged prisoner. Of all the severe instructions brought by Yazykov, only one remained in force: she was forbidden to have contact with her son and vice versa. And first Moscow and then Saint Petersburg made sure it was obeyed.

The appearance in Suzdal of a wandering peddler, redhaired Yankel, had created a real sensation—as if an Indian prince in a diamond hat had ridden into town on an elephant. The city of Suzdal had never, since the day of its founding, seen an Indian prince or a Jewish peddler—Yankel was the first. And while the locals may have had a glimmering of diamond princes, the appearance of a side-locked, red-haired peddler in black stunned them like thunder out of a clear sky. Children ran after Yankel, showering him with pinecones and small stones, while adults crossed themselves and surreptitiously spat over their left shoulder. The black-clad visitor reminded them of the devil somehow. They didn't recognize him as a Jew at first, and they didn't know who Yankel was and from what distant parts he had come—but this mystery added pepper to the groats.

The whole town was talking about him by the time he set up shop at the market. His wares—inches of spices, crosses made of olive trees from the Holy Land, turquoise earrings and rings, framed mirrors—were very popular. As he approached the peddler, Captain Stepan Glebov—a man who had seen the world, who had been to Moscow and Saint Petersburg more than once, and who had entrée for ten years now to Elena's cell—suddenly stopped, gently slapped himself on the forehead, and said, "Why, he's a Jew!"

The discovery did not affect anyone particularly: so he's a Jew. As they crowded around the peddler, the citizens chuckled. They had taken an ordinary Yid for an important foreign bird. Of course, it was interesting to take a look at a Yid too.

From the market, Yankel headed for the wealthy houses after lunch. There he showed other wares too: silver crosses, golden rings. Before nightfall, still accompanied by a crowd of kids, he knocked at the convent gate.

They were waiting for him here too, warily but curiously. Abbess Pelagya was offered plain crosses and crucifixes in ivory or silver, as well as chains of varying length and price. Yankel presented her with the longest chain and the most beautiful cross. "Holy wares aren't spoiled even by Jewish hands!"

Pelagya agreed with Yankel after a moment's thought and accepted the present, but she still asked him to remove his wide-brimmed black hat for a moment. Not finding any horns underneath, the abbess allowed the Jew to display his wares in the small gallery before the meal. Captain Glebov found Yankel there, beckoned to him, and led him away.

Elena's cell was on the second floor, at the end of the hall. Yankel crossed the threshold and silently bowed to the still stately, handsome woman, who was reading a book at a simple table covered with an expensive brocade cloth.

"Here's the peddler I told you about!" Glebov said in response to the lady's surprised look and, huffing, sank into a chair by the door: the stairway was steep and the captain was heavy.

The room, with its tall, vaulted windows, little resembled a cell. The wide bed was covered with a fox-fur blanket, and the floor with a Persian carpet. Under the window stood a large wardrobe made in Vologda. Logs crackled lazily in a tiled stove. To its right, in the corner, an icon stood in the shimmering candlelight, its gold cover and precious stones sparkling.

Standing before the lady, Yankel pulled a worn leather casket with brass corners from his sack and set it on the table. A padlock hung from the casket. He fished for the key for a long time, bending over and rummaging under his shirt, and finally caught it with a sly, satisfied smile. These actions amused but also worried Eudoxia; she accepted the tiny filigree key with curiosity and anxiety. Under Yankel's urging eyes, she unlocked the padlock and opened the lid. In the casket, on a piece of red Chinese silk, lay mirrors, strings of gray river pearls, round silver jars with face powder and rouge. Unhurriedly going through the goods with her short, sleek fingers, Eudoxia looked questioningly at the peddler. Jerking his beard in the direction of the wheezing Glebov, Yankel put his red, soot-stained hands into the box and with his quick, bony fingers pinched the edge of the red Chinese cloth to lift it. Under the cloth, on the bottom of the casket, Eudoxia saw a package and recognized Alexis's seal. She dropped the lid, as if to avoid a blinding light—Yankel barely got his fingers out in time.

"The things are marvelous," Eudoxia said, without letting go of the box. "Leave it here for now. I'll make a selection . . . Stepan!" Glebov turned, making the armchair creak. "Take him downstairs; he has so many other wares. And stay there with him, stay!"

Glebov, with a sigh, rose heavily to his feet. It was not easy being the bosom friend of a czaritza, even a former one.

When Vice-Chancellor Schönborn had exclaimed "It's not hard to avoid war!" he had been joking. Peter's sending Tolstoy—diplomat, spy, and terrible man—was the last drop in a cup that was filling quickly. If Tolstoy failed, Field Marshal Sheremetev and his troops would not. Too bad nothing was working out with that nice, pathetic czarevitch, with this whole charming adventure. But it was even worse to place Austria's ribs under Russia's fists. Peter, apparently, was a very strict father, and basically he was right: his son's trip could have cost him dearly. And now Alexis would have to pay instead.

As he placed all these thoughts in their cubbyholes, Schönborn left a space for Veselovsky. The resident was in big trouble; he would be recalled and replaced by someone else. Who? How would the change, this whole business in fact, affect the relations between Peter and the Austrian court? Veselovsky's future didn't worry Schönborn a bit: for the vice-chancellor, the not-stupid Jew's existence ended with his service in Vienna.

After the extremely unpleasant conversations with Tolstoy, after the czarevitch's secret departure for the Neapolitan shore (Schönborn had made sure that the route was known to Tolstoy and that Alexis had not deviated from it), the old Jew showed up at Veselovsky's house on the Grabenstrasse, this time calling himself a seller of dead birds. The letter from his uncle Peter Pavlovich told Veselovsky in anxious tones that his conversation with Czarevitch Alexis in Schönborn's house was known in Saint Petersburg; that Veselovsky should not return to Russia under any condition and should avoid at all costs meeting Captain Yaguzhinsky, who would be sent to Europe to catch him and bring him back to Peter for trial and punishment. Veselovsky gave the old Jew a gold coin, sighed, and called for coffee and rum.

As his eyes lovingly roamed over the books, paintings, and expensive knickknacks that now ought to be hurriedly packed and taken somewhere, Veselovsky automatically repeated the phrases from Shafirov's letter, guessing at what was between the lines. News of the conversation with the czarevitch would inevitably lead to an investigation in Suzdal, and that would threaten their "Jewish mail service." If he returned voluntarily to Russia or if Yaguzhinsky's undertaking was successful, the role of his uncle could surface—especially what he had revealed about Tolstoy coming, or about Yaguzhinsky, not to mention about the possibility of war between Peter and Austria. So where could he run, and where could he hide? The sensible thing would be to go to London first, to his brother Fyodor; but Fyodor wouldn't be patted on the head for giving refuge to him. It would be better if Fyodor didn't return either; he would lose his head for having known about his brother's plans and not reporting them. Oh, it was all suddenly falling apart, going to hell! How many people would Alexis drag after him if he didn't get out of Peter Tolstoy's hairy paws! It was lucky, at least, that the Veselovskys weren't chained to Mother Russia, that Jewish roots could take any soil—in London or in Berlin, and best of all, in quiet, Protestant Geneva: he'd build a house on the lakefront, convert to Protestantism, and be a successful merchant . . .

Once more he looked over the room, now with a businesslike air, deciding which things had to be packed first. He stopped at the portrait of Peter against the background of a raging battle—and with a smile, as if thinking of something very remote, he recalled the battle of Poltava, and himself, the czar's adjutant, and how he had galloped to Copenhagen with the news of their victory over the Swedes. . . . Mysterious are Thy ways, O Lord! And what luck that we are not chained, not nailed to Russia.

Things were not going well for the czarevitch. On the way home to Russia, he'd had to part with his pregnant Efrosinya, who stayed in Berlin to give birth. As they got closer to the Russian borders, Alexis grew sadder and more remote, no longer sharing with Tolstoy his plans to live a quiet life in the country, and he listened indifferently to Tolstoy's bittersweet stories. Only when he sat down to write to Efrosinya did he feel calm, humming softly to himself, his eyes turning warmer; he tenderly begged the mother of his future child to take care of herself and not be thrifty: she should order medicines in Venice or Bologna, or best of all in Germany, where the pharmacists were artful, and not lose the prescription.

Sitting down late at night to write his letters, listening to Tolstoy's sleepy wheezing behind him, Alexis doodled—sturdy country houses alternated with scaffolds, swords, and axes. He did not really trust his father's promise, as conveyed by Tolstoy, that if he came home voluntarily, he would be allowed to live with Efrosinya in peace and quiet in some distant corner. In despair from Schönborn's polite, empty hints, having received no replies to his appeals to the Russian senators, the Swedish king, or the Turkish sultan, the czarevitch was prepared almost wholeheartedly to renounce the crown and settle in a village in the woods near Suzdal.

At the same time the first detectives, like the first swallows, had arrived in Suzdal. Walking in the marketplace, sitting in taverns, they asked the simple folk about any strangers who had appeared in town recently. Red-haired Yankel was the first one named. The specialists from the capital discounted him: who would use a Yid in something this important? After the swallows came the hawk, Captain Skornyakov-Pisarev, with personal orders from the czar. "Go to Suzdal and there in the cells of my wife and her favorites examine letters, and if you find any suspicious ones, arrest those whose letters they are and bring them and the letters with you, leaving a guard at the gates."

The investigation was widening. The first group of prisoners was sent off to Moscow. From Preobrazhenskoe, where twenty years ago Ivashka Miloslavsky's bones had floated in the blood of the Streltsy rebels, Peter commanded: "Bring my former wife and whoever is with her, as well as her favorites, and her mother . . ." Skornyakov-Pisarev tried hard, acted quickly, and in accordance with the czar's capacious phrase "Whoever was there at the time and whoever knows about it, bring them all," group after group headed out from Suzdal along the Moscow road. Stepan Glebov was transported in a covered two-horse carriage and tortured three times in the Secret Chancellery, but he would not admit to a conspiracy against the regime either for himself or for his lover, Eudoxia Lopukhina.

By then—February 1718—Czarevitch Alexis had reached Moscow. Their meeting, in keeping with his father's wishes, was ceremonious and solemn. The affair had gone far beyond a family quarrel, and this had to be known not only in Russia but in Vienna and in Turkey.

Peter met his son, who had waited for an audience for three days outside Moscow, in the big throne room of the Kremlin, surrounded by senators, generals, and the high clergy. Against this golden background, Peter's plain gray clothing lent him an icy grimness. Alexis, dressed just as modestly, with a pale, haggard face, looked amazingly like his father.

The czarevitch entered the hall with a slow, steady pace. Not looking around, he approached the czar, immobile on the throne, fell to his knees, and handed him a thick piece of paper rolled into a tube. Without unrolling it, Peter handed the letter to Shafirov, standing to his right. Accepting the document with a bow, the vice-chancellor skimmed the text and, bending to the czar's ear, whispered, "Nothing important, Your Majesty. . . . A plea for mercy."

"What do you want to say?" Peter asked harshly, inclining his head. "Speak!"

"I ask Your Majesty to allow me to go to the country and live there without ever leaving it to the end of my days," Alexis said by rote, in a tired, lifeless voice.

Without looking up, Peter chuckled. Shafirov had spent three days with the czarevitch, drilling every word of this conversation into his head.

"By your desire," Peter said, raising his voice, "you of your own free will deprive yourself of the right to inherit our throne. Sitting in the countryside until your death you will not learn statecraft. Are you willing right now, on your honor, to sign a decree of renunciation of your own free will?"

"I am," Alexis muttered, with a spiteful look at Shafirov.

"Louder!" Peter roared.

"I am willing to sign!" Alexis said, getting up from his knees.

"And now come close to me and tell me who advised you to run," Peter said, leaning back comfortably in the throne. "Well, come here!"

Avoiding Shafirov, Alexis came around the throne from the czar's left, leaned against its golden armrest, and whispered something in his father's ear. Peter leapt to his feet like a young man and strode quickly, pulling his son along, to the inner room. A few minutes later, Shafirov was called in.

They returned to the throne room a quarter hour later—first came Alexis walking stiffly with hands clasped behind his back, then Peter and Shafirov together. The vice-chancellor was waving the decree of renunciation before him, as if to dry the ink.

"You handle my family affairs excellently," Peter said with a half smile, leaning down to Shafirov. "I won't forget this . . ."

The praise and the promise made Shafirov weak in the knees and gave him a lump in the throat. Staring without seeing as Alexis signed the decree, he kept repeating to himself: "First Prut and now this. . . . Good God!"

The investigation broadened. Messengers galloped between Moscow, Saint Petersburg, and Suzdal. The first heads had rolled, the czarevitch's counselor Kikin had been quartered, and fat Stepan Glebov had been impaled. Cleverly crafted rumors spread through Russia's taverns: behind the silly czarevitch were experienced conspirators, who wanted to kill the czar, who planned to give Russia up to the Swedes, Turks, and Germans. And Alexis wasn't the czar's son at all; that was known for sure now, and Eudoxia had been exiled to Suzdal for adultery. And since Alexis had renounced the throne, he would certainly lose his head; you can't execute the heir, but you can your son, and certainly your stepson. After all, the czar must have approved the whipping Alexis got. The czar himself had come to the torture chamber, and with him Prince Menshikov, and Peter Tolstoy, and the Yid

Shafirov: all the most important men.The traitor got twenty-five blows, and that was just the beginning! There were those who felt sorry for the czarevitch—but on the quiet.

Czar Peter, who destroyed his enemies and those who surrendered or resisted, those who were strong or were weak, wanted the death of his son. He didn't believe all those stories of a quiet life in the country, all those tearful written promises to renounce the throne. If he were in his son's place, he would not have stayed in the country long, nor would his followers have let him; and when his father died, he would have forgotten all the solemn decrees he had signed and made a dash for the throne. That would swerve Russia from her new road, from her Petrine prospects. That could not be allowed to happen. For the sake of his grand experiment, which had already demanded tons of human meat, Peter had sacrificed at Prut the thing, so laughable in politics and so stinging under the blanket—his honor. Now the time had come to sacrifice his son. There simply was no other way, and there was no point in seeking one. And that meat, that blood, would be for the good of the experiment.

After the torture of Czarevitch Alexis, Peter did not let master of the knout Vytashchi leave; he sat down to a game of chess with him. Planning and calculating his moves, the czar listened distractedly to his son's groans as he lay in the corner on a bed of straw. Chess always soothed him, cleared his head. He won, flicked his fingers on Vytashchi's head with pleasure, and asked, with a glance at the corner, "Will he survive?"

"Anybody can survive twenty-five strokes of the knout!" Then Vytashchi added, "Now if it were fifty, and dragged out—that's another matter . . ."

Peter got up, kicked over the chess table, and strode quickly out of the room. Vytashchi hurried to pick up the amber chess pieces.

The same day, before evening, Shafirov dropped in to see Lacosta on his way home. They had not seen each other in a long time, and just before he got to Lacosta's hut, the vice-chancellor suddenly felt embarrassed. Lacosta was one of his own people, and yet he lived in the middle of Saint Petersburg in a hut like a simple muzhik. He should have taken an interest, helped out. And that miserable business with the daughter . . . With a heavy sigh, Shafirov knocked and entered.

The owner of the house was at the table eating fish. Hearing the creak of the door, he was about to take off his yarmulke, but recognizing Shafirov, he merely adjusted it. A pile of gray fish bones bristled on the table like a wintry bush. With the side of his hand, Lacosta neatly swept the bones onto a tin plate, wiped his fingers on a napkin, and moved up a chair for his guest.

"I don't hold a grudge, Peter Pavlovich," Lacosta said with a smile. "Sit down, sit down! I know you're much busier than I am, and I don't want to bother you without a reason either. It's silly, of course: we haven't seen each other in over a year. But I know how things are with you; Antoine tells me."

"Yes, yes," Shafirov agreed with relief. "Life is like that, so busy. . . . But I know about you too, just by hearsay, of course. How's Mashenka? Is she in Germany?"

"She no longer exists," Lacosta said, staring into the plate of fish bones. "She died of consumption last year in Hamburg."

"Forgive me," Shafirov moaned. "Forgive me . . ."

"What's to forgive?" Lacosta raised his eyebrows. "It's life and it's death. Everything in order. It's no one's fault. And

I'm the way I was twenty years ago—not with my Riva, but with her little boy. As if those twenty years had never happened . . . Yakov!" he called. "Yasha!"

A large-eyed, curly haired boy stumbled out of the other room, brandishing a wooden sword.

"So that's what we're like!" Shafirov said in a sweet voice. "How old are we?"

"Going on three," Lacosta said. Shafirov moved aside the wooden sword, which the child was aiming at the diamond star in his ribbon.

"We'll have to enlist him in the Preobrazhensky Guards," Shafirov said, watching the boy's hand tensely. "So militant."

"We'll see," Lacosta said evasively, hugging the boy to his knee. "Only noblemen are accepted there, anyway."

"Well, you and I know what kind of noblemen they are!" Shafirov laughed. "The Serene Prince Alexander Danilovich . . ."

Lacosta said nothing, caressing the boy's cheek.

"Yes, it must be done!" Shafirov pressed the issue. "I'll arrange it, have no fear. . . . Do you remember that Passover"—he leaned his head to one side and stared into the distance—"and that crazy Jew from Smolensk, and how the czar suddenly came?"

"I remember," Lacosta replied. "His name was Borokh Leibov."

"And that night on the Prut"—Shafirov was practically moaning—"the night, the noise, and his dead, silent tent, and you went there—remember?" He shook his head, and the curls of his wig trembled. "I'm here with another favor to ask, Yan."

Lacosta unclasped his hands, and the child ran off.

"You know that . . ." Shafirov furrowed his brow. "Vytashchi, the master of the knout? He tortured Alexis Petrovich."

"Yes, I know him," Lacosta said. "I won't say he's my best friend, but he is a miserable man in his own way. And then, he and I are colleagues of a sort."

"Exactly!" Shafirov moved closer. "It's very important what I am going to ask you. No one could do this except you—only you!"

"What are we talking about here?" Lacosta asked dryly.

"The czar," Shafirov said. "The czarevitch. Russia . . . You love the czar, don't you—like me, like all of us?"

"Yes," Lacosta said after some hesitation, "I really do love him. He is miserable in his own way—just like Vytashchi. I don't like happy people—they're either stupid or blackguards."

"Czarevitch Alexis must die," Shafirov whispered. "It's decided, because Russia needs it. But a shameful public execution is not in the interests of Russia or of the czar. . . . You know this, Yan—the great Peter is not made of iron or stone. It is hard for a father, impossible, to say, 'Go kill my son.' I know that the father awaits help from us, and you . . ."

"What can I do?" Lacosta's head flew up. "I'm a jester, the royal jester!"

"And I'm not?" Shafirov interrupted. "We're all jesters—you, me, Menshikov, Romodanovsky—all of us! And I want to be the jester of Peter the Great, because his greatness rests on our jests. . . . Yan, go to Vytashchi, he'll listen to you. He must tell the czar what the czar is waiting for, what the czar doesn't want to and can't say himself: 'I'll kill him . . .' "

"Now if it were fifty strokes, stretched out," Vytashchi muttered from the doorway. "And I didn't stretch it out . . ." Lacosta had explained everything carefully to him, and he pitied Peter, even though it was very frightening to pity the czar.

Peter sat hunched over his paper-strewn desk, looking at his jester and master of the knout closely, but as if he were not in the room but in Vienna: on top of all the other papers there was a report from Yaguzhinsky that the Viennese resident Veselovsky had fled to London and that the British were refusing to send him back.

"Yes?" Peter said, resting his palm on the report. "What are you talking about?"

"Well, sire, Your Majesty, I want to do what's best," Vytashchi went on. "Look at yourself, you're exhausted—terrible to look at! That has to be understood . . ." His mouth went awry, he blinked fast, and something between a sob and a roar escaped from his throat. "I will kill him and put an end to it . . . Your Majesty!"

Peter rose slowly from his desk, staring deep into the murky, tear-filled eyes of Vytashchi. Hearing that long-awaited phrase, he couldn't understand at first who was weeping—the half-mad jester or himself, the father. Then he realized it was both of them.

He came over to Vytashchi, took him firmly by the ears, struck his forehead with his own, kissed his cheeks, and said, choking, "Do what you said . . ."

They were almost the same height.

XI

Hell's Kitchen • 1722

President of the Berg-Collegium Yakov Williamovich Bruce was extraordinarily worried: they had been expecting Peter in Olonets for two days now, the welcoming torches along the entrance road had been lit for three false alarms, and the people, exhausted by waiting, were getting drunk. Besides which, a horrible thing had happened: a villain had stolen the oilcloth protecting the triumphal arch decorated with welcoming words that had been erected by the gates of the iron foundry. An investigation revealed that the guard had gotten drunk and fallen asleep, and the daring thief had taken advantage of the fact. The guilty party, still not quite sober, was whipped outside Bruce's temporary office; this had added a bit of color to the waiting.

When he left Saint Petersburg for Olonets the week before, Bruce had intended only to shape up the two foundries, Alexevski and Povenetsky, under the Berg-Collegium, for inspection by the czar. But once he had arrived, foundering in spring mud and slush, Bruce decided to clean up the town as well; the arch was erected, and torches were placed in the fir trees outside town. A look at the city wharf, on the Svir River, saddened the neat and order-loving Bruce. The czar would certainly want to come here too, and then there would be no way of avoiding the storm. The main thunder and lightning would naturally fall on the head of General Admiral Apraxin, president of the Admiralty Collegium—but Apraxin was far away and Bruce near at hand. And the czar's fist was heavy and in anger struck without distinction. So the wharf needed improvement, and a hundred men, urgently collected in the villages, were sent under convoy to the Svir to clean up and to make fir wreaths to decorate the ship frames.

It was only at the last moment that Bruce remembered the Olonets healing waters, opened on Peter's orders three years ago and until then known locally as Hell's Kitchen. Bruce berated himself for that. He might miss other things, but the czar certainly wouldn't skip the waters! They were searching all over Russia for mineral waters like those in Karlsbad, and the czar, with his love of medicines and operations, kept a personal eye on the search. The sight of the stinking stream, reeking of swamps and rotten eggs, lazily pouring out from beneath a decaying snag, bewildered Bruce. There was no question of erecting gazebos and halls with benches and bathtubs—but would they have time to knock together a decent-looking shed?

Fifty half-drunk and festivity-minded citizens were snatched up in yards and taverns and brought to the source, not without some struggle. Near the snag, in the icy mud, they found some rotten boards—all that was left of the old kiosk built for the triumphant opening of the waters. Peter had been there and watched with satisfaction the long line of Olonetsians grimly waiting at the entrance. Those who didn't appear were threatened with the knout; those who appeared and swallowed a mug of the stinking hogwash were promised a mug of vodka. The czar himself, out of curiosity and a desire to set a good example, drank a goblet of the warm, nauseating liquid, found it satisfactory, and ordered the locals, regardless of sex and age, to take the healing waters internally, and to bathe in them if they desired, no less than weekly, to maintain their health. Having given the order, Peter went back to Saint Petersburg, and the Olonetsians drank the promised vodka, cursed, and forgot the road to the source. Soon the hall grew dilapidated and fell apart, to the great relief of the locals.

As Bruce approached the snag, he wrinkled his long, sharp nose and spat discreetly. The sight of the smelly, opaque water made him sick. It really was Hell's Kitchen! The men who had been brought there angrily chewed sunflower seeds behind him.

"Well, come on, come on!" Bruce shouted. "What are you standing around for! Carpenters, over here! I want a bathhouse here no later than sunset; this big!" Pulling his tall boots out of the mud, he paced off the parameters. "And build boardwalks with railings—you can drown in here!"

As he was leaving, he thought it might be nice to have an appropriate saying colorfully painted over the entrance, but he searched his memory and couldn't come up with one.

Along with the title of Emperor, the Great, and Father of the Country, the Senate gave Peter a covered sleigh, roomy and luxurious. Upholstered in soft leather with many pouches, the sleigh had windows and copper flasks to fill with boiling water for heat. At the back there was a bed with a wolfskin cover, and at the head of the bed the traveling medicine chest with a first-aid kit. The imperial sleigh was powered by horses harnessed in tandem, and it could seat five, though tightly. Peter liked the sleigh, which combined indisputable conveniences with the latest in technology. He traveled around in it all winter and used it to go to Olonets in the late snow.

Dragoons galloped around the imperial sleigh, and the retinue followed in all kinds of smaller sleighs. Lacosta and Vytashchi traveled with the chef at the tail of the procession. The wind blew snow through the cracks of their conveyance, and the jesters and the chef huddled close to one another under sheepskins.

"Shove over a bit!" Vytashchi said. "I need to get at my box."

Lacosta moved his legs from the wooden box, in which Vytashchi carried his instruments: knout, pliers for pulling out nostrils and smaller ones for pulling out fingernails, and three branding irons. There, wrapped in the knout's tail to keep it from breaking, was a bottle of vodka.

"Here!" Vytashchi said, wiping the neck on his sleeve. "It's cold!"

Lacosta had a drink and passed the bottle to the chef, who also drank. The chef felt uncomfortable in Vytashchi's company.

"Here, have some!" Vytashchi broke an onion into three parts and held the pieces in his hand. "Damn it, forgot the salt."

The chef's head was drooping; he was asleep, or pretending to be.

"Huh, so tired!" Vytashchi said snidely, not surprised by the chef's discomfort. "The hell with him. We'll manage by ourselves."

"Travel, travel," Lacosta said, once more resting his feet on the box. "We're always traveling somewhere."

"Why not!" Vytashchi responded. "We serve the czar. Where he gallops, we follow on foot. How else!"

"Once upon a time, long long ago," Lacosta went on, paying no attention to Vytashchi, "I had a friend. A very close friend. . . . And she tied a silk ribbon to a basket. But when, where? I didn't know a thing about it, and I would never have done it on my own. But she tied the ribbon. That meant she had her own life, and we were totally different people, she and I. . . . But why I remember that incident, Stepan, I just don't know either."

Vytashchi listened closely, without moving, his shoulders hunched like a giant owl. Then he shook himself and said, "You know, I get all kinds of incidents in my mind, too: how I broke my grandmother's pitcher when I was little. Or my father dividing up the bread on the table, and all us children sitting and watching. . . . Strange! And then I think about it, and I feel sorry for all creatures: a sheep, even a bug."

"What about yourself?" Lacosta asked. "Do you feel sorry for yourself?"

"You're right about that," Vytashchi said grimly. "Sometimes I feel so sorry for myself I can't sleep. I just lie there. I get good pay and have my own house, but I can't sleep. . . . Believe it or not"—and he leaned close to Lacosta and mumbled as if confessing something shameful—"I want to become a little child again. I really do! But I can't."

"You can't," Lacosta said with a sigh.

They grew silent, shaking their heads and regarding each other amiably.

In the damp gray twilight of early morning, the torches blazed on the sides of the road, the flames trembling as if in a long, low-ceilinged corridor. The wind was playing in the crowns of the firs and pines. Above the thick fog were patches of blue; fair weather could be expected by day's end.

Bruce galloped up to the royal sleigh on a dark mare and was admitted. Peter looked grim as he rubbed his twitching cheek.

"I know, I know!" He waved Bruce away. "You've repainted the foundry! How many cannons on the lathes? Six? Well, that's fine. Thank you. . . . We'll go look after lunch."

"Lunch awaits, Your Majesty," Bruce reported. "The town's head—"

"No!" Peter interrupted. "First we go to the waters, and we'll have a snack there. . . . Do you drink the waters?"

"I do, Your Majesty," Bruce lied.

"You're a fine fellow," Peter said. "Let them give each of the workers in the factory a glass a day. That water gives strength and improves the spleen."

The jerry-built pavilion protruded from the swampy shore like a chimney in a burning house. The dragoons who had galloped into the snow-dusted swamp had to restrain their wallowing horses.

"Why isn't anyone around?" Peter wondered, looking suspiciously at Bruce and at the lonely terrain. "Where are the patients? I ordered everyone, everyone to drink the water no less than once a week!"

"Because of Your Majesty's visit the men and women were forcibly chased away," Bruce said, thinking quickly. "Others drink too much and drown in the swamp."

"What do they drink too much of?" Peter asked suspiciously.

"Vodka!" Bruce explained, realizing that he had overdone it. "They come here with vodka, as if to a picnic."

Leaving the sleigh, Peter stepped onto the boardwalk and headed for the pavilion. His retinue, stretching their legs, followed. Bruce stayed behind to give orders for a table, wine, and food for a second breakfast to be brought.

It was warm and quiet in the pavilion; a bench of freshly cut wood encircled the snag, which was cleared of seaweed and mud and decorated with gold foil, like a chicken leg on a platter. Peter sat down on the bench, stretched his long legs, and took a deep breath of the sulfurous air. It didn't smell this bad, he thought, at European spas.

He filled the tall glass mug, threw back his head, gargled noisily, and spat into the runoff stream in the canal. Then he refilled the glass to the brim and drank it slowly and thoughtfully. Barely suppressing the urge to vomit, he spat again, rubbed his eyes, and shouted at the open door.

"Hey, who's there?"

The small room was instantly filled with people, breathing cautiously. A human circle formed around the czar, who sat on the gilded snag; everyone wanted to move away from the wall or door to be closer to the center, but no one wanted to separate from the crowd and end up inside the circle, face to face with the grim Peter. A minute or two passed this way.

"Well, why aren't you drinking?" Peter asked at last. "Drink!"

The circle shuddered visibly, the ones in front backing up, their eyes lowered.

"Too bad Kabysdokh died!" Peter said bitterly. "Or he'd pass it around." He jumped up, shaking a heavy walking stick of black wood. "It's for your own good, you fools! How long will I have to teach you? Drink, or I'll pour it down your throats!"

The circle was falling apart. The people in the back had gotten out by then and stepped off the boardwalks in the crush. Now they cursed as they stood in the icy mud. The rotten smell of Hell's Kitchen reached them anyway.

Vytashchi, his head pushing against the ceiling, stood by a wall and gazed loyally at the czar. He had no intention of leaving until he was sent out. He bore the stink patiently, like a light punishment.

"Hey!" Peter called him over.

And while he pushed his way to the czar's side, the people in the back cleverly got out the door.

"Here!" Peter said, handing a mug to Vytashchi. "Drink it! It's good for you! They don't understand a thing."

Vytashchi took the mug, sniffed it obediently, frowned, and made the sign of the cross over his mouth. Then he breathed out, shut his eyes, and poured the stinking liquid into himself in one fell swoop.

"There, you see!" Peter said in a lecturing tone. "Go on, Vytashchi, have another. Rinsing the intestines relieves the heart and pulls the blood away from the head. Every man should know his anatomy. It is enlightening and protects from disease. . . . Drink!"

Vytashchi did not bless himself or breathe out. With clenched teeth, he brought the mug to his mouth and forced himself to sip the contents under the czar's encouraging eye.

"Well, how was it?" Peter asked after Vytashchi placed the mug upside down on top of his head, to indicate that there wasn't even a drop left.

"So so . . ." Vytashchi muttered in muffled tones. "Your Majesty, give me permission to vomit . . ."

"No!" Peter shouted harshly and struck his staff on the floor. "You have to bear it! Otherwise there's no benefit! Drink, you fool! More!" He filled a mug himself and handed it to the jester.

Vytashchi took a sip, began reeling, dropped the mug, covered his face with the crook of his elbow, and ran out. On the boardwalk he quickly stuck two fingers down his throat and leaned over the railing. The flimsy wooden railing shook under him.

"A spoiled man," Peter said, listening to Vytashchi's roar. "His stomach is irreversibly rotten. Even healthful waters won't cure him; he should have started earlier."

Vytashchi straightened and went to his carriage, where he got the bottle of vodka from his box. He drank a long time with his head thrown back, looking at the pretty blue stretches of sky above him.

Between the picnic and the dinner at the house of the head of town, they went to look at the foundry. Before they reached the gate, at the decorated arch, the sleepless guard stood at attention in front of the imperial sleigh and a group of sturdy, red-cheeked girls wearing new bast shoes piled out of a hole covered with fir branches, as if out of a cave. Prancing and crying out a song, they plucked their balalaikas, while Bruce, who had come up with the idea, sighed in relief: the czar seemed to be pleased.

Peter examined the arch closely, knowledgeably. Painted the seven colors of the spectrum, it represented a rainbow over the road. At its zenith, on a wooden platform, stood a toy bronze cannon, the size of a dog. The banner, as if quoting the cannon, read: "With an artful bombardier, I can fire as far as Persia."

Against the instruments' music and the girls' song, Peter twice circled the arch and nodded in approval to Bruce: looks good! No one had the slightest doubt that the artful bombardier was the Emperor Peter himself, who was planning a campaign against the Persians, because they were brazenly hurting the Azerbaijanis. And as a result of this campaign, with the help of the cannons of Olonets, great Russia would free the oppressed Azerbaijanis, the wild Caucasian tribes, and other Armenian types. Simple and beneficial.

The foundry was good too. The masters were skillful and the workers diligent. Peter put on an apron and ran all over the shop, drinking kvass from a ladle, giving advice, teaching, checking, joking, swearing, and fighting. Old Bruce barely kept up. The czar's cheek had stopped twitching. The physical tension and bustle had put him in a good mood, as usual. He forgot about his plan to make the workmen drink the water; he grew flushed, his glistening round eyes looked lovingly at Bruce. Before personally breaking the form and releasing the molten metal, he insisted on going up to the blast furnace along the narrow, winding staircase made of wood. Bruce flushed with worry. He had not anticipated this possibility; it had never occurred to him to reinforce the worn, rickety planks. But a direct appeal to Peter's common sense was useless, and he knew it.

"Those stairs are intended for people made of flesh," Bruce said cautiously, "and you are cast iron, Your Majesty. There's no one in the entire foundry with your weight, and, by the laws of physics . . ."

Peter put his foot on the bottom step and looked around—he was at least a head taller than everyone else. Only Vytashchi, leaning against a wall as usual, was almost his height—and broader in the shoulders.

"Hey, Vytashchi," the czar called. "Run up to the top there. Hurry up!"

"And stomp around up there; stomp hard!" Bruce added anxiously.

From below they watched, heads back, as Vytashchi carefully placed his feet on the flimsy steps. Finally he reached the cramped platform, three boards wide, and as ordered, stamped and jumped.

"It's hot here, Your Majesty!" he repeated joyfully, as if he had made an important discovery to be proud of.

"Now come down!" Peter said, twisting his head impatiently.

The very first plank Vytashchi stepped on cracked and broke under his weight. Waving his arms, he caught hold of the edge of the furnace, but his fingers slipped, and bent at the waist, he flew head down onto a mound of iron bars piled up at the foot of the furnace.

The first to reach the fallen man was Peter, who bent over him and looked grimly at the bloody face. Then, straightening abruptly, he turned, looking for someone. Lacosta stood before him, muttering to himself and looking at Vytashchi.

"A physician, Your Majesty?" Lacosta asked, guessing the czar's wishes.

"Bring my medicine chest from the sleigh," Peter ordered. "And get him outside; it's dark in here."

They carried Vytashchi on some matting, carefully: the wounded man groaned softly, and there was no hurry. People abandoned their work and discussed the event in whispers.

"He drank that rotten water in Hell's Kitchen, and his head started spinning!"

"That snag has to be buried and covered with a stone. Let the water drain into the swamp: let it drain away!"

"Silence, silence!" Bruce commanded. "They'll handle it without you!"

They expected a miracle from the czar, instant healing. The appearance of Lacosta with the medicine chest added faith. The shiny lacquered chest with silver corners and its multitude of drawers and compartments was an impressive sight. The crowd parted for Lacosta and then closed ranks. People craned their necks and waited in silence.

Vytashchi lay at the czar's feet, in the snow dusted with soot. He was on his back, and his large white face, blackened along the edge with blood, stared at the hard, faraway sky. The wind had scattered the clouds, and it was cold and dry.

Peter threw back the lid of the chest and spread out several surgical instruments on the lid as if it were a table. The sight of the instruments provoked anxiety: scissors, knife, needles, and a small mirror on a long handle. He wet a cloth with something from a crystal flask and wiped Vytashchi's forehead and temple, then cut off the bloodied hair and examined the wound. Bending low, he pulled back the lips and eyelids. Then, holding the short, silver-handled knife comfortably in his hand, he cut open the caftan and the shirt in one long, light movement from throat to below the waist.

"Closer, come closer!" he shouted at the crowd, without looking over his shoulder. "We'll look at anatomy now."

"He's still alive, Your Majesty!" Lacosta whispered, never taking his eyes from the strip of light steel in the czar's hand. "He's breathing!"

"Almost not breathing," Peter determined, after bringing his ear to Vytashchi's mouth. "The remaining air is coming out. . . . He was a useful man, and his death is useful. Everyone must be of use—he, you . . ."

He slid the blade along the skin and then with the second pass widened and deepened the cut, opening the abdomen. Steam rose from the black slit and dissipated.

Struck dumb with horror, Lacosta stared at the spot where the terrible cloud had floated above the body and then looked down into the slit, as if it were a gaping crevasse that had opened at his feet. Peter put his hands in the slit, and with light grumbling, spread the walls apart. Feeling something smooth and slippery, he tugged at it, snipped it off, jerked it angrily, pulled it out, and stood up with a bloody lump in his hands.

"What is this?" he asked, showing it to the crowd.

The crowd stood in deafening silence.

"Hey you!" he addressed a thin man with rheumy eyes who stood nearby. "Answer: what is this?"

"Guts, Your Majesty," the man replied uncertainly, snuffling.

"Fool!" cried the czar. "It's the liver! You must know these things!"

He put the lump on the snow and plunged his hands into the slit again, tugging and jerking.

"What's this?" He shook a heavy red sack under the nose of a bald grandfather wearing a long coat.

"It's guts, of course!" the old man said with a brazen look. "What else would there be in the belly!"

"Many things are located in the belly besides guts," Peter explained to the crowd. "And you, Grandpa, get fifty lashes for being lackadaisical. . . . Well, let's move on!"

Next came the spleen, a chunk of lung, the heart.

"And what is this?"

"A heart, Your Imperial Majesty!"

"Correct. A glass of vodka for you."

The gall bladder, the stomach, the large intestine followed. The switch and the vodka followed. It was basically useful instruction.

Stuffing everything back into the slit, Peter wiped his hands on the edge of the apron and said, "Everyone should definitely be knowledgeable in anatomy."

Leontiev, head of the town, was rightly considered a big eater but not in the least a gourmet: he preferred black grouse to hazel grouse because it was bigger. Leontiev had the same approach to drink, cowberry vodka being a favorite.

Having learned everything he could from Bruce about the czar's culinary preferences, Leontiev decided to show off not only the amount of food but the wit with which it was presented: in the midst of meats and fish, kashas and pickles stood a centerpiece, an engraved Tatar platter holding a small deer with gilt horns and hooves. The legs were spread out to the edge of the platter, the head bent and lying in a bucket of wine. A silver chain stretched along the table from the deer to the czar's place, and Leontiev planned for Peter to pull the chain at the right moment.

Chilled in the foundry yard, the guests took their seats noisily, staring at the amusing deer and then at the czar, to see how he liked it. Peter took a goblet of cowberry vodka from his host and drank it down in one gulp, followed it with pickled mushrooms, and having no doubts about the meaning of the chain, started to pull it; people were waiting to see what would happen, and Peter was curious himself. Leontiev, who had planned for this moment to occur in the middle of the banquet, hurriedly rose to his feet.

"Your Imperial Highness!" Leontiev began. "The prince of the forest, so to speak, brought this gift in his belly, for you, the Great Ruler . . ."

Without listening to the host, Peter pulled the chain. The deer's belly opened and the organ meats, roasted in butter, fell out onto the platter: cut intestines, kidneys, the heart. The guests buzzed in delight.

Lacosta saw his colleague Vytashchi as he looked at the steaming mound, and saw Czar Peter with a scalpel, not a chain, in his hands. "Today him, tomorrow me," Lacosta muttered. "This mad genius will degut all of Russia the way he did poor Stepan, to see what's inside. . . . Hell's Kitchen! God have mercy!"

The next day, just before their departure, Lacosta was called to see Peter in the sleigh. Peter was lying down, his hands behind his head, on a bearskin blanket. The interior smelled of fresh hay and was warm: the copper radiators had just been filled with boiling water.

"I was watching you yesterday," Peter said, indicating a place next to him to Lacosta. "You're sad, Jester!"

"I am old and pathetic," Lacosta said. "And then, I've never heard of happy jesters."

"What do you mean?" Peter sat up to hear better.

"A jester must be funny, not happy," Lacosta said. "I wouldn't have called Kabysdokh a happy man either."

"Well, Kabysdokh wasn't a man, but just . . ." Peter said. "What about Vytashchi?"

Lacosta said nothing and stared off to the side.

"First the anatomy and then those deer giblets—how do you reckon that?" Peter asked in a whisper, sitting up even more.

"A coincidence," Lacosta said after a pause. "Simply an unpleasant coincidence."

"You're lying," the czar said, as he sank back on the bed. "You're afraid to say it."

"I am," Lacosta said. "Jesters are allowed to be afraid."

"Vytashchi was also afraid," Peter said thoughtfully. "You're afraid. That's reasonable. . . . But how did that happen, really, the anatomy and then those roasted giblets? Eh? Don't be afraid; speak."

"I am afraid, but I'll tell you," Lacosta said. "If you hadn't done a demonstration of human giblets, Your Majesty, then the sight of the deer's wouldn't have bothered you in the least. And Stepan Vytashchi might be alive today."

"You can't possibly understand that!" Peter interrupted. "I've studied medicine and you haven't. Vytashchi would have died anyway, his neck was broken." Peter suddenly rose up on one elbow and moved closer to Lacosta, who was sitting hunched on the bed. "Do you know how many necks he broke? And whose? And now his time had come."

"Then the deer tripe was something to eat, and nothing more," Lacosta said with a crooked smile. "Like a pie or kasha."

"And if he had remained alive," Peter continued, "he would have led many more to death. Perhaps even you."

"We have a saying," Lacosta said, hunching down even lower. "Don't stare long at the sun or at the czar. After Prut, Your Majesty, I live every day as a fortunate accident. I shouldn't still be alive, but I am. At that damned river, I crawled too close to the czar. It was frightening but beautiful, and I should have been turned to ashes. And I am not the only one."

"And you are not the only one," Peter said, and it wasn't clear whether he was agreeing or merely repeating it. "New grass has grown on that river, and Shafirov's path is covered now; no traces left. And the Turks are lying low, lower than grass and quieter than the water in that river, while Russia is full of glory and majesty."

"What about the Russian people?" Lacosta spoke up. "What does that majesty give them? New boots? An extra piece of meat?"

"Now you seem to be a smart man, but you see things only from your own little burrow!" Peter chuckled and flung himself back on his pillows. "Russia is a diamond and little people are clay. And the czar, the leader makes what he wants and what he can from that clay: however many model soldiers he needs, however many learned men or, say, merchants. . . . And as for what the little people wear, that's up to me to decide too: boots are better for a soldier, while bast shoes will do for a peasant. And what people wear or eat does not make the Russian diamond any bigger or more brilliant."

"A leader leads people into war," Lacosta countered grimly. "A leader doesn't live without war . . ."

"And who would have given me Saint Petersburg or Azov without war?" Peter asked ironically.

"What for?" Lacosta whispered. "For the sake of diamond Russia, for the sake of national interests? But the national interests are new shoes and an extra piece of meat. Have the Russian people become any happier from the fact that their czar conquered Azov and Saint Petersburg? Stepan Vytashchi, your faithful servant, did he become any happier?"

Peter huffed angrily and then asked, after a pause, "How many years have you lived in Russia?"

"Twenty-five years, soon, Your Majesty," Lacosta replied.

"But you're a stranger!" Peter shouted. "You measure everything with your Yid measuring stick! If you had a true czar and homeland, you'd think differently, and all your talk leads to is harm and confusion. Be off!"

It was roomy in the wagon now. The taciturn chef huddled against the wall and stared warily from his sheepskin, and Vytashchi was carried in an open sleigh, in a plank coffin. After giving the chef a sidelong glance, Lacosta put his feet on Vytashchi's box and shut his eyes. He assumed that the post-Prut mistake would be rectified as soon as they returned to the capital. There was only one thing he had to do: take Yasha to Shafirov. There would be room in the vice-chancellor's palace for the grandson of Yan Lacosta. Of course, as the czar had said, "You are not the only one."

XII

On the Block · 1723

From the cellar window of the Preobrazhensky Department—a narrow, barred, slit opening on an inner courtyard—the urine-soaked, stale snow looked like fresh, crustless bread to Shafirov and the chunks of gray February sky like a precious merit star, unattainable. Sitting chained in the cold, filthy cellar, Shafirov did not damn anyone and did not forgive anyone; he wondered whether the czar had written his pardon yet and why they bothered with the stupid bear chain—he wouldn't have left the place.

Peter Pavlovich Shafirov had not been beaten or tortured. After his argument in the Senate with Menshikov and the subsequent establishment of a special Investigative Commission, the vice-chancellor's future seemed to lose all connection to his words and actions and was directed only by an extraordinarily evil external spirit. No one asked Shafirov any serious questions or listened to his explanations, as if everything in the case were clear to the One Who Wanted It. And the One Who Wanted It returned from his Persian campaigns and heard out Shafirov's congratulations aloofly and distractedly and Menshikov's with a beneficent smile. And that led to conclusions of a not very consoling nature.

Chained up in the rotten straw, Shafirov thought how the real cause of his misery was neither Menshikov nor, of course, the sheep Skornyakov-Pisarev, who had been given the position of Senator Ober-Procurator for galloping quickly to Suzdal and handling Eudoxia Lopukhina in her convent. The blockhead didn't even realize that this whole business would eventually turn on him too. He led the investigation in Suzdal, and stuck his nose willy-nilly in the czar's business—and they'd chop off that nose and maybe his head, too. Meanwhile Menshikov, damn his soul, merely lit the fuse with his denunciation: he reported that Shafirov was swearing and cursing in the Senate and was a thief who had paid his brother an illegal salary for six months.

Tossing and turning in the straw, Shafirov sincerely regretted not having choked Aleksashka to death, back then in Kitai-Gorod in the Polish Rows. There would have been one less tramp and robber in the world. He didn't do it then and he'd been paying for it all his life and now he was going to the execution block. Of course, it would be wonderful to drag the serene prince along with him; but his time had not come.

Time made the choice, and Peter pointed his finger: "You," "you." To the wheel, to the execution block, into exile. And what difference did it make which excuse was used—whether you stole a million or overpaid your brother by three pennies? Now Bogdan, the brother of Captain Skornykov-Pisarev, had allotted many spoils unfairly to Menshikov during the division of the Pochepsky lands—and so what? Shafirov reported it to the czar—and where was his reward? Here it was: the chain and the block. The czar knew that ever since then Menshikov had hated Shafirov more than ever and wanted nothing more than his ruin—but he appointed Golovkin, another bitter enemy, to the Investigative Commission. How could Golovkin ever forget that damned night on the Prut River, when Shafirov had so undiplomatically boasted to his superior: "Tonight I saved Russia! I did!" So he saved it . . .

Of course they wouldn't take off his head. Peter would put off the execution; this chain and this stinking straw were only props in the play called "Justice Triumphs." The playwright was the czar. The acts: investigation, trial, retribution. And what awaited the lead actor after this cheap, stupid comedy? Poverty, shame, death. And a place in history, as immutable as a notch on an ax handle. . . . Damn it, what did an ax have to do with it! The czar's pardon must already be in Makarov's pocket.

His certainty in the pardon was unshakable. Without that certainty Shafirov would have been gnawing the iron chains and banging his head on the walls. Peter would not chop off his head, would not take away his life. The sentence was nothing but a farce. . . . But it was so hard to live through this night.

He had sent his wife and daughters off to Saint Petersburg the day before, assuring them of a happy resolution. Either way he would have to face the shame, and he did not want to have his family see him shamed. Now, in the middle of the last night, he regretted being alone, without a soul. Thinking about his pathetic loneliness, on that damned straw, he felt a warmth and heaviness in his eyes. He wiped the tears with the sleeve of his ratty fur coat and swore wearily: "I've really gone soft! They haven't lifted a finger against me, they allow me to have visitors—everything will be fine!" Rattling the chain, he turned on his side and tried to fall asleep, to kill time. But sleep would not come. With his fist under his cheek he lay on the spittle-covered floor—but for some reason he did not feel the damp cold of the stones or the weight of the collar, as if that fat, well-tended body was no longer his body and had nothing to do with his soul. His soul was in the buttery moonbeam falling obliquely through the barred window, and in the bushes near the Prut River, and in the library of his palace in Saint Petersburg, and in the Polish Rows in Kitai-Gorod—everywhere. And here, on the chain, too.

"Peter Pavlovich, my dear!"

On the doorstep, bending in the low doorway, stood Anna Danilovna Menshikova.

"My Antosha sent me, and here I am," she chattered, looking around the cellar in horror. "He said that he himself couldn't come, he simply couldn't . . ."

Shafirov understood that and accepted it without pain. If Divier were in his place, he would not have gone. And probably he wouldn't have sent his wife either.

"I was calumniated," Shafirov said, sitting down. "Anna Danilovna, dear lady, you must know this: I was calumniated and ruined by your brother."

"I know!" Anna whispered and waved her hand. "Antosha told me everything, how it happened! Alexander Danilovich is nasty, and he's aiming to use his claws on us, too."

"He shouted at me," Shafirov said, returning to the scene in the Senate, boiling with rage. " 'Don't you choke me!' So that I wouldn't choke him, ha!" He laughed and shook his head. "And I replied loudly, so that everyone could hear: 'You're the one who could kill us all!' And that's the truth, everyone knows it."

"It's true, it's true," Anna repeated, her voice barely audible. "But you be quieter, Peter Pavlovich, dear. Antosha always speaks quietly about that."

"Yes, yes, you're right," Shafirov agreed and raised his voice again, moving around, rattling the chain. "Skornyakov got a bribe from the prince, a hundred houses, and Skornyakov, that thief, offered me thirty out of the hundred, for me to shut my eyes to the Pochepsky business! But I wouldn't agree, because they're all my enemies! They wanted to usher me, Shafirov, out of the room! Me! The sergeant at arms grabbed me by the lapels!"

"Quiet, Peter Pavlovich, quiet!" Anna patted the shoulder of Shafirov's raggedy coat. "Take care of yourself. It will all blow over!"

"I know," Shafirov grumbled angrily. "I know it will blow over. But what will happen to my daughters? They'll take away everything except the remainder of my life. That's my reward for my labors."

He grew silent. It was a shame that Divier hadn't come after all. He could tell Antoine what was on his mind, but not Menshikov's sister. "My reward for Prut." She wouldn't understand anyway. Divier would get it, and so would Lacosta, but Lacosta was in Saint Petersburg; you couldn't lure him out of his hut all the way to Moscow. But his turn might come too: "The reward for Prut."

Shafirov shrugged, and Anna removed her white hand. It would be good to be alone again, and shut his eyes, and slide up that cold moonbeam—to Smolensk, and to the cozy palace, and to his library with its soft leather armchairs.

He did not hear Anna leave and did not know how much time passed before Lacosta appeared.

"It's you," Shafirov said, awakening. Standing in front of him, Lacosta cut off the moonbeams with his agile black-clad body, and the connection with the world was severed, and Peter Pavlovich was back in the cellar, chained up. "You know, I wanted you to come. Especially you."

The bristles on Lacosta's cheek showed silver in the flickering candlelight. His eyes, deep in their sockets, looked like dried tobacco leaves.

"I thought that perhaps you might like it," Lacosta muttered. "And I . . . you understand . . ."

"Listen," Shafirov said. "The worst does not threaten me. The czar must have signed the pardon by now."

"Thank God!" Lacosta said, his arms flying up like wings. "Thank God! Do you know that for sure?"

"As surely as there are still certainties in the world," Shafirov said and smiled condescendingly. "It's not so easy to chop off Shafirov's head. And just between us, the czar with his penchant for amusing jokes could have used a golden chain for me."

"You're so courageous," Lacosta said, after a thoughtful pause. "I don't think I'd be able to joke like that . . ."

"In my place, is that what you were going to say? Why not? If you're talking about this place, it's just temporary, until tomorrow. As for my real place"—Shafirov straightened and his face took on a cold and haughty expression—"I worked on it for two decades. Another would have slipped and broken his neck long ago, but I held on. And they send me—me!—some lousy little officer, with a ridiculous name . . . Why are you smiling?"

"I'm pleased for you," Lacosta said. "After all you've been through, you still have the strength to get so angry!"

"You know what that scoundrel dared say to me?" Shafirov continued waxing indignant. "That I, Baron Shafirov, was the son of a boyar's serf named Shayshka, and a Yid at that! He said that to me."

"But your father, of blessed memory—" Lacosta interrupted.

"My father's name was Pincus, or in Russian, Pavel," Shafirov said sternly. "And tell me, what's it to that little officer? That Skornyakov-Pisarev? He calls me 'Yid' as if I were lame or cockeyed and he was laughing at me. I'm not lame or cockeyed. I'm like the rest of them. Do you understand me?"

"No, Peter Pavlovich, you're not like the rest of them," Lacosta said softly but with conviction. "You only want to think so, and it seems to you that it is so. To your friends you are a Jew and to your enemies a Yid."

"But I'm baptized!"

"So what!" Lacosta shrugged. "What does that matter to Skornyakov-Pisarev? Or to you, for that matter, just between us? Well, it's served you: without it you couldn't have become who you are."

"And does it matter to you?"

"Not at all," Lacosta said. "So you're not a rabbi. But you're a real, full-blooded Jew, miraculously saved from a horrible death."

"But Skornyakov-Pisarev," Shafirov said, growing angry again, "he hates me as a Yid and as a baptized Jew. That's meaningless, after all! Aren't I right?"

"Why do we always seek to be loved as Jews and not just as people?" Lacosta said, without answering Shafirov. " 'Russians don't like Jews,' 'Germans like Jews.' . . . If some Moshe is a robber and a thief, he's a robber and a thief not because he's Jewish but because he is a bad man. And if Moshe is a hero and everyone loves him, that means he's a good and wise man, and his Jewishness has nothing to do with it."

"Only we can understand that," Shafirov said doubtfully.

"If we only did!" Lacosta said. "If we understood that, we'd be spared a lot of misery. On the one hand, we want to be like everyone else, and on the other hand, we're scared to death of it. . . . Czar Peter once said to me: 'If you had a true czar and homeland, you'd think differently.' Until we have our own land, we can't be like everyone else. And if we do get our own country and our own czar, we will become like everyone else, but then we will stop being Jews. . . . Would you be a jester for your own czar—a Jew just like you? I'm not sure, Peter Pavlovich, that I would."

"What do you mean?"

"I remember what you said: We are all jesters of the great Peter, and his greatness rests on our jests."

"Yes, yes," Shafirov said, lowering his head as far as the collar allowed. "And it makes no difference whether you're a Yid or Skornyakov-Pisarev. Aleksashka is as Russian as can be, but his turn is waiting for him, and God willing I'll laugh at him. This isn't only a question of Pochepa!" Shafirov raised his head in its unkempt wig and started shouting. "It goes deeper! It was Menshikov who was embezzling at the lard and fish enterprises in Arkhangelsk and wanted to drag me into it! I wouldn't let him. I got out of that clean!" He was shouting and shaking his head, and the moonbeam no longer beckoned and Lacosta's presence did not restrain him—he had forgotten Lacosta was there. "His serene prince is a thief, he's been stealing since he was a child! He thinks he's gotten the better of me—the hell he has! He offered me thirty houses. Why, I wouldn't sell myself to him for a thousand houses. I've got three thousand of my own. I'd rather enjoy the sight of his shame, his lousy death! They've pardoned me, but that cur won't be pardoned!"

Finished ranting, and breathing heavily, Shafirov turned to Lacosta and did not find him. Then, shivering, he wrapped himself more tightly in the thin fur coat and leaned against the wall.

It was getting light.

The sleigh was ordinary and black. It was generously heaped with hay, and sitting in it was almost comfortable. Shafirov took that for a good sign.

A powerful horse dragged the sleigh from Preobrazhenskoe past the gates, down the small streets of the outskirts toward the Kremlin, to the execution place. The entire square and its perimeter was crowded: it wasn't some tramp or robber who was going to lose his head today—it was Vice-Chancellor Shafirov. That was worth crowding and jostling and freezing for. And even though all executions, like all women, differed very little from one another, how honest folk itched to taste the delights of a noblewoman and to see the head of a baron or prince roll! The flesh was the same and the blood was the same, but it was interesting nevertheless.

Passing the marketplace in Kitai-Gorod, where the crowd began, Shafirov turned in the hay and grumbled: line up, line up, you fools! Your hopes will be shattered. The baron's head will remain on his shoulders. Now what does that crooked degenerate want, pushing through with his filthy sack from the market to the square? Or that snot-nosed woman with the child in her arms—has she forgotten something on the square? She just wants to smell noble blood! Why doesn't she stick to her wares, rags, pies, whatever they are? . . . He suddenly remembered the merchant Evreinov's shop, and himself at the counter, and he smiled. And seeing the smile on the face of the condemned, the snot-nosed woman gave a high-pitched scream and giggled.

The closer they got to the block, the more soldiers there were. Shouting and waving sticks, they pushed back the crowd, clearing a path for the sleigh and the convoy. Two priests with crosses in their hands walked alongside the sleigh, without looking at the condemned man. The executioner in a bright red cotton shirt stood idly by, resting his shoulder on the block's stone wall, staring contemptuously at the crowds.

The sleigh stopped, and Shafirov, supported by two soldiers from the convoy, clambered down into the snow. His wig had slipped over his left ear, and before moving toward the block, he used both hands to adjust it. The tall, luxurious wig looked incongruous with the shabby fur coat.

A steep, narrow staircase led up to the block, and Shafirov panted and groaned his way up. Secretary of the Senate Makarov was waiting for him on top—the man who would read the sentence and the pardon. Shafirov tried to catch his eye, to read "pardoned by the grace of the czar," but Makarov stared emptily into space. The executioner, spitting through his teeth, scraped snow with the side of his hand from the block. The crowd grew hushed, and thousands of eyes focused on the accused.

Makarov stepped forward with the unfurled pronouncement in his hands.

"Guilty of disobeying . . ." Shafirov heard, "of arguing the reverse, of violating the decorum of the Senate . . . of appropriating large amounts . . . of violating the established order . . . of not reporting runaway peasants within the proper deadline . . ."

Dry snow fell from the sky and dusted the block again. Shafirov thought that it would probably be pleasant to press his overheated face to the cold wood.

"For these crimes," Makarov went on, "he is sentenced to losing his ranks, titles, estates, and his very life by beheading."

Rolling up the pronouncement, Makarov stepped away. Czar Peter was clever, so inventive! Announcing the pardon now would be too easy, too boring and undramatic! It's much more exciting to bring it to the very last moment, to the crowd holding its breath, the executioner dancing with the ax in his hand! Say what you will, but the czar never missed the opportunity for a big effect . . .

The executioner's assistants tore off the fur coat and pulled off the wig. Now the crowd saw not Vice-Chancellor Baron Shafirov, but a bald old Jew with short legs, disgustingly fat. And that was interesting too.

Shafirov approached the block from the side, got on his knees with difficulty, and put his head in the indentation. The comedy was dragging out a bit! The snow-dusted wood cooled his cheek. Why wasn't Makarov saying anything? How long was this going to drag on, for God's sake?

The executioner's assistants silently jumped him, and pushed him down on the log that rested against the block. It was uncomfortable lying on the block; his belly got in the way. One of the assistants sat on Shafirov's outstretched legs at the ankles. Out of the corner of his eye, Shafirov saw Makarov give the sign to the executioner. Spread-eagled and flattened, Shafirov at that instant realized that there was no pardon, that Makarov had read the whole pronouncement. He also saw the executioner's legs, bouncing in place. Then the legs stopped, and the executioner took a big swing and rose on his toes. The crowd's exhalation coincided with the executioner's "Khah!" Shafirov did not feel any pain; he only heard the dull and horrible crunch of the ax. Amazingly, the picture before Shafirov's eyes—the block's rounded edge, part of the scaffold, and the people below—did not change, but merely lost its sharpness and intensity. Sounds reached him as if through cotton.

"By his Imperial Highness's mercy," Makarov creaked, and looking around, Shafirov saw the ax, deep in the wooden block next to his neck, "for services rendered to the state, the death sentence is commuted to exile in Siberia."

The assistant jumped up from his legs, another helped him up from the log and plopped the wig on his head, a third draped the coat over his shoulders. Shafirov wept, twisting his mouth. He was led down the stairs—practically carried—and brought to the Senate to hear congratulations on the czar's mercy. His legs would not obey; his head trembled and shook from side to side. At the Senate, in the familiar long corridor, his strength gave out completely, and muttering something and pressing his hands to his chest, to his heart, he sank to the floor. The court physician Govi bled him. Staring at the flow, Shafirov spoke softly but clearly, and was heard. "It would have been better to let the blood out of my large artery, to put an end to my suffering."

It was a rhetorical statement: the czar's mercy, like his wrath, could not be reversed.

Fedya the parrot puttered in his cage, jumping nervously from his perch to the floor with his clumsy human feet, giving his master a baleful eye. Divier had not said a word to him all evening, had not scratched his blue breast with the long-handled silver scratcher in the shape of a hand with a pointed index finger. The parrot was unhappy.

Divier was unhappy too. Leaning back in his chair, his strong-muscled legs sprawled out, he watched the hands of the clock. On the side table next to the clock stood a pitcher of ginger beer and a mug, from which Divier drank from time to time. Lacosta was due any minute. The talk he had to have with him bothered Divier.

The issue was perfectly clear; the only possible way out

had been found in time. The document had been written up with extreme clarity and gentleness. But how to explain it all to Yan? How to prepare him? "Dear Yan, circumstances are such that . . ." No, that was too dry. "Dear Yan, it's better to lose your wig today than your head tomorrow . . ." That was no good—too playful and biting for Lacosta, a gentle person. Maybe he should begin with Yasha and his future? But what future could there be for him now? Damn this whole evening and this conversation!

Seeing Lacosta smiling placidly, Divier sat up in the chair and set his lips in a tight line.

Then he spoke. "Sit down, Yan, my dear fellow. Some beer? Here's a mug. . . . I have to prepare you for an unexpected turn of events. You're going into exile in Siberia. I managed to arrange it for you."

Now Lacosta was smiling suspiciously. His eyes glimmered anxiously above the mug.

"If you don't leave for exile today," Divier continued angrily, "tomorrow you'll lose your head. Well, next month. I know what I'm saying."

"But for what?" Lacosta asked, setting down his mug.

"What's the difference!" Divier was astonished by Lacosta's lack of comprehension. "I arranged that you be exiled for lackadaisical work. Last month you left for Moscow without permission. In another week you'll be accused of going there for a secret meeting with the state criminal Shafirov."

"But he was pardoned by the czar!" Lacosta was bewildered. "And then . . ."

"He was pardoned, but you won't be," Divier interrupted. "Peter Pavlovich isn't in Siberia, he's in Novgorod, and, I think, he won't be there long—he'll be back. But for you, Yan, exile is a life preserver."

"Do I have to go for a long time?"

"Until your release," Divier said moving closer, and lowered his voice. "Shafirov has been sentenced, the Veselovskys are on the run, now you. . . . It looks like I'm the only one left, and that's too conspicuous. I don't know how long I'll last."

"Yasha. What will happen to him?"

"He can live with me for now," Divier said. "When Shafirov gets back, the boy will live with him. That's the best for everyone."

"Where am I going?" Lacosta asked. "And when?"

"Here's the order," Divier said, taking it from his pocket. "Voskresenskoe village, on Lake Baikal. It is far, true, but almost completely safe: no one will remember you're there, God willing. You've been given a not-too-large allowance, so that no one will notice."

"You really are saving my life," Lacosta said, putting his hand on Divier's shoulder. "Five more days," he said, reading the order. "It must take two months to get there."

"Closer to three," Divier said. "You'll travel by wagon, with two men in convoy. I can't do anything about that."

"Will I be chained up?" Lacosta inquired meekly.

"No!" Divier chuckled. "I took care of that. And the guards are my men; they won't bother you."

"Is this all because of Prut?" Lacosta asked hesitantly.

"Not only," Divier said quietly, looking away. "Prut, Vytashchi, Shafirov. Too much. . . . The czar sometimes loses control, that's the problem. The czar is sick, Yan, very sick."

"It was his order to . . ." Lacosta managed to say.

"Luckily for you, no! But there were people to remind him of you and your role."

"I didn't think I had enemies."

"Those people don't want to do you harm. They wanted to do something good for themselves. The czar's wrath brings harm to some and benefit to others. The ones who reminded him hoped to be rewarded for zeal. . . . Next week I'll report to the czar that you have been punished for poor service, and the matter will rest there."

"And you will have another enemy, Antoine," Lacosta said. "The one who will not get a reward."

"That's not so terrible! My hour hasn't come yet. And when it does, what difference will one enemy more or less make?"

They fell silent, each lost in his thoughts and staring ahead: Divier at the hour, not here but rising before him, Lacosta at the village of Voskresenskoe on the shores of Baikal. He was glad he could travel there without shackles or a bear chain.

"What about Shafirov—was that over Prut?" Lacosta asked with the burning curiosity of a saved man. "If you can't tell me, Antoine, don't."

"Because of Prut," Divier replied, frowning. "The Reward for Prut, that's what he called it, and to his misfortune, he repeated it, often and loudly. . . . I warned him, Yan. But those Polish Jews are so independent, and so feisty! They like to show off too much!"

"He had a bad time," Lacosta said. "In the cellar and on the square . . . Horrible!"

"Yes! That was a bad joke. But"—and Divier automatically shifted to a low whisper—"a royal one! I'm telling you, Yan: His Majesty is sick. Arguing with him means putting your head on the block. He suspects everyone, including the empress. He loses control for two or three days after every domestic argument, and then heads fly. And the head of Catherine is also held by nothing but her neck."

"That means?" Lacosta said, reaching for Divier's elbow.

"That means that it would be better for me not to know any of this, and for you too. And it also means that I'm as hungry as a thousand devils, and you and I are going to eat and drink now, eat and drink a lot. And why are we sitting in the dark? Hey! Someone! Light the candles! Dinner!"

Anna Danilovna entered the room swiftly and silently.

"Just one little minute, Antosha!" she said. "Everything's been ready a long time! Well, thank God, you're hungry; that means you're healthy. I was beginning to think that some pox had befallen you."

The servant quickly lit the candles. Fedya the parrot, blinking and shaking his pink comb, stuck his square black tongue out of the side of his beak, clucked, and gave a juicy pirate whistle.

The wagon pulled by two horses left Saint Petersburg before noon. The late April sun was pleasantly warm, and the heavy mud had dried up and was covered by a thin, fragile crust. The air over the Moscow road was imbued with the scent of fresh pine and that special hint of decay and conception that makes young people think of the eternity of life and old people of the proximity of death.

After a quick glance at the road leading through the forest to the Spruce Lodge, Lacosta turned away. What difference did it make, really, why he was going into exile—for lackadaisical work or for the murder of Chevalier Reńe Lemort! All of it—the work, the chevalier—was behind him now, in a different dimension, where the living were entwined mysteriously with the dead. And every passing hour and every milepost became part of his past forever. . . . And yet there was something attractive in this long and strange trip to Voskresenskoe on Baikal: he no longer had to work as the sad jester, and the guards were much less frightening than Czar Peter. The horse did the pulling and he just sat in the wagon. This was probably the first time in many many years, perhaps the first time in his life, that he was traveling completely free, without any responsibilities—they were all over, loved and gone, and there was nothing to do about it. Yes, yes, free! No one would call him to see the czar, no one would force him to do what he did not want to do. He was alone, not counting those nice guards, who were total strangers, talking about some man named Elisei Zhubryak he never heard of. He was born again, a marvelously irresponsible man without roots and without a past. The horses pulled; he went. This must have been the feeling Stepan Vytashchi had wanted to experience when he spoke of wishing to be a child. Three months on the road, three months of freedom. And then— "until his release," release from exile or release from life. And if it were his fate to pass once more along this road in the opposite direction, past the Lodge and back to Saint Petersburg—he would obediently and impatiently return to his past, where the living were so irrationally and cruelly separated from the dead.

Epilogue · 1738

On Saturday, July 15, on Admiralty Island, at the market square opposite the new Gostiny Dvor, a large crowd of Saint Petersburgers watched the red-shirted specialists lay bundles of dry birch logs, clumps of kindling, and armloads of straw around the base of a tall pole. The specialists worked diligently: the business was scandalous and the punishment had been approved by Empress Anna herself. The festive crowd munched pies and chewed sunflower seeds. Sweaty vendors hawked kvass. Women and children sold apples by the piece. A pickpocket on the edge of the crowd had been knocked down and beaten.

The criminals had not been brought in yet, and people kept looking at the passage guarded by soldiers leading from the prospect under construction across the square to the pole. The kindling and logs were piled rather high, almost up to the round platform where the convicted prisoners would be placed, to afford a better view for the public and to let the flames burn higher and hotter. One of the specialists had climbed onto the platform and held on to the pole with one hand as he caught blocks of wood tossed to him from below and stacked them neatly around his feet. Spectators jokingly warned him about falling off. If he did fall, of course, that would amuse the crowd and make the waiting, which was getting tiring, more fun.

The appearance of the prison cart was met with a roar of animation, which subsided quickly; the event demanded attention and concentration. The cart was open and without sides. There was a block of wood in the middle, and two men were shackled to it—a portly old man with a fluffy white beard and a tall, middle-aged man with reddish-blond hair and a bruised, swollen face. The beaten man stood calmly, apparently not quite realizing what was going on, while the old man tore fiercely at his chains. Before reaching the stake, the nag pulling the cart came to a stop, and the executioner unshackled the two men. Their hands were still bound, and the old man shook the manacles, while the beaten man walked without prodding, taking small, scuffling steps: one of his eyes was swollen shut, and the other had limited vision. Beside the steps leading to the stake's platform, the two men stopped and were immediately set upon by the guards and executioners. They hauled the old man up first, put his feet on the platform, and attached his manacled hands high above his head to a hook in the stake—the man's toes barely touched the floor. There was a lot less trouble with the other man.

The quickly muttered death sentence interested no one—they all knew it anyway. The chief executioner checked his subordinates' work and moved slowly around the stake, lighting the kindling. A light blue smoke curled up, and yellow streams of flame licked the pile of artfully placed logs. The crowd, with bated breath, waited for the first screams.

In the hushed, quivering silence a peasant wagon approached the empty market rows. It held two hog carcasses, covered with matting, and a skinny old man in bast shoes and rough trousers, his face as hairy and wild as a forest spirit's.

"Hey, wild man, we're here!" said the driver, a pockmarked peasant with high Tatar cheekbones. "Pay up!"

The old man dug around in his pockets and gave him a copper coin, blackened with age.

"There," the old man said. "As agreed."

"Add a bit! You see, there's no business, they're putting people to death again and everyone is off watching. . . . Add a bit!"

"Where will I get it?" the old man asked in surprise and cooled off the driver with a look from his dark brown, piercing eyes. "As we agreed!"

"All right, all right. Don't if you don't want to. . . . Don't stare like that. You're a forest spirit, not a convict."

"I'm not a convict or a forest spirit," the old man said with a placating smile. "You drove the free old man Yan Lacosta. Here's a half-kopeck to celebrate that."

Lacosta turned away from the pockmarked man and headed for the square. Over heads and backs, he looked at the fiery whirlwind, in the heart of which two human figures showed black, and then asked, "Whom are they burning and what for?"

"The Yid Borokh Leibov for perverting retired naval captain Voznitsyn into the Yid faith," Lacosta was told. "The Yid is on the left and Voznitsyn is that one over there."

The fire was raging, and the Yid and the captain were no

longer discernible. Staring into the flames until it hurt, Lacosta tried to find Leibov—and saw the cellar in Shafirov's palace, and the seder, and Leibov, offering Czar Peter a yarmulke with the nerve of a madman. . . . So that was Borokh on the left. Poor Borokh.

Leaving the crowd, Lacosta went around the square, took one last look at the fire, and walked along the river. It wasn't far to Divier's, and Lacosta was in no hurry. The past revealed itself on his first day—death on the left and right. Czar Peter had been in his grave a long time, but fires still burned in the square. "The Yid Borokh Leibov for perverting . . ." It was 1738, yet right in the middle of Saint Petersburg inquisitors were dragging people to the stake. Two hundred years ago, the ancestors of Lacosta and Divier had fled Spain to get away from inquisitors—and now their descendants fell from the frying pan into the fire. God only knew how many other bonfires would follow this one and who would burn in them. Lacosta? Or would the old man be lucky enough to die a natural death, and would it be his grandson, Yasha, who would be burned instead? In blessed Hamburg a Jew had to worry about trouble from his fellow Jews, and that was in the order of things—but it would never occur to anyone to kill you simply because you were a Jew! That was impossible! Yasha could have become a respected doctor or lawyer there and no one would have sent him into exile or to the stake.

Divier's house had not changed over the years—still sturdy and handsome, its tall windows looking down welcomingly at the water. A young, fancily dressed servant opened the door and, without letting go of the knob, regarded Lacosta haughtily.

"I need to see Anton Manuilovich," Lacosta said. "Divier!"

"Are you crazy, old man?" The servant laughed. "Go to Siberia, to hard labor, to see Divier. Come on, get out of here!"

So much for Divier. That left Shafirov.

Lacosta arrived at the back entrance, and the cook looked suspiciously at his pants and bast shoes.

"Did you bring some fish?" the neat cook asked, once she had looked him over.

"Then, Peter Pavlovich . . . is here," Lacosta said, gasping for breath from the unexpected agitation. "Tell him Lacosta is here. La-cos-ta!"

Shafirov ran out on his short legs and embraced him. Then he adjusted his wig and dabbed his fingers at the corners of his damp eyes.

"My God, it's you . . . My God!"

"Forgive the way I look," Lacosta said, afraid to sit down. "I just got in today."

"The last time we saw each other I was in no better shape." Shafirov smiled. "And once more I have titles and rank. . . . But what am I doing? I'll have them bring you clothes."

"Just one question. My grandson—he's—"

"He's here with me," Shafirov said. "Divier brought him."

"Antoine is at hard labor?"

"In exile! And do you know who else is there? That bastard Skornyakov-Pisarev! I knew it would happen! And Menshikov, His Serene Blackguard? Dead! In exile! In poverty! While I came out of it fine! The empress gave me Peter the Great's own sword! For my services! . . . Why are you smiling?"

"You're still the same, Peter Pavlovich!" Lacosta said. "Time doesn't touch you."

"Of course," Shafirov said and turned to the mirror. There

in the clear Venetian glass two old men smiled at each other—one with a victorious smile, the other with a kind and pathetic smile.

On Shafirov's orders, enough garments were brought to clothe five naked men. Out of that pile, glistening with silver and gold threads, Lacosta pulled a roomy, mouse-colored caftan, brown trousers, and sturdy traveling shoes.

"If I didn't know that you had returned today from exile, I would have the impression that you were headed there," Shafirov joked, pulling a long face. "What do you want with those horrible shoes? Put on these light ones, with buckles!"

"I'm just returning from exile," Lacosta said, tugging at the caftan. "I still have far to travel . . ."

"Where?"

"Hamburg."

"You've lost your mind," Shafirov said angrily. "Why Hamburg? . . . I'll get a fine salary for you and an apartment. And think about Yasha—it's time for him to marry!"

"I have thought of him," Lacosta said stubbornly. "I was at Gostiny Dvor this morning."

"So?"

"I saw them burn Borokh Leibov."

"So what? He was crazy, a maniac! You remember how he made Peter wear a yarmulke? I almost had a stroke! And why the hell did he start up that wild business with the captain! We live in Russia, after all, and we have to remember that!"

"When I lived in Hamburg, I didn't have to remember," Lacosta said. "But now I recall it frequently."

"But why are you so upset about that Leibov? Who's he to you—a relative, a friend? And how many times have you ever seen him, anyway—once, twice?"

"Today him, tomorrow me," Lacosta said, shaking his

head. "And it's not that I'm so mortally afraid; that's not the whole point. It's just that in these last years I've forgotten how to live in constant terror: that some thug will come and drag you into the dungeon because you're a crazy old Jew. Therefore, only two paths are left to me: return to Voskresenskoe or return to Hamburg. You must agree that Hamburg is a more reasonable choice."

"But you'll leave Yasha here?" Shafirov asked uncertainly. "He's almost Russian, after all."

"No," Lacosta said. "Yasha goes with me."

They set out that same day, before evening—the old man in sturdy new boots and the youth in traveling clothes. Shafirov's coach carrying a trunk waited for the travelers at the fourth milepost on the Lithuanian road: Lacosta was determined to embark on his voyage to his homeland on foot, and if there had been any ashes handy, he would have sprinkled some on his bald head, so that his grandson would not see. A return home after forty-six years of wanderings, frivolous and horrible, should not take place in a luxurious coach. Actually, this wasn't even an ordinary homecoming—this was an escape, and the first steps of an escape should be on foot, exhausting. Exhausting himself before getting into Shafirov's coach was particularly significant to Lacosta.

The coach was supposed to bring the travelers to the nearest way station, from where they would travel by public transportation. After three hours on the forest road, they approached the station in total darkness. When they knocked, the sleepy host opened the door, scratching his unkempt head.

They followed the host, who was carrying their trunk, into a cramped cubicle with plank walls that did not reach the ceiling. No one else was there. The host, reeling with sleep or drink, dropped the trunk on the floor by the wide bed covered with a faded quilt. And nothing would have changed if the grandfather and grandson had learned that it was under this quilt that Masha Lacosta had hid that morning when the unkempt host rummaged through her trunk, picking out clothing to pay for René Lemort's enterprise.

They were lucky. In the morning they struck a deal with a passing merchant delivering rawhides to Smolensk, and he let them ride in his wagon.

They saw the spires of Hamburg's churches two months later, on September 19, 1738.

On August 25, 1943, Yan Lacosta's direct descendants—the men Josef, Johann, and Henry, the women Hilda and Rosalinde, the children Hans, Hubert, and Minna—were killed in the gas chamber and burned in the crematorium of Buchenwald in Germany.